SOME STORIES JUST HAVE ELLIPSIS...

YOU CAN FIGHT THE WORLD FOR THE PEOPLE YOU LOVE,
BUT YOU CAN'T FIGHT THE PEOPLE YOU LOVE.

RAKSHITA S.

Made with ♥ on the Notion Press Platform
www.notionpress.com

To every love story that lived its eternity,

and all those who loved through that eternity.

Some stories,

They don't have commas or full stops, they just have...

ellipsis

Contents

Contents

Preface

Some books begin with answers.
This one begins with ellipses...

This isn't the kind of story where people say the right things at the right time.
It's messy. It's full of almosts, maybes, and unanswered texts. It's about people who walk in, people who walk out, and the strange ache that follows when someone leaves- but the memories stay.

These pages were born out of moments that didn't fit into a clean narrative.
Moments that hung between decisions. Between "yes" and "no."
Between who we were and who we're still becoming.

I didn't write this for a happy ending. I wrote this for the girl who sits in her car after work, wondering if she's still allowed to dream.
For the boy who felt too much too early, and broke quietly when no one noticed.
For everyone who knows what it feels like to be almost chosen.

I wrote this for the survivors of feelings that never quite found a place to land.
And maybe...
for the version of me who needed someone to whisper,
"You are not the only one who feels this way."

So if you find yourself in these pages- somewhere between Iana's storm, Zayne's longingness, Hella's fire, or Zeeshan's silence- I hope you know: your pain is valid, your softness is powerful, and your story, even with its ellipses, is worth telling.

Let's begin at the part where most people stop talking-
Let's begin where it still hurts.

Rakshita S.

For all the stories that never ended.

Acknowledgements

To put this story into the world has meant opening up parts of myself I once kept tucked away. This book- its messiness, its longing, its soft hope- isn't just fiction. It's a collection of shadows and echoes that I've carried within me for a long time. And I couldn't have brought it to life alone.

First, to the version of me who felt everything a little too deeply- thank you for surviving long enough to tell the story. For choosing to write instead of staying silent. For making sense of chaos through words when nothing else worked.

To my family, for loving me in their own way, even when they couldn't always understand the things I chose to write about. Your quiet support, spoken or not, has held me up more than you know.

To the people who broke me, thank you. You gave me the fragments I needed to build something whole. You gifted me pain that turned into paragraphs. Even if we'll never speak again, your presence echoes through these pages.

To my readers, especially the ones who find pieces of themselves in these characters, you are the reason I wrote this. You are the reason I kept going on days I wanted to give up. If this book gives you comfort, or makes you feel seen, or just makes you feel less alone... then it's done what I needed it to do.

To the nights I stayed up writing,
to the heartbreaks I tried to make sense of,
to the songs that played on repeat,
and to the healing that came slowly,
thank you.

And finally, to the story itself, for choosing me. For knocking on my ribs and refusing to leave until I wrote it all down. I hope I did you justice.

With all my love and strength,
Rakshita

Prologue

"Why can't we just talk it out? Why it has to be like this..."

"Because it is meant to be like this..."

"No, it isn't. You *choose* for it to be this way."

"I won't correct you if you really think it to be this way."

"When did we go like this? What did we do wrong to get here? I just need my answers... I guess I deserve this much at least. You can't just pretend for it to be so normal..."

"It is normal, it is as normal as it can ever be... I don't know why you're trying to look through and find something which isn't even there! Come out of your fictitious world and *see!*"

"Why?"

"What why?"

"Everything..."

"Can you please be straight? I can't understand what you want to say?"

"You *can't* or you probably don't *want* to?"

"Ghosh! Please stop, why do you want to make it more difficult than it already is? We knew this would come up eventually, so guess it's best that..."

"Best that we flee? Take the easier way which let me point out very clearly to you sir is no easier for me, and I won't go too far to say that it isn't easier for you because now..."

"Now what? Say it..."

"...now I don't really know if it really is easier for you."

I could hear him sigh, I didn't really know anything that was going on, but it wasn't meant to be this way. It was supposed to be better, perfect, just like I had always imagined, just like we always talked about, it had to be other way, it had to be...

I don't know, just, different...

"I... I can't say anything much now..."

"Did you ever?"

"Why do you want to take it this way? Can't we just keep it normal?"

"For heaven's sake can you tell me even a bit of it which is normal?"

"What do you think, I don't wish for it to be different? I don't want things to be different, to be the way we talked, the way we planned, the way we imagined?"

"Apparently, not enough."

"How am I supposed to make you understand, I know it's difficult, but this is how it's meant to be. And we can't help it even if we want to, that's how life goes. We don't always get to choose. And God knows had I had the choice, I'd have chosen you over and over and over..."

"Then why not now?"

"Because... I don't get to choose."

"We can fight it together, whatever it is we can, it's just time, I know it'll pass..."

"The thing is, you can fight anyone and everyone and all the odds and all the things but you can't fight your own people. I give up. Am sorry, I just can't..."

"...is that what you really want then?"

"I just... I don't know, it's just too..."

"Is that what you want?"

"I just want you to understand my..."

"For god's sake give me a clear answer now, you can't just keep me hanging like this."

"I don't want to, but I guess I have to..."

The static beep from my side shouldn't have astounded him, I guess. He knew me well enough to know that that was a goodbye we both couldn't have said. I just wondered how different it would have been had we not met the way did, had we not known each other way we did, had we not felt for each other the way we did, had we not fell for each other the way we did or perhaps,

Had we not born into the circumstances we did...

CHAPTER ONE

IANA

The town looked so pretty from here, everything below looked so celestially pretty. The lights looked like the diamonds that fell from the Archangel's bag while he strolled through the gardens of heaven and he, too careless to bother to collect them back left them there as if to let mere human existence have the pleasure of some of the heavenly source of beauty. Only, it was a pity that not many had the chance to really see it that way, or rather, they did *have* a chance but didn't care enough to *take* it. And not out of ostentatious gratefulness but a rather genuine acknowledgment of the fact that he gave that source of light not just for mere pleasure but for much more than that. That that we failed to understand until we really put our minds to it, I couldn't help but look beyond where all those lights ended and everything seemed to melt into the oblivion of darkness and somehow all of it fascinated me to an extent that I wondered if someday even those dark parts might light up. Even if they wouldn't what if I might find a way to light them up at least for me... I had before... found ways to light darkened things up, then maybe this time too I could.

I noticed that I had been drifting off to myself a lot lately, but it felt nice, to be by myself, in my head. After all of too much that had happened since last year, it seemed like I needed it much.

I looked at my phone screen, it showed 4:51 a.m. I was two minutes earlier today. I had been pushing myself, bit by bit every day, and I wasn't doing too bad. The sun hadn't started to rise yet and the trees down the valley cast shadows which might have terrified someone who at first glance would have definitely mistaken them for outlines of some kind of unknown oblivious threats and perhaps devils those humans feared within. Just that they'd have seemed physical manifestations of the fear we often carry within. Yet I didn't fear them, in fact, they seemed soothing, mysterious, and somehow intimately connected. Maybe because the shades of darkness matched those that I myself carried within. All of it was too heavy for someone who might look at it that way for the first time, but I was used to it. I didn't know why, it's just that there was always something more that I wanted things to have. I always looked for more, from everything which it possibly had to offer to me than just on the face of it. I wanted to look beyond it, beyond the face of it. Sometimes it didn't even make sense, but then it isn't always rationality that satisfies a soul. It might satisfy the *mind*, but not the *soul*. Soul asks for things beyond reason, things that keep one *alive, going*.

The morning breeze was cool enough to let my perspiration evaporate and soothe my troubled breathing, probably from walking at a slope and against the wind flow. But it had been almost two months now since I'd been measuring the slopes of these mountains which had been here since eternity but I didn't quite find an occasion to wander and explore them, their sides which not even folks who here every day knew.

The paths had been reconstructed since I had last been here, the streetlights worked more often than not, and it was quiet mostly at the time of morning when I woke up to the beep of my alarm and scrapped my shoe souls against the rough high roads. But it wasn't just my shoe souls that wore off, somehow, day after day, since I started walking up this hill and seeing those twinkling diamonds it felt as though a part of me wore off too... no, not in the slightest of negative way, the part of me that wore off was that weaker one which I should have let go of a lot earlier, but somehow, I couldn't. But now it was, wearing off. And I was glad about it. Even grateful. I was learning, and after whatever happened last summer, I was growing, at least I was trying to grow. But it still hurt, it still plagued me in my nightmares.

The phone beeped in my right pocket, it was 5:15, time to get going. I had to be down before the other alarm went off, which I had set for exactly twelve minutes later. I had almost forgotten about it, lost deep in my reverie. The music seemed too loud for such a quiet morning but I didn't really care because the fast beats of music kept my feet going at a pace I otherwise might have failed to keep up. There were four more songs left in the playlist before it'd have started to repeat and I was sure that before that happened, I'd be back below, so I kind of skipped the other two songs in a row and played the one which I liked the most because apparently my human tendency to hear what you like more, took over and I definitely wanted to listen to that one before I reached back home. I connected to the song, it felt like it was made for me, to help me keep going. I knew it was silly of me to think so because it had come out long before I could have even fathomed what it possibly meant, but now I very clearly could not just make out what it meant, but *knew* that it was something to make me want to hold on to things for a while longer...just keep going for a little more time...

What doesn't kill you makes you stronger,
stand a little taller,
doesn't mean am lonely when am alone...
what doesn't kill you makes you fighter
must've seen how lighter,
doesn't mean am over 'cause you're gone...

I couldn't help wondering what possibly made Kelly Clarkson sing that tremendous song. But whatever it was I knew it was something that broke her enough to make her come back that strong. I knew because I myself was trying to come back strong after whatever happened last year.

I could see the sky turning orange, the sun had almost lit up the dark sky, driving out shadows of dullness that the night had engulfed the world around with. It looked like the world was waking up to its beauty and agility which had been veiled momentarily by the quilt of inactiveness of night. And all of it

looked so pretty that for a moment, I didn't want to return home...
I felt like this was my home...this place full of light, and possibility,
this place which made even darkness seem so pretty, this was my
home...I *wanted* to make it my home.

I glanced at my phone screen; it showed still two minutes left
for the alarm to go off...not bad! I took the last few moments to
adore the heavenly beauty and then clearing my mind, I tightened
my shoelaces set my ponytail which had been messed up like I had
been out, fighting a war, and jogged down the pavement and streets,
back home.

#

The lights were still off and though the sun had risen to its full
glory, the environment at my place felt damp and gloomy. I pulled
away the tight scrunchy that had been holding my hair in place for
a while now to set them free. The ease that came rushing as they
fell loose on my shoulders felt like a rush of fresh air after a long
while of holding breath. Fiddling with the rubber band still in my
hand I walked across the room and pulled away the curtains, letting
the day shine fill the room. The city had already woken up and was
about. People at their jobs, locomotives with their engines revving,
ladies with all their fancy outfits out for work, men hurrying for
their work... everyone running an invisible race, not for winning,
but just not to be left behind. The serene image of quiet nature
flashed in front of me and suddenly my heart ached for that calm
again. It had started to feel empty a lot. For a while, I thought it
might go away with time, the feeling of emptiness... and it did, or
possibly no, it didn't. It was only that I had gotten too engrossed
that I forgot to acknowledge it for a while. But it was there, all the
while. I wondered if I would ever really not feel like that anymore,
if it was even possible that I'd feel whole again.

"What on earth are you thinking now?"

"Nothin' just usual philosophical thoughts, too heavy of a shit for
you, kiddo!"

"Ghosh Eea! I am not a kid anymore!"

I very well knew the fact that she wasn't a kid so small anymore. It's just that it felt nice to bother her that way sometimes. It reminded me of times that were much simpler for us. But surely Hella was a grown teenager now, the girl I hid my secrets from, was my secret keeper now!

"I know kiddo!" I chuckled as her sharp features twisted with sheer annoyance.

"Shouldn't you have gotten ready twenty minutes ago? I guess you don't get an upset stomach worth missing your college every day, do you?" I eyed her questioningly.

"I surely don't, but I do get a day off *after* having an upset stomach."

"Jeez Hella! You'd have bunked all your lessons had it been in your hands! Only, thank God it isn't."

"I am not *bunking!*"

"No, you're not. You're *missing!* Which's far worse!" I shot the cushion lying nearest to me at her.

"Damn! You know you sound like old nuns at convent sometimes. We didn't come this far from home and family to just live boring nine to five lives. C'mon Eea learn to *live!*"

"Yeah, why not. But for now, I guess we should probably get going. And if you aren't going to college anyway, then get the laundry done." I said slipping into the bathroom to shower and get ready for work.

"Fine!" she shouted from the kitchen.

The water felt cool on my skin and for a while, I didn't even want to come out of it. It felt like I was being filled up with new energy as those tiny, pious droplets washed the sweat and dirt of the labor of the early morning off me. It was indeed rejuvenating. 'Learn to live' I couldn't drive these simple words of Hella's out of my mind. I knew they meant far more than they just portrayed, but how? What? I didn't know! I wanted to but I didn't. I tried living once and it was shattering! And though I longed for that feeling again, I was too afraid by even the thought of it and questioned myself every day that could I take that pain that accompanied it all over again? I didn't know. And I guess I didn't even want to. I turned the faucet off and stepped out of that comforting little space of mine. I stood there in front of the mirror, staring at the girl who looked back at me with the same intensity with which my gaze was set upon her. *She* was so different from the girl I knew years back. *I* was so different. Half the things that had happened, I guess none of us knew we were capable of facing them. But here we stood, staring back at each other, trying to build ourselves. I caressed the girl in the mirror for a while and then swiftly closed the distance between us as if wanting to keep some secret of ours'. I whispered,

"I love you, honey, you're strong. Thank you for being me. I love you." Yet the emptiness lingered somewhere deep within me. Like it shouted to be fed, to be looked after, to be...filled.

I walked into the messed-up room with my wet hair still held up by a towel, and just with a look, I knew Hella had been up here searching for matching jewelry for my day's attire. I didn't know what pleasure it gave her to plan my outfit almost every day no matter whatever the occasion might be. It had become some kind of a ritual now, which she never failed to complete, not even on her worse days. I remember last summer when she was going through a very bad breakup, even then she didn't fail to plan my outfits. In fact, she did it with more passion. Was it out of anger or just out of a need for some kind of distraction, I didn't know, but I surely wouldn't have been the smartest intern at the Muses and Caerus publications had it not been for her planning my outfits so precisely.

But none of it could justify her creating such a ruckus in my room. It looked as if all the 'Little man' and 'Fat boys' had been dropped here instead of Hiroshima and Nagasaki. And I could foresee a war surely about to be fought here right now as I shouted at the top of my voice,

"Hella! Here. Right now!"

"Comin'."

She came strolling stealthily as if she knew what was going to be the sequence for the next few minutes, which she actually did know, but still... it gave her no right to not come running at my first call full of angst!

"What in the hell happened to this room?" I eyed a here furiously.

"Hella happened to this room." She giggled at her own joke. And however, it also kind of made me want to smile, I held back my desire and refused to give in to that sinful temptation lest it might have made her not take me seriously. Which she already didn't.

"I want all of it cleaned up before I return home. I believe I've made myself clear enough."

"Oh really! that's not the way you talk to your kiddo sissy who takes so much pain to get your outfits arranged. That hurts!" she made a real sad face half-jokingly.

"I intended it to. Now, did you get me?" I asked sharply, though I had given in to my temptation of smiling and was almost smirking at her.

"Yeah, yeah. Your dress is hanging by the wardrobe door in my room. I like today's especially. Good job, me." She patted herself as she started to clear the mess she had made of my room.

"Thanks, though, kiddo. I love you." I ruffled her hair like I used to when she was too young and had a bob-cut which made it all the way more fun.

"Love you too, Eea! And stop being so serious. Get a life sissy!" she shouted from the room behind me as I ascended the stairs.

#

The outfit was really *amazing*. Sometimes I wondered where on earth did, she get *that* talent from. It indeed was pretty amazing. No doubt she was the hot sizzling Diva of her college. The matte olive lipstick seemed too much when Hella insisted that I added it to complete my look, but it pretty much went with the look. I gave her extra points for that one at least.

I shifted my gaze from the back mirror of the car to the side one. As I adjusted the seat to fit into it and as I pulled the seat belt and hit the gas the engine burst to life, and inertia of rest jerked me back a bit before I was set into motion for the place where I had always dreamed of working and was now finally working at.

It was like a dream come true, had I not always dreamt of it? And being so young, and achieving it to measures that were possibly more than anyone of my age I should have been the happiest person alive. At least a happy person alive... but no, it was still there, that feeling of emptiness.

I drove past the Broadway and St. Louis' Street crossing toddlers holding their mom's fingers lest they might get lost, young children pushing their skateboards with bags full of books which might have seemed useless burden to them, and wondered what having a *life* would *feel* like.

Crossing the last traffic light and taking left from Garner's field side I drove into the parking of the lavish building of the world's one of the most famous publications. The valet greeted me with a smile as he helped me with the parking and my stuff. I walked slowly to the stairs and unlike every day when I used to take the elevator which would drop me directly to the thirty-second floor where my cabin was, I took the stairs and headed to the ground floor. I climbed with a steady pace lest tripping in my extra half-inch tall stilettos which Hella was too adamant about to let me wear flats and ruin her extra special look. Climbing the stairs in those heels seemed more difficult than the run I had this morning to the hilltop and God! Finally reaching the ground floor gave me no less pleasure than looking at the rising sun.

I took a deep breath and walking out of the main door of the reception, I stood there, taking my own time before I finally turned around to face the skyscraping building of one of the specimens of large successes that the world had witnessed in the past few decades. The words leaped from the digital board that hung to the left of the building displaying in large the salutation by which that success was owned... '*Muses and Caerus Publications*'. It was strange that after all this while since I had been working here, it was today that I really cared to look at this place so clearly and ponder upon the idea and desperation with which I once had *wanted* to be where I so luckily was now. But still, Hella's words somehow refused to leave my mind. And though I knew she hadn't said it with even half of the seriousness with which I was perceiving it, I couldn't help thinking why all of it felt so empty just because of someone who never even meant what I thought he did. I stood there, staring blankly at my hollow achievement as it still rang through my mind,

'*Get a life...*' it's just that I didn't know,

how...

CHAPTER TWO

ZAYNE

"Can you just explain it to me once?" I couldn't hide the anger which had started to rise after what happened today in the gym.

"I don't think that I need to explain anything to you..." How could she be so casual about it? Like it didn't matter.

"Sorry? I deserve to know Jacey, I... at least you should've told me that..."

"Told you what Zayne? It isn't like we two are really dating that I need to tell you everything that goes on in my personal life. And even if we were dating even then I wouldn't be answerable to you" She was right, we weren't dating, but I thought it was something more special than just 'normal'. How could I not care when I...

"But I guess we were at least close enough that you could have at least *said* or *talked* about it once."

"We are, but that doesn't mean I've got to tell you all that I do or everyone that I talk to."

"Goddamn it Jacey, stop fucking me over, once you say you find me to be the most special one you've ever found and a few weeks later you find your 'most special one' in someone else, that too from someone of my company? Who are we trying to fool here?"

I didn't want to sound too harsh but after what she did, I thought it was justified to demand answers.

"Damn. Jesus Zayne, will you stop being so mad. See? That's the problem with you Indian guys, you people believe in 'true-life-long-love'. Take it easy, and stop creating an issue out of nothin'."

I just didn't know what to say after that, she had left me speechless. I had always been a person with a bad temper and God knows what I wouldn't have given for her not being in front of me right then lest I didn't know what I would have done. She was wrong, about most of the part about Indian guys and that 'true-life-long-love' thing. But was she really wrong about *me* being like that? I didn't know... but she was wrong, very wrong.

Or probably it was just my fault? That I had started thinking and feeling too much too early. But I just didn't know why it had to be like this... I knew I was too young but I couldn't help if I felt too much or too deep.

I logged in to my snap account and scrolled the pictures we had together, there was something so magical between us, anyone in the room could've told it, I didn't know why it had to be with her when it didn't with anyone else earlier, not here, not back at home. I didn't know why it had to be with her when all of it was nothing but some kind of distraction for her.

She was smiling through the camera with her baby blue eyes crinkling at sides and I... I looked like some dumbass who had forgotten that one was supposed to smile when being clicked. Really, was it so casual? Because for me it surely wasn't, but what seemed pretty evidently, for her it was. I knew it wasn't wise to go over it again and again but how could I not? How could I've helped myself?

I pulled off my vest and smashed the phone into the side pane, I knew I'd regret it later but I didn't care, I needed something, anything. The screen was still lit up with our happy faces peering through it. I turned the shower on and cold water sprayed on my face, washing away unshed tears which found a crevice to vent out, hidden behind the water. I could feel the heat of emotions that had started to rise in my ears, on the back of my neck as my whole body physically ached from the heavy emotions which ruthlessly pressed themselves upon me. My vision blurred, the last thing that came before my eyes was the red fluid running down my hand. Darkness took over my senses before everything became numb and my vision went completely blank.

#

The light in the room was so bright that it made me squint. My head hurt like someone had smashed it hard. It felt like I was walking through burning coal as my whole body felt like it was on fire. I lifted my left hand to see an enormous white bandage wrapped around it, stained at places with red and yellow. I remembered seeing the blood flow, but nothing after that. Something felt very wrong, like I didn't remember all that had happened. I knew the look of puzzlement must've given me away cause when my elder brother walked in to the room with a tray full of proteins and medicines, he held his hand up, gesturing for me to not say anything before I could even speak something.

"Smashed the mirror in your anger. Doc said you'll be fine. Just don't work out for a while. Maybe take some time off from the gym."

Zeeshan was always too distant and cold, but I knew he loved me, he had been my father, my friend, my brother, everything. He always did more than he could in the capacity of being my elder brother.

"I can't it's okay. I'll be fine!"

"For just a moment will you stop acting so immaturely like you always do? When will you show some sense? Just a little. Is it too much that I am asking from you?"

"It isn't easy, am trying, it's just... it was too hard last night, it never happened before..."

"I know it's never happened before and that's why I'm more afraid Zayne, I am. You can't just go smashing glasses and bleeding the shit out of yourself every time it happens."

I wondered what he meant by *every time...* because I doubted it'd ever again.

"You've got to keep your nerves junno, you're growing, life is not always easy. And at the pace you're going, I can see you ending up in a hospital in the next few years, with broken limbs." He punched me playfully on my arm. I realized how strong he was. I held his hand before he could pull away,

"Seems like you've got a lot of experience," I smirked at him.

"You bet." He laughed, pulling his hand free.

I wonder what I would have done without him. He wasn't too playful kind of a guy, maybe the responsibilities which came upon his shoulders at such a young age had made him so, but I could see how hard he tried not to give in to whatever it was that bothered him so much. I wish it could've been different, and I wished I could've done something about it.

"Did you love her?" his voice rang in my ears,

"What?" I was astounded.

"The girl, whose picture your phone showed when you smashed it to the pane. Did you love her?" he said nodding towards my damaged phone which lay dead by the bedside.

"I... I just felt a lot for her... I don't know what it really was and how it really is, it's just that... I don't know..." I looked out of the window where everything looked so vibrant and lively like the earth was smiling while *Allah* graced her with his mercy and *love*. I wondered if I'd ever be able to feel that way again, if I'd ever be able to feel *that* kind of *love*.

"It's okay, you'll learn. Happens. Just don't hurt yourself Zayne, that's silly. No one's worth that much." I looked at him as he took the empty tray from the bedside table and got up to leave.

"I didn't do it because of her..." I looked in the direction of my broken phone.

"...I just, I was missing the feeling of her..." I pointed towards the direction of the sky where stars had started to show up, not many though, but I guess it was enough to make him understand who I was talking about.

"It's okay. She'll always be there. Just have patience, she wouldn't have liked this." he turned slowly and I heard the door close behind him. There was a finality to that shut, I didn't know how, or why.

I pulled the duvet aside which had been stained a little from my sweat, and put my feet down on the floor, it seemed like I was suddenly a hundred kilograms heavier than before in just a night.

My bodyweight seemed too heavy for my feet to carry. Slowly I supported myself to the window with my right hand. It took a while for the heaviness to fade away. The city looked so pretty from here, everything so divine. So beautiful, just like her...

I remembered what Zeeshan had said, "You can't just go smashing glasses *every time* it happens.", I wondered if it would happen *even once* again, let alone *every time*. Though I wished that it did happen, I wished to fall, and to be fallen for. Because...I didn't know... I just wished for it to happen. Though I didn't know,

If it ever would...

#

I didn't know if I could have faced her at the gym or not, the memories of last day's events were all too fresh to not think about it, to even *pretend* that everything was normal. I still remembered how she had come in running through the doors, leaving them dangling open while she ran to beat the minutes she had been running late by. It never failed to make me smile, and the pictures of last week...they didn't fail to overwhelm me. It was strange. Strange that how you could feel everything for someone and them, not even a hint of reciprocating feelings. It was annoying, it was... unfair.

I rode past the last traffic light and taking left from Garner's field side rode a mile straight to Willard Street and took left. The guard was off duty today, so I had to open the building before the people started to pour in. I was pretty on time, some old men just drove in when I was unlocking the door, punching in the code, and putting in the key to turn on the power supply. The housekeeping had been here before. I knew because the gym was cleaned up and the dustbins had been emptied. I kept my duffel in the cabin and headed for the locker room. It had been cleaned too, I switched on the exhaust fans and opened the ventilation windows. Strolling back to the cabin to have a look at the empty place, except for few retired people working their old limbs to keep them going, and wondered how much Kratos' Fitness Training Centre had meant to Zeeshan. It had been three years ago that he took on the responsibilities and pains of staying away from the family to help them keep goin'. I was angry at him, for pulling me into all of this with him, but how could I not? I missed home, I missed our family. But I loved him. And I knew it wasn't easy for him to do that to any of us. But he had to. I didn't blame him.

The door swung open and there came the ever so chirpy Liz. Liz had been at Kratos' since the start. Even when everyone thought that there wasn't even a hell of a chance that an Indian fitness center would hit-off in this part of the city, she believed in it, in us. What had she not done to help us in any way possible that was within her power, sometimes even out of it. We never could have thanked her enough.

"Hey Zayne, how're you doing?"

I stood frozen for a while; it seemed ironical, because I didn't know the answer to that question myself.

"You fine?" she asked, concerned.

"Oh yeah, absolutely. Just short on sleep." I fumbled a bit, giving her a silly smile.

"Um hey, Liz..."

"Yep?"

"Can I ask you something?"

"Shoot."

I suddenly didn't know what was it that made me say that to her, but she was nearest to what I could consider as family so far from my family. Maybe that intimacy made me wanted to talk about my tumultuous thoughts with her.

"Is it wrong to feel too much?"

She looked up from the screen, astonished. The sudden change of topic confused her.

"Well...um,"

"You know what? Fuck it. I am sorry," I waved my hand in the air clearing out imaginary commotion which was not so imaginary in my head, "it's fine if you don't want to answer that one. I'm sorry." I said, feeling stupid.

"No, it's nothing like that. It's completely fine." She said with a sorry smile on her face.

I looked into her eyes for a while and turned away, to walk to the balcony. I could see happy couples down there from here. It just made me want to feel it even more desperately. Only, I didn't know if I ever would.

"It isn't wrong to feel too much Zayne...'

I turned, shocked. Liz was standing beside me, watching in the direction I had been looking just a while ago, she knew what I was looking at. She eyed me with her eyes full of softness that I remembered seeing in that of my sisters'.

"...it isn't wrong to feel too much, it's just wrong to feel too much for the *wrong* person."

I looked at her in awe, a tear might have fallen from my eye, cause I could feel her hand very delicately brushing it off my cheek,

"How am I supposed to know who's wrong, Liz?"

"I don't know how you're supposed to know the wrong one but..." she held my hands softly into hers. I could feel calluses on her palms from lifting weights.

"But?"

"...but you'll *know* when the *right* one comes along." I looked at her, confused, not knowing what she meant.

"Give yourself time Zayne, it'll be fine."

"Did you know?"

"Know what?"

"Did you know how I felt for Jacey?"

She nodded slowly.

"Did you know that it wasn't the way she felt for me? Not even near?"

She sighed and the way she did, I knew she knew. I knew she could see through both of us.

"Why didn't you tell me?"

"I... I just couldn't."

"Why?"

"I don't have every answer you want me to have Zayne." She pulled in a deep breath and then letting it out she finally said,

"Somethings, you've got to learn yourself." She walked back inside and retired to her work.

I couldn't help wondering what it was that had to be learned, but more than that I couldn't help but wonder how the *right* one would feel.

I wanted to feel it...

That feeling...

That *right* one...

I *wanted* to...

Desperately.

CHAPTER THREE

IANA

The day had started to exhaust me already, there seemed to be a heap of work piled right next to my desk when I reached into the cabin, five minutes late... busy watching... introspecting. I wondered if someday too much of this thinking might even cost me my job! Jesus! It'd be too high of a price to pay for *getting a life*. I definitely couldn't afford such an *expensive life!*

I turned on the computer, the screen came to life, asking for my employee ID and password. I couldn't help while a smile crept to my face and a single tear rolled down from the corner of my eyes accompanying it while I typed in the password, I just wondered how silly it seemed now when all of it was over, but for some reason, this was a small piece of it I was still clinging to. My fingers still trembled as I typed in the last *y* of the *infinity* in the password space.

The screen came into focus at complete brightness with the official logo of the company, I brushed my fingers across the screen, tracing the lines of the perfectly designed piece of imagination which had been so beautifully brought to reality. What would have I not given to be where I was sitting now... I knew what I wouldn't have... but somehow it didn't matter now, because what I wouldn't have *given* was anyway *taken* now. Breaking the unpleasant chain of thoughts, I pulled my chair closer to the working station and set off for the day's work, it was going to be a long day, there were a few new submissions, some were from pretty young writers, I liked it. I remembered how I had once been there too, and smiled to myself. I went through all of them meticulously, making sure I did justice to their effort. One of them particularly caught me off guard, the title itself made me gasp, '*even if it's not meant to be forever...*' it was by a writer who was yet in her college but wanted to become an author, damn! so impressive. The raw and genuine emotions that leaped from her work made me long to have that way with words too, it made me want to express myself that way too. Unconsciously, I had started to envy her. It was kind of funny, how I envied someone, who a while ago, I didn't even know existed. I read the proposal letter and the sample, and unlike the conventional response period of a minimum of fifteen days, I immediately wrote back to her, showing our interest to work further on the project, and added the manuscript to the database to be considered by a senior editor.

I went through other works and proposals, considering which could be taken up for further evaluation, sending humble apologies to ones which won't fit into the requirements, knowing that each apology slaughtered some hopes attached with the simple electronic mails. But I couldn't do anything because that's how it went. That's how you *got* things in this world. Working, struggling, trying, falling, getting rejected, still not giving up, and trying again. *Trying again*...my head got stuck there, trying again... how could I? Try again?

The clock buzzed at 12:35 p.m. I turned the sleep mode on and stretched my arms and raised my head to peep to the other working heads in the room. Almost everyone had been out of their cabins for the break, only, not Eign. He was standing next to my cabin, like always, waiting for me to join him to walk together to the cafeteria. I had first met Eign when I had joined Muses and Caerus as a junior. He was supposed to be my mentor, guide me, which he did. But more than that, he was a friend, a friend I could never thank enough to have. He had been working with the firm for five years, started too young I guess, because he wasn't much older than me. He had been there when I was going through that terrible time last summer. All the while, he was there, just a call or a text away, never judging me for having such breakdown. I secretly adored him for that and I guess he knew it too.

"So, how many submissions today?" he asked zealously, typically Eign.

"Quite a few."

"Anything super amazing?"

"Um...yeah, this one from a teenage girl, all the way from India."

"Wow, that sounds interesting, tell me more about it."

"Well, I don't know much, but as far as the proposal letter suggests, she's just 19, and has just started college."

"Indians are damn talented I see," he smiled at me an all-teethed grin.

"Umhm, they pretty much are. But it's pretty rare you know, someone so young being so motivated about their passion, and more than that, knowing their way about getting them. It's just amazing."

"I am not surprised though; I have an example in front of me." He said, pulling the chair in front of me at the same spot that we occupied every day in the cafeteria.

"So, what's the story about? I mean the title?"

"Unfulfilled love..."

Eign rolled his eyes at me and watched me closely, narrowing his eyes to give a sheer look of disapproval.

"GOD! That's why you like it? Jeez, Iana no, please. Don't get yourself back there."

"Damn, no Eign, this one's different. And I am not getting myself *anywhere* near it. So, chillax. The title, it caught me..."

"What's it?" he sounded genuinely curious.

"'*even if it's not meant to be forever...*'"

"Wow! That is some heavily creative shit I see. No wonder why it attracted you so much. Would've caught anybody's attention."

"I know, right. I hope the senior editor likes it. I see the potential in it."

"You see a story you *want* in it." I was taken aback by his answer, I didn't think him to be capable saying anything like that. But what scared me was that he wasn't completely wrong. Maybe yes, I did *want* that kind of story for me... but no, I didn't want mine to have that ugly comma in my story, I wanted my story to be whole. He saw me go silent and suddenly changed the topic,

"Anyway, you look amazing today!"

"Oh, thanks." I tried to contribute to his effort towards making it less awkward.

"Think Hella's been perfecting her skills quite a lot lately."

"Seems so." I smiled at him.

"Hey, I and Sasha are going clubbing this eve after work, want to join?"

"Uuuuhhhh, sorry, Hella's got some plans. Have to be with her. Next week maybe. Have fun though."

"Oh! Cool, yeah. You too."

My phone buzzed; it was mom. I looked at the screen for a while and then eyeing Eign, excused myself to the empty corridor as he nodded at me gesturing for me to go on and take it.

"Hey mom, how're you?" I let out a short breath.

"Am fine. How have you been? You didn't call after we last talked. I was worried."

"Sorry mom, I was just a bit occupied, I'm fine, nothing to worry about."

"You're coming home this *Diwali.* aren't you?"

I had completely forgotten about it...

"Oh what... yeah, totally!" I tried to hide the hollowness in my assurance.

"It has been a while since you've been home. At least come on *Diwali.*"

Her voice failed to hide pain and expectance, which she surely didn't want to show.

"I'll try mumma, let's see how it goes. Talk to you later. Bye. Take care."

"Bye, take care, and call soon." I heard the line go still and waited for a while before I walked back to the cabin.

I couldn't and didn't even want to go back. After whatever happened last year, I didn't know if I could have taken it. I had been trying to avoid everyone, even my family. Though I knew it wasn't fair to them, but I needed it for myself.

I let out a deep sigh and looked at the tiny figures moving down the streets, from the window. I didn't know how much time I needed; I just knew I needed a lot of it. Taking a last look at my phone screen, which showed 1:10 p.m. I turned it off again and running my hand through my messed-up hair to settle them down a bit, I walked back to my cabin, to get the day's work done.

#

It took a while for even an elevator to descend thirty-two floors. I looked out of the glass wall as the elevator descended, seeing things zooming in to their actual size as I neared them, making me feel like being pushed back into the realities of the enormous world. The elevator finally came to a halt, the screen displayed basement, and the automated voice chanted 'basement one'. The elevator dinged as the doors flew open and I walked out of them. Nearing my car, I saw the last person I could have expected to be here at this time. She looked up from her phone screen and seeing me closing in, turned the phone off and tossed it inside her bag. I got near the car and unlocking it I eyed her with a look that must have been sufficient to make her answer my unspoken question.

"I was going through the list of these 'to-do-things-to-get-completely-over-shitty-breakups'," I eyed her sarcastically even before she could complete herself, giving her my deadliest look but she ignored it as she indulged into a soliloquy.

"Hear me out before you get mad at me," she said, stopping me before I could even say something, like she knew that I was about to argue against it.

"Okay, shoot." I surrendered. I was not in the mood of putting up a debate with my only family in this huge unknown town and also, I was too tired after the day's work.

"I did find some pretty interesting stuff, but one that particularly caught my eye was getting into a specialized training program for body toning." I looked at her, making a face that might have looked disgusted because her features tightened.

"Seriously? You want to enroll me in a specialized training for body toning program?"

"Not you, us." She said too cheerfully, giving me a goofy smile.

"You can do all that you like for yourself, but one thing that's for sure is that *I* am not being part of any kind plan you have. Not this, not any."

"You surely are, big sister. Take left." She grabbed my hand and turned the steering wheel to full nine o'clock. It startled me as the car swayed and we almost leaned out of the windows. I screamed at her, trying to get in control of the wheel.

"What in hell are you doing Hella! Where are you headed for?"

"Well, *we* are headed towards Kratos'"

"And what the hell is that?"

"The best fitness training center down the city and the better part is that it isn't even far from your office. So, you can very well hop in for your sessions after getting off work." She stated these facts as if they would make it any better for me to be dragged to such a place by sheer force and not taking into account my unwillingness.

"As if that matters," I said rolling my eyes at her.

"It does. And oh, I even checked its rating, it's got a fucking four-point-five stars. Now that's some real serious shit you see."

"I don't care, I am not going there, or for that matter anywhere..."

"Yes, you are. You've got to trust me with this as you do with your clothes. Please."

I saw a look of genuine concern in her playful eyes which were dead calm now, and I hated it. Because it always meant me giving in to her whims and fancies, which though were better than what I could ever think of, but were always at the times when I perfectly wouldn't want to do them even for a million dollars. But I had to do it, all of it. Not for a million dollars, but for her.

"Fine!" I rolled my eyes at her, "for how long will you make go through this torture?"

"Three months at least, after that we'll see to it. Stop!"

"What? We're here?"

"Yep!"

I looked at my left and lifting my head higher I couldn't help as gasp escaped my mouth. Okay, with bare honesty, this seemed some real amazing shit. I felt a tinge of excitement finding its way through my annoyance.

The parking was almost full! I guess I should've expected it, after all, a fucking four-point-five rating ought to have meant something grand. The elevator clicked open and we hopped in, Hella pressed the button to the first floor. There were two more girls with us, one was in her casuals, the other one looked pretty much ready to hit the weights straight away. She was pretty. I realized I had been staring at her unconsciously, her almond eyes with baby blue shade and her hair tied in a perfect bun like they had been arranged by some expensive hairstylist made her look crisp and...hot. She looked confident and so familiar around to the place that it gave me an impression that she had been training here for a while now. It would've been no surprise to know that half of the guys in the gym might have already been crushing on her and the other half would have already made move in some way. The elevator opened into a big hallway, walls filled with tough motivational quotes as faces of fitness stars, wet with sweat, peered at anybody who walked in there. The girl, with blue eyes, moved out ahead of us, carrying an attitude which said *after me girls*. The old me would have taken it on her ego, but now, I didn't really care, I stood back and let her walk out a good few yards away before I finally exited the elevator. Hella led the way to the reception, following the girl who had been walking just ahead of us. She stopped briskly, making me and Hella almost bump into her. Hella managed to stop few steps behind just in time to not go crashing into her. Though we two collided, but it was something I could've happily taken rather than making an awkward scene even before I practically joined this new jail for me. I pulled back and followed Hella to the reception desk, rubbing my head which had bumped into Hella's, she didn't seem to care much. While I rubbed my head, I noticed the girl giving an ice-cold look to a guy standing near to the receptionist. It looked as though the two of them knew each other enough to have something bad enough happen for the guy to have earned *that* kind of look. I turned my eyes in the direction of the girl's gaze to find who the lucky winner of such an icy glance was. My eyes landed on a tall, lean and extraordinarily hot guy, the kind whose picture could've been a perfect fit for an erotic novel cover. He might have been six feet or so. He seemed to have been working out for long enough to have that kind of body. I was just looking at him when his eyes met mine for a brief while before I abruptly turned my gaze, embarrassed, caught stalking a guy whom I wasn't really stalking, but he might have thought that I was stalking. We reached the reception desk, and though the guy had departed to talk to someone in the nearby waiting parlor, he was still awfully close in range to make me feel uncomfortable after that short meeting-of-eyes event.

"Hey, this is my sister, Iana, and I am Hella. I called you this noon." Hella, punched me lightly on the arm to bring me back from my wandering. I suddenly turned, blank for a while, then gaining my composure I smiled as I replied to the blonde girl behind the screen,

"Uh-Oh, hi." I smiled, embarrassed a bit. She might have noticed my discomfort because she gave me a warm and humble smile to ease me out a little. And it did work. Even though it felt more like 'it's-okay' smile

"I want to turn my baby sister into a super-hot Greek goddess, Liz," Hella said with a smirk on her face, talking to the receptionist like it was some kind of ambition that she wanted to fulfill with the help of one of her old friends which, in this case, was not so old until it was fine to count five minutes of acquaintance in that category.

"I see," the girl, Liz as I figured out was her name, said with the smile still pasted on her face, nodding in my direction. Damn, Hella had been working on it seriously. I thought it was just some shitty thing that'd slip off her mind soon. But for now, as it seemed, it was serious than that. And I doubted it was not going to go off hook before a while. It wasn't good news. I let out a sigh while I thought about it.

"So, I thought you might be able to help me out with this one," Hella said, smile left her face and voice sounded different, taken over by her *'let's-talk-business-now'* tone.

"Sure. It'd be a pleasure to help you with that." Liz replied with her constant humbleness.

"So, may I know how shall we proceed with this?" Hella asked.

"Yeah, Zayne will tell you more precisely about it." She nodded, calling past us into the hallway, not too loudly. While she did that, a six-feet tall, all muscles and shredded-bodied figure crossed us to take his place near Liz, only stopping briefly to shake hands with both of us formally.

"This is the owner and trainer of Kratos'. Zayne." Liz looked at him and then at us. "He will answer all your questions miss Hella, and miss Iana."

The guy looked in my direction when Liz said my name, and I could feel the heat rising to my cheeks while I felt the color filling my face.

It surely wasn't too comfortable to have the first person to encounter be the very guy who caught you stalking him.

I looked back modestly at him, trying to act as normal as I could, hoping that he didn't notice the blush on my face.

"Hi, nice to meet you." Hella, nodded at him formally.

"Pleasure." He replied in his husky voice.

"I wanted to talk about a specialized personal training program for my..."

"Um, sorry to interrupt, but I... maybe Liz can show me around? I just wanted to have a better look at the place while you two talk about the technicalities?" I said, interrupting Hella. Zayne, seemed surprised just for a brief second, and then gaining back his calm look, he nodded at Liz.

"Sure," Liz said, as she crossed Zayne and came out from behind the desk and led the way towards the hallway.

"See you guys in a while," Liz said, while we moved down the corridor, putting some distance between me and Zayne.

It was only after a while when I was sure we were pretty much out of their larger vicinity of earshot or even sight, that I relaxed and finally breathed. I suddenly realized I had been holding my breath for those entire twenty long minutes for which he was there in front of me.

CHAPTER FOUR

ZAYNE

I had been keeping a look at my watch, it was almost time for her to arrive. And I surely didn't want to face her, at least not right now. I was about to leave when I just for a while stood back, I didn't know why. But just at that very minute elevator doors swung open and there came Jacey, with her *'I've-got-this-shit'* aura. Her perfect gym bun bobbed as she took confident steps in my direction like she wanted for me to see her on purpose.

But it didn't matter, for it wasn't her who caught me off guard. My eyes traveled past her as I saw a quiet and calm figure emerging out of the elevator. She walked delicately like she didn't want to create more than necessary effect on the surface. But there was something more to it. Her walk didn't look hesitant. She was pretty confident. I couldn't help but look at her in awe. The formal suit suggested that she had been to work, but she looked too young to work somewhere to dress so formally. Her shade told that she and the other girl with her, surely a few years younger than her, probably her sister, were Indians too. There was something very different about her. Her olive-green shirt and trousers looked crisp and gave her an edge which despite her delicacy made her look beautifully flawless. The olive lipstick marking the beautiful contours of her lips looked just as perfect as everything else on her. I saw the way strands of her black hair escaped her messy braid and fell on her shoulders, making the curves of her beautiful face stand out even more vividly. She chwas beautiful. There was something in her calmness that made me want to keep looking at her, talk to her.

I was so lost, watching her that I almost didn't notice Jacey giving me an icy look which radiated sheer disgust and annoyance. I didn't care about it though, not now. But she must have seen it. She saw the way Jacey looked at me for I saw her eyes follow Jacey's gaze in my direction. And for a very brief moment, our eyes met, before she turned them away, embarrassed. She

might've thought I was stalking her, which I realized I was. I wanted her to stop and not to turn away her gaze, to watch into her eyes for a while longer. Though, I sensed that she was embarrassed by the sudden eye contact. I could tell because her cheeks had turned red and blush had rose to her face making her look even more beautiful. Though I didn't want to, but I walked the other way into the hall, pretending to talk to someone, when she neared the reception to talk to Liz probably. I didn't want to make her any more uncomfortable than she already was. But I made sure I had her in my vision range. From what I could make out from her face, it was pretty much evident that she had been dragged here quite involuntarily. Suddenly I felt nervous, I didn't really know why. Maybe the idea that what if she didn't really come here again, made me feel so. I felt stupid thinking like that for a complete stranger. For a girl, I didn't even know existed five minutes ago. For a girl I might not have even seen, had I walked away to avoid Jacey. But a deeper part of me knew that I was grateful that I didn't.

I was just trying to work my way through all my messy thoughts when I heard Liz's voice from a distance, calling me, to probably fill in the new clients with the proceedings. I felt a tinge of excitement as I closed in on the distance between her and me.

"Zayne, this is Hella," Liz said nodding in the direction of the younger girl. I shook her hand formally.

"...and this is Iana..." I heard her name. It was beautiful, just like her. I took her soft hand in mine, it was warm, the fingertips were callused, like she had been holding something for long. We shook hands briefly and I tried to hold her gentle hand for a while longer before she finally pulled it back. For the time that her eyes were locked on mine when we touched for the first time, I felt a strange tingling of current run through my bloodstream while my heart pounded faster inside my ribcage for the whole while I felt the heat of her touch against my skin.

"Zayne." I said smiling at her.

She didn't say anything, just nodded with a hesitant smile. God! She was even more beautiful up close.

"He'll fill you in with the proceedings," Liz said to the younger girl. Different. Interesting. Younger sister bossing around elder one. I couldn't help smiling at the thought.

"I wanted to enroll my sister for a specialized personal body toning program." Said the younger girl, Hella, as I had figured out was her name.

"Oh, I see," I said, looking at her once again.

It was her sister who did most of the talking all this while, I didn't get to hear even a syllable out of her mouth. It was quite after a while that she finally spoke, asking Liz to show her around. I was pretty much sure that it was possibly more to not be there so close within my vicinity for so long than really wanting to see around. She must've gotten too uncomfortable about that eye contact over Jacey's icy look. I nodded in Liz's direction in affirmation. They both stood up and headed towards the hallway. I saw her back until she was completely out of sight. And a pang of desperation hit me right through the chest as the longing to hold her back and make her stay right here in front of me, took hold of me. It was a completely new feeling for me. I couldn't remember feeling this way *ever* before for *anyone*. Not even *Jacey*.

#

I walk to the third floor where my next training session would begin. Though there was still good half an hour before that. I simply pulled out my phone and opened my Instagram, not really thinking I typed the name in the search bar... *Iana Singh*. The app buffered a bit before it displayed a list of all the Ianas out of the seven billion people out there. I scrolled down through the list, scanning each one, trying to find her. I could find nothing which even remotely matched what could've been her profile. Two or perhaps three profiles did seem like they might've been her, but I wasn't quite sure. So, I gave up on my quest for searching a complete stranger girl whom I had just come across. But something nibbled away at the back of my mind which made me restless and jittery. Something that I couldn't really chuck out of my head even if I tried. It was her. Her eyes, her footsteps, her hair falling carelessly on her shoulders...everything made me not being able to forget her. Rather, it made me remember her more vividly. *Wanting* to remember her just like she was here in person.

I heard footsteps approaching and shut my phone and was just keeping it away, expecting the next batch to spill into the room when what I had least expected happened. Jacey walked, pushing past the doors, a cold look spreading across her sexy features.

Jacey was beautiful, but not in the most innocent way. She was that badass kind of beauty that made one wanting to be careless. But the moment one let their guard down around her beauty they'd be done even before they could know what hit them. Her beauty was sensual, dangerous, nothing like *her*...

She came glaring, straight at me, and before I could gain my composure and push aside my surprise, she pinned me to the wall. I was too surprised. Out of all the million possibilities I could have thought in my head, I didn't see this coming for sure. She kept her hands on my chest, all her force in her strong arms, and bringing her face very close to mine she hissed in my ear, "Silly little boy, well wait... not so little though, but does it matter..." she looked straight into my eyes, "you can have all the feelings in the world you want to have for me. But let me get this very straight, there isn't a chance in the hell that you've got a shot here. So, better keep this thing straight for yourself as well as..."

I could feel the anger rise to my face as I pulled her hands away with force, turning her swiftly and pining her in the place where I had been, just a few moments ago,

"Listen to me," I almost glared at her, "you didn't want to talk about it, fine! You acted like you didn't care, leaving all those questions unanswered, fine! But now, you don't get to make an issue out of this. You wanted to leave this matter alone like nothing fucking happened, so now just stop creating a scene out of it." I could feel the acid in my words as they came pouring out from inside, probably pushed by the suppressed anger.

"You..." she opened her mouth to say something but before she could, I pressed her back harder into the wall, my grip still firm on her hands. Drawing my face so close that I could see right through her baby blue eyes I opened my mouth to speak. To my surprise my words came out like I was hissing at her, "*You* don't get the last say here, Jacey, no. Not this time." I released her hands and turning around, I walked straight outside, not waiting even a moment to see the look on her face that followed my last words to her. I had never imagined, the day we had met first, that this would be the way we'd end up. But I didn't care, I wasn't feeling hurt, surprisingly not. I was just angry. Not at her. Well, yes at her too, but also for something else... for feeling too much for the wrong person.

#

I could see the lights, sparkling at a distance, and for once I wished to be out there... doing anything. I missed *Ammi* now more than ever. Even though it had been too long, I still remembered her smell, her smile. Everything. It all felt just like yesterday.

I was so deep in thought that Zeeshan's hand on my shoulder startled me. I didn't know for how long he had been standing there, quietly beside me, but I knew that he knew what I was thinking. He let out a deep sigh and ruffled my hair, just like he used to when we were kids,

"It's okay Zayne. It'll be fine. She loves us. She always has, and always will." He said in his usual elder-brotherly tone.

"I know, I just miss her too much sometimes."

He just nodded. I had noticed him; he had gotten quieter. It was like something was eating away at him. But he wouldn't let it out to me, and that hurt. I wanted to be there for him, but he wouldn't let me. It was like there was this invisible wall between us, always. One which I ached to break through, ached to cross desperately to reach out to him.

"What's the scene with that girl?" he said, pulling me out of my head.

"You talked to her?" I turn to look at him.

"Not really, just a short chat doesn't count as 'talking'," he said, still looking out of the window at the distant sky, darkness.

"Damn *bhai*, why!"

"What? It's no big deal. It wasn't even a talk."

"It's nothing, forget it. Let it be."

"You smashing glasses and breaking your phone surely isn't nothing."

I sighed, not saying anything. It wasn't nothing *then*. Butit was surely as good as nothing *now*.

"I just wanted to make sure you're fine. At any cost." He looked at me, a look of concern made his young features look aged.

"Am fine. It's okay. It isn't her fault."

"I know, but it isn't yours either."

"Let it be." We stood there, looking straight into the dark sky, at the stars.

"*Bhai*," I shifted my gaze in the glass to meet his eyes in the reflection.

"Do you ever kind of just randomly feel drawn to a complete stranger and even though you've just met them, not even met, just seen them moments ago, does it happen that you feel like you want to just hold on to that person?" he looked at me for a few moments, it looked like he was trying to figure out the most suitable answer to my absurd question. He opened his mouth to say something but then maybe changed his mind and just muttered instead.

"Umhm,"

"I...I just don't know, I was just kind of wondering how it might feel, to... you know, stumble across your *right* one like that. Like you know..." he cut me off and I tried to hide the eagerness and desperation in my voice while I asked him these absurd questions which gave away my inner turmoil.

"It's okay, Zayne. It happens. You'll be lucky to feel that way someday, to really be able to hold on to that person..." his eyes met mine and I could have sworn that I saw sheer hurt in them. He turned away quickly, waving away my any chance to clearly make out what it really was.

"...Though I doubt it's worth that trouble." He laughed at his own joke, trying to ward off the tension that had built up. He turned to walk away and I just looked at his reflection crossing the room and holding the door open when he paused,

"Everything need not *be* right, it should just *feel* right to you," he didn't wait for me to answer. I heard the door close behind him.

My mind involuntarily drifted to her. That hesitant smile came into my vision while millions of questions swam through my mind.

I didn't know if it was right.

Was it really, right?

Was she the right I had been searching for all along without even knowing what the definition of right was until... she walked out of those elevator doors?

I didn't know, not everything.

I just knew that

She wasn't just right,

She *felt* right.

CHAPTER FIVE

ZEESHAN

I saw him standing and looking into the void, again. I knew he was missing her. I missed her too. For once, I wanted to let him know it, but I couldn't. I knew he was having a tough time. And after what he did last night, I knew he wasn't taking it too well. I wished I could've told him that it was fine, it was going to be alright. But I couldn't tell him something which I myself knew wasn't true. I wanted to tell him, that love was not always the pretty road, the way it's portrayed in movies and songs. I wanted to tell him that there was a lot more to it, a lot more to sacrifice, a lot more to pay, a lot more to *lose*.

But he looked different today, not grieving over Jacey. It was like suddenly she was far too less important to think about, in front of something that had occupied his mind. I didn't know what it was. Nor did I care to know. I knew it was too early for him to grieve too deeply. But I could *feel* the road he was going down on. And God! Who would've known better than me how much I wanted to hold him back and push him there at the same time. I wanted him to feel it, to live that life. But I knew it asked for more than it ever gave. And I didn't know if he would be able to take it. After seeing him lying unconscious on the bathroom floor, knuckles split, bloody, it was like I could feel my heart come in my mouth. I couldn't see him like that, but I didn't get to control that. I couldn't control it for myself, how could I for him? I just wished, and hoped, that he didn't get to pay the way I had to. He didn't get to *lose* what I lost to destiny.

CHAPTER SIX

HELLA

I knew getting enrolled into a personalized fitness training program was the last thing Iana would've wanted to do, but I knew some deep hidden sporty part of her would like it. And maybe she would soon start to take it much more seriously than just a burden imposed on her by me. But I had to do it. It had been almost a year now since that thing with her ex happened, she had definitely become strong, or at least she tried to show that she had, but I knew there were issues, still, that she was facing, alone. And I knew she wouldn't let it show, she'd always been hard-headed. I admired her for it. But this time I had to get her out of it. I had to let her know that life wasn't over, that she was so young and beautiful, and smart. That she was all the more worthy for all those amazing things and people out there, far better than her stupid asshole ex. Enrolling her in this program was the best thing I could think of to at least distract her from that shit for a while. Maybe being around sexy and hot demigod type guys would do some magic (though I found it quite unlikely) but still...maybe. I thought I already caught that hot trainer stalking her. The way he was looking at her, God! Only I knew how I controlled my laughter and barely managed to keep my formal tone on. But damn, I already liked the idea of them together. He was cute, and hot, and sexy, and tall and far far far faaaaaaaaaar better than Iana's shitty ex-boyfriend. Though I knew it was too early to think anything like that but still, I couldn't help wondering about the possibilities. Ghosh! I loved her so much; I just wanted her to be happy again. I wanted that carefree and insane sister back;

I wanted the girl from before all that shit happened back. And I knew I'd get her out of it. No matter what.

"What are you thinking?" Iana's voice startled me as she crossed the room to sit next to me.

"Trying to fly with one eye open," I shot at her sarcastically.

"Hahaha, quite funny." She gave me a cold look

"Am trying to complete my assignment, only if someone would leave me alone..." I tipped my head towards the door, to let her know that she had outlived her welcome in my room.

"With no papers and pens and paraphernalia, I doubt it's the best way to try getting any assignment completed."

"Para- what?" sometimes she could be a complete nerd which meant you'd literally have to use dictionary to be able to make out the shit she threw your way.

"Forget it. Tell me what you are *really* doing." She asked, narrowing her eyes at me.

"I was about to start it just the moment..."

"...I dashed in?" she said, shooting her one eyebrow up.

I nodded at her sarcastically.

"Damn, Hella. When will you start being a bit polite, you know you'd be grounded..."

"Yeah, yeah I know I'd be grounded had I been back in India for this shitty behavior and blah blah but who cares! The fact is that we are not in India and this is how I am." She rolled her eyes at me. I knew she couldn't argue because she herself was this belligerent once. And I knew that part of her was still alive, just buried somewhere deep down there. And I was pretty determined to get it out.

"Fine!" she held her hands up in surrender. She never fought me. I knew how much she loved me. It had been her who took my side to move here for my higher education. Had it not been for her, I would still, have been stuck somewhere in a college where I wouldn't have even wanted to go. And for what I was sure about was that I was going to get my witty and humorous and bellicose and awesome old sister back.

"Eea," I called for her just as she started to leave for her room.

"Yep." She paused and turned, but didn't cross the room to close the distance between us.

"Did you see that guy at the center?"

"Which center?" she asked a bit confused. A look of recognition spread over her face after a while as he mind figured out what I was really talking about.

"Um, nope."

"Don't tell me you didn't even see that hot trainer!" she rolled her eyes at me.

"Stop! Hella!" she tried sounding annoyed, unsuccessfully trying to hide her blush that had started to color her cheeks as if she had remembered something embarrassing. That too at the mention of that trainer, welllllllll, it was a start for sure. And I was pretty excited about it.

"What! See you're blushing!"

"Damn no! it's just that," she stopped short

"Just what?"

"He caught me looking at him and he might've thought I was stalking him, which I wasn't really, but then he suddenly caught me looking at him. It might've looked...." She seemed so conscious and cute that it made me want awwwwww at her.

"Wait, you *were* looking at him?" I asked her, raising my eyebrows.

"No. I mean yes. But not like that." I might have looked confused cause she stopped for a moment took a deep sigh, as if trying to gain her composure, and spoke with more precision, like she was trying to clear herself from some kind of accusation.

"I was looking at the girl who was with us in the elevator and was just admiring her when she walked to the reception side and she gave this very icy look to someone, and I swear Hella that look was so damn murderous and cold that I couldn't help my curiosity of finding its recipient and it was just then when my eyes followed her gaze and landed on him that he caught me looking at him. God, it was so embarrassing." She did seem pretty embarrassed about it.

I could figure it out from her voice.

"Eea, just calm down, it's no big deal."

"Yeah, I know, that puts a *full stop* to all your 'there's-a-possibility' thoughts. Okay?"

"Not really," I smirked at her gleefully.

"Hella, I guess she was her girlfriend or something because it seemed pretty serious. So, stop being unreasonably optimistic." Ghosh! For once why couldn't she talk *normally!* All that heavy philosophy and vocabulary sometimes made my head spin. No wonder why she was so bad with guys even though many guys had a big crush on her.

"I am not saying anything!" I held my hands up in surrender this time. She rolled her eyes at me and was just about to slip out of the door when I added,

"I am just not putting a complete full stop there though," she stopped, astonished.

"What?"

"Am saying there's not a complete full stop there, maybe an *ellipsis,* I guess. You never know."

She didn't say anything, but I could swear I saw a faint smile as the door finally closed behind her.

It was nice,

the idea of ellipsis...

IANA

All this fitness program thing seemed so shitty to me. I didn't even know why did I agree to it in the first place, but then it wasn't about me, it was about Hella. I loved her too much to not let her have this one. I knew what she had on her mind when she wanted me to go there. I just didn't know how could I have made her understand that it wasn't about finding someone new to feel okay. It wouldn't make any difference if I dated anyone new until it was me who really did the job of moving on and not care about what happened last year. I wanted to let her know if she already didn't, that I was trying. That I didn't need any such distractions. But she was too adamant. And it didn't seem that bad after all. Maybe I could've found some hot guys to stalk at least. It'd been a while since I took interest in guys anyway. I didn't know if I wanted to even now. But trying wouldn't harm.

"A duffel with so sexy pencil skirt doesn't go. Where was Hella when you were being part of such a huge catastrophe?" Eign spoke from over my shoulder, almost startling me off my feet.

"Damn, you scared me shitless." I sighed, trying to calm my racing breath. "She was the one who push me into it."

He gave me a confused look.

"She enrolled me into a personal fitness training program. She thinks it'll help me..." I had to take a deep breath before I could speak. It still scared me to say it out loud. It was still too much to be able to speak about loudly, "...to get over."

He nodded as if he understood even half of what I had been going through. But then, he was there, he did know if not understood, how difficult it had been, it still was for me.

"Damn, I love this girl. She's just amazing!" he said with a bit sincerity and a lot of excitement, trying to change the subject to something less awkward.

"Seriously?" I raised one eyebrow at him.

"Hell yes. She loves you Eea, for once just let it go her way, she knows pretty much. You've got to agree to that." I did. But I hate to admit it.

"Fine! Besides, that's the only option, at least for now."

"Way to go..." he sounded unnecessarily extra excited. I almost smiled at him.

The elevator dinged and just before we parted ways for our cars, he nudged at my arm like he always did when he had something very serious to say,

"You know we love you, don't you?" he looked at me as if wanting to hear my obvious answer aloud.

"I do."

"Don't be so tough on yourself, Eea. Just let yourself get out of it. Don't rob yourself of all those seconds and thirds and a lot more chances that you are worth. Please don't." he didn't wait for my answer, I guess he knew I didn't have one. He just went straight, not stopping to say goodbye even. I watched his car roll out of the parking and wondered since how long had I known the fact myself which he just said out loud to my face. It's just that it wasn't that easy, and that I was trying. I needed that chance; I wanted to give it to myself. But I didn't know how... maybe I did know. It's just that there lie a big ellipsis.

#

I looked at my phone, 5:10 p.m. it showed. I still had exactly twenty minutes to change and be at the cardio before my session began. I dashed to the changing room, took a quick shower, and made sure to put my formals meticulously folded lest they might get ruined, all thanks to the gym rush. I walked out wearing the outfit which Hella had planned out with extra effort and care, to make 'perfect first-day impression' she had said. I didn't even know if there was any such thing like that, but "who cares?" she had said and waved me off.

I looked at my phone, five minutes to 5:30. I walked slowly to the cardio section. I could see him standing there. He was so tall and muscular that it was practically impossible to ignore his presence. Just before I could open the door, I was almost taken aback...

Heartbreak songs? Seriously? In the gym? What the fuck! I would've literally puked. I tried to straighten up my features, trying my best to not show my sheer annoyance and disgust. I opened the doors and greeted him with my sincerest smile. Well, the sincerest smile I could manage with that kind of song playing in the background.

"Evening, sir." I shook his hand, which he had extended before I had even said anything.

"Zayne, call me Zayne." I simply nodded with no intention of changing my acknowledgment to him.

"What is it?" I was a bit confused by his question. I surely hadn't expected it.

"Um... I'm sorry I am not very sure about what you're asking." I tried to sound polite but I guess my voice came out more like what-in-the-hell-you-expect-me-to-answer-to-that-random-question.

"I mean you don't look too comfortable." I guess he wanted to say that I looked pathetic with all those awkward expressions on my face but decided against it because of it not being the politest way to talk to a client and a girl, even if she was the girl he had caught stalking him the first day she came in to talk, but still.

"Uh-oh, no. it's nothing like that...it's just the...um," I tried to search for words that wouldn't make me sound like I was throwing a tantrum. Damn! I didn't know why I even touched that topic. I could've simply said it was fine. Before I could say anything, he broke the awkward silence, as if reading my mind,

"The song?" he looked at me with... I don't know, tenderness, or maybe I was just hallucinating or something. There could be no way on the earth that he could be thinking anything like that for a girl he practically just met once. Not even really *met*. Thanks to me, I ran off, to avoid it. Shitty me.

"Is it?" he asked again softly, as if trying to remind me that I wasn't alone there.

"Oh, well no, sorry I was just... I mean yeah. Yeah, the songs I mean." I stumbled over the words. Shit. I couldn't have made it any worse.

"Even I don't like them." He said, with a look that said he meant it and wasn't just saying it out of courtesy.

"The guys play them by themselves, so we don't really tell them to change, you know, whatever they like. But to be honest, even I kind of find them annoying. They suck."

"I'm not annoyed," I said defensively, "It's just this isn't the right place or time. You know, I mean the songs aren't bad, it's just that they're bad for the moment."

"Yeah, I know. Sorry."

"You don't have to be." Though I wasn't sure what he was sorry about. For saying that the songs were bad? Or maybe for making it awkward for both of us? Or maybe both. I settled for the latter one.

"Do you like them?" I asked him, not really knowing why I was even doing that. I could've just moved on with the session, not really caring. But I didn't know why I felt like wanting to know more about him.

"The songs? Sad ones you mean?" he asked.

"Not really sad, solemn ones maybe."

"There's a difference?" he asked, amused.

"Not that it really matters."

"It kind of does I guess, if there really is some." He said, trying not to smile too much at me. I guess he didn't want to look stupid by doing so.

"Hm."

"I just listen to them when am alone, at night. They hit, you know, different. I like feeling them."

"That's depressing." The words were out of my mouth before I could've even given them a second thought. A look of shock crossed his face.

"Why, I didn't..."

"Oh, not like that, it's just..." shit. I was making it worse than it could have ever been. Damn.

"...all those emotions are too amplified at night, and facing them bare, with those songs," I pointed in the direction of speakers which played *moral of the story by Ashe*, "it's kind of brutal."

"Well, we can't ignore them forever, can we? So why not face them at their ugliest..." he said, making small circles with his feet, keeping his eyes fixed on them. I knew he was right. I had done it ample of times myself. I just thought it was too silly, but now, after talking to him, I didn't think it was.

"Fair enough," I said, holding out my phone with dial pad open to him. He looked confused for a while and then took it from me and typed his number on it.

"I guess I was supposed to do just that?" he said, handing back my phone to me.

"Could you've done anything else?" I smirked at him sarcastically. I surely was getting more comfortable than I was when I'd entered to that grand welcome song.

"I guess not." he smiled shyly.

"Get started, shall we?" I looked at my phone. We were fifteen minutes late.

"Oh, yeah, sorry."

"Are you always so sorry?"

"Yeah, no. I mean no, just sometimes. I mean not really until...ugh...sorry." he let out an exhausted breath as he gave up and we both stood there laughing hysterically.

I looked at my phone screen once again, we were twenty minutes late for my session, but I didn't really care. It felt strangely nice. It was the first time since what happened last summer, that I actually was feeling up to talking with someone. Like *really* talking and not just because I was supposed to do so.

"I guess we shall get started?" he said, trying to sound business-like but failing miserably.

"Oh, yes."

"We shall start with light, first day you know, let's start with running?"

"How much?"

"What?"

"I mean for how long?" I said, explaining myself.

"Oh yeah, sorry, twenty minutes, we'll do complete cardio in an hour and then some abs. Sounds fine?" I wanted to laugh out loud again when he said sorry, but decided against it.

"Pretty much." He escorted me to the treadmill, the blue-eyed girl was already there on one of them, sweating like she had been there for more than an hour. She shot a look of sheer hatred to him past me. I knew it was something pretty bad to be like that, and one thing that I was sure about was that I didn't pretty much want to be part of any of it. So, I quietly went on to start with my first training session which I had already been late for.

After completing the one-hour cycle of cardio, I looked like I had bathed in my own sweat, not to say anything of the smell and the utter mess that my hair was.

I wiped the beads of sweat off my forehead as I searched through the glassed rooms and corridors for sir to move on with my next session, the strength training. Well, I just didn't know why I called him sir, but I couldn't do anything against my deeply entrenched habit of calling almost anybody who taught me, sir or madam out of sheer formality and respect.

I was just crossing one of the random rooms, finding the place too difficult to decipher when he suddenly appeared from nowhere, like one of the jump scares in those horror movies, and almost knocked me off my feet.

"Wow, shit."

"Sorry, I didn't want to startle you," he said, helping me regain balance, preventing me from falling on the floor stumbling.

"Oh, it's fine. I was just looking for you,"

"Me?" he asked questioningly,

"Oh, I mean looking for you to know what to do next? I mean am done with the cardio, so what's next?"

"Oh okay," a look of disappointment crossed his face like he was expecting something else.

We went on for the rest of the session not talking much.

The workout was tiring, but I felt nice. The sweat and stuff, it didn't feel like a burden like I thought it would. In fact, it felt nice to do something different, something which I hadn't done in a while. Now I wasn't feeling as bad as I was when I had first walked in.

I walked to the changing room and after a quick shower, I changed into my formals, to my relief they weren't crushed. Though my hair refused to give in to any of my efforts at making them look a bit sober and not a complete mess like I had been at some kind of war but it was fine. I walked out, carrying all my stuff and took stairs instead of the elevator, I didn't know why. Maybe because I suddenly kind of got more health-conscious to the slightest of bit. I was just about to land in the parking when I saw him coming upstairs, it wasn't the place I had expected to cross him, but then it was none of my concern even if seemed pretty awkward. He smiled at me and stopped, he just stood there looking at me for a while, all the playfulness and carefree look from earlier, gone. He looked exhausted, but I didn't care to bother him with that, I didn't quite know but I was guessing it might have been something to do with that girl in the cardio section. He held out his hand to me and I suddenly realized that he had been holding it out for a while, I smiled embarrassed, and took his hand for a brisk shake. "Oh, thanks." I said, chewing on to my lower lip, embarrassed.

"Done with the day? Liked it?"

"Not bad at all I must say." I said, trying to smile more freely, maybe to get his spirits up a bit, I didn't know why I even cared about it, it wasn't like it was any of my business, but still, I just felt like I *wanted* it to be my business. Strange. I hadn't wanted anything like it for a while now.

"Oh, I'm glad you liked it."

"Thanks," I said nodding.

"See you tomorrow?"

"Umhm," I said so softly that I doubted he would've heard.

I didn't know why I was just sitting in my car seat and staring at his number on my phone screen. I wasn't sure if I should do what I was thinking about, but surprisingly, I wanted to take this chance, I didn't know why but I wanted to.

I guess maybe just to know what possibility that ellipsis held.

CHAPTER EIGHT

ZAYNE

I saw her walking to her car, I wished I could just ask her to stay some more, why, what for, I didn't have a reason, and even I didn't know why I wanted it in the first place. I just knew I wanted it. I walked to the cardio room and suddenly her smell hit me straight in the face and I felt an ache of nostalgia, which was kind of funny because I barely knew her to feel so intimately about any of it. But I couldn't help. I replayed the events of the evening over and over in my head and each time I saw them sliding past in front of my eyes, I could feel myself there. I could feel the *rightness* of the moment. I looked past the crowd in the gym, at the sky, it had started to get dark and I could see the stars had started to come out, despite the commotion that was there in the room, I could still hear her voice clear in my head, the song that was playing, which miraculously got us to talk, something that I had been wanting so bad, unconsciously. The speakers were blaring upbeat workout songs now, I guess they were in Latin or some other language like that, I couldn't make out the words, I didn't care to. I could still hear the song that was playing when she had entered the room, in my head. I wish I could go through that moment again, and again, and again, and ever again. I looked at my wristband, it was already nine. I had to get done with my workout, I couldn't let things with Jacey mess with me. But it wasn't really Jacey who was actually messing me up, it was her.

I washed my face to clear my head before I hit the weights. Zeeshan was there, training his clients. Most people had left, only the late office personnel were still working out. Even they'd leave in an hour so, it was already near closing time.

"She came in for the first session today?" Zeeshan said, from behind the smith machine, supporting a lady who had been our client for long enough to know us both personally, I didn't know her much, I could not even remember her name.

"Who?" I asked, not sure whom he was talking about. For a moment I thought he might as well be asking about Jacey but no,

"That young Indian girl, who came to join in the day before. Did she come?" Iana, he was talking about her. I wondered how he knew her; he wasn't there when she had come the other day to enroll or more precisely to get enrolled, by her bossy sister.

"Yeah, how do you know? I mean you weren't..."

"She works under one of my friends' dad. She called in to make sure that she was alright. Just worried about her."

"Oh,"

"Hm,"

I couldn't imagine how we both had been so strangely connected all this while, and how we never really knew about it. Strange, how you could know someone, be connected to them all the while except not really knowing them until one day you actually come to know that you've known that person or at least have been connected to them in some way all along, funny.

My phone beeped, I could see its screen light up and then go back dark again when I didn't check it. I put on my wrist supports and got back to my chest workout. I had been distracted quite enough for the day.

I had just finished my last set of chest press when Zeeshan gestured for me to turn off the lights and come downstairs. I looked at my wristband, it showed ten thirty, it was already half an hour past the closing time. The gym was empty, Liz had left an hour ago, it was just Zeeshan and I in empty the place. I went on to change and pulled on my sweatshirt just before leaving the changing room.

We locked the center and while on our way down to the parking I checked my phone, which I had almost forgotten about until just now. There was a text from an unknown number. I didn't open it straight away, random texts from unknown numbers weren't new, people often texted or called to inquire about fitness programs or customers whom I planned diets for, it wasn't like there was anything much interesting about any of them. I clicked the phone shut without seeing the text and putting on my helmet, and adjusting the side glass for one last time, I hit the race and pulled onto the calm highway route. I just wanted to be away for a while, from all the chaos. I wanted to be away, alone.

The town looked so pretty from here, the lights, just like diamonds. I didn't remember how many times I have been here, but no matter how many times it might be, the place always brought the same relief. It always felt nice to be back. I sat there on the edge of the low sidewall, my feet dangled sending some stones rolling down the incline of the hill, making a soft rustling sound in an otherwise calm surrounding. I pulled out my phone and scrolled aimlessly for a while. After a while when I was just going through my playlist a text popped up. It was from the same unknown number. I wouldn't have cared to look at it if only the notification hadn't read 'try these, you'll like them'. I tried remembering any stranger who might send me something that I might like, at this hour of the night. I couldn't remember anyone who it might be, except... her. I pulled out of Spotify and clicked into the texting app. And tapped the latest text,

Try vibing to these, must add to your late-night vibing playlist.
It was sent two minutes ago. It was her. It was *her*.
There was another one, from earlier when I was working out.
Fomenta
Damn, it was her playlist, the songs, the ones that we were talking about in the gym.

I opened Spotify, it still had my playlist on display, I pressed the search bar and typed in the first song on her playlist. The music filled in soon enough to take over the silence of the place. It was nice, it had been long since I heard something so beautiful *and* Bollywood. The music was just amazing, I wondered from where did she get to know about it. I wanted to put the song on loop but I went back to the playlist and looked at the next song, and searched for it, it was a less famous version of a very famous old Bollywood song. Damn, her taste was pretty good. I could picture her putting on her earplugs and getting lost in them, not caring if others around her liked the same kind of music or not, or judged her for liking that kind of music.

I could hear the words, I could feel them, and even though they were sad songs, I felt happy. With all those tiny lights in the distance of the city hustling eternally despite knowing their inevitable transience, and all those stars above, which twinkled so calmly but had been there since eternity and would be there till eternity and with her music, which was filled with so much more than one could ever possibly feel all at once, I felt strangely happy. A sad kind of happy. I remembered the first time I saw her, small yet warm brown eyes, dark messy hair. I had noticed her trying to set them down, trying to make them look a bit less messy. And only I know how bad I had wanted to hold down her hands and tell her how beautiful she looked in those messy hair. I had wanted to tuck that loose strand behind her ear every time it escaped and fell across her face. I didn't know how could I feel so intensely for someone I had known for just two days, but I did, feel. It all seemed like a miracle, *she* felt like a miracle. She felt so much like the feeling I had been craving for all this while. She felt *right*.

I didn't know if it was right or not, and surprisingly, I didn't care. I remembered her face, twisting in annoyance just before she entered the cardio room this evening when the heartbreak song was blaring at its loudest. I remembered her soft but strong voice when she had asked if I liked them, I remembered the bare sarcasm in her voice when I'd told her that I didn't really like them but I heard them at night. I could see her face when we laughed together, over me fucking up our first conversation by saying sorry more than anything else. It was new, I had never cared to observe anyone so much before her. I used to observe Jacey, but not like I observed her. I didn't care to see if her hair were a mess or not, though they never were but still. I never wanted Jacey to just stay in the same room even if we didn't talk or even looked at each other. But

I wanted it with her, I wanted it with Iana. I wanted to feel her presence around me. I remembered what Liz had said, and what Zeeshan had said, and I could feel it now, I could sense it through me while I heard the songs which seemed so intimately close to her. All the songs felt like she was trying to tell something through them whenever she insisted to hear any of them, waiting just for that one person to pick up the hints and decipher them and reach out to her and tell her that they understood. Everything that the song said, and everything that *she* wanted to say through them. I checked my phone, it was two in the morning, the city was asleep but the lights were still there, the stars were still there, and her music was still playing in my ears, the sound of her laughter from yesterday accompanied the melody of the music. I looked at her number on my screen and wondered what she might be doing right now, wondering if she would be thinking about me the way I was thinking about her. I tried to look for any clue those digits might give me, hoping they would somehow make her appear here, right in front of me. I saved her number, not knowing what to do with it. I checked in on her playlist once again just before pressing the home screen and going for the text app. I let out a deep sigh, I didn't know what I wanted to say, because honestly, there was so much of it that I wanted to.

I started typing, then backspaced.

Then again, backspace.

And again, backspace.

It was far more difficult than I thought it to be. I shut my phone, exasperated, and just sat there, listening to the voice that felt nothing like hers. I wondered if she could sing, if she would ever sing for me. I would want to hear her.

I just didn't know why, but I was imagining all sorts of wild things, all kinds of pretty pictures.

None of them made sense, especially the fact that I could picture none of them without her.

I sighed and looked down at the text I had been trying to structure for the last half an hour, I didn't know how fine it was or whether it was what I really wanted to say, but then it wasn't completely false either. So, before I could backspace it for the zillionth time, I pressed the send button. The song, the one which was playing right now, became my favorite. I heard the singer take the last soft note before the music faded until it died completely and there was complete silence, I pulled over my helmet and taking a last look at the skyline and the lights below, I headed back home.

ZEESHAN

Jeane had called in the day before, it had been long since we talked, but it was nice to hear from her after a while. Though it wasn't completely for checking-upon-an-old-friend, still, it was nice talking to her after so long. She had called in to ask for looking after some new client who had apparently enrolled that day. It was some girl who worked under her dad in his firm and was good friends with her. I must not have been there when she might have come to inquire. Although, I said that I would take care of it, I didn't get the chance to catch up with her. I had been caught up. It was almost after a year that Easha had called. I didn't know how long it lasted, how long we talked, but it still felt so much like the old times. She sounded so much like her, all the comfort and softness and care, just like her. I wondered how it would have been, had it been different. Different than how it was now. I wished I could stop those moments. Even though I didn't want her to get upset about it, but I did want to hold her and tell her everything, how it was.

Nobody knew about it, except us. And honestly, the only person I wanted to talk about it with was her, but I couldn't. I knew it hardly mattered now, but the thing is it never gets easier, does it?

My phone chimed as I opened the can of soda that I had almost crushed in my hand, it was Jeane, wanting to know if I checked up on her friend. Iana, pretty name.

I tried to catch up with her today, but she had left before I was there. Zayne had looked after her session though, I guess it was fine anyway.

I'd look after it some other day. I needed time to sort my shit out first. I just hoped I got over with it soon. I couldn't let it drag me down again, but then I didn't control it. Nobody does. Because even if you know something isn't right, but if you have your heart at it, then there's no going back.

The heart wants what it wants.

CHAPTER TEN

IANA

It was there in the morning when I woke up. But I wanted to take my time before I really said something which I wouldn't want to regret later. All the way up to the top I couldn't for once, stop thinking about the text that lay unread in my inbox. I wondered if he liked them or not. I loved those songs, and if he couldn't vibe to those, I guess there was a big full stop already. Would there be really? The full stop? "Of course, not" I could hear myself whisper, I didn't know what or how I really felt about all of it, but I did know that it had started to affect me already. Even If it was only the slightest bit, still it did. I had been thinking a lot about the ellipsis thing, surprisingly, in the way Hella had said.

The sky was still dark, it still looked like it was midnight and I wouldn't have known it had I not been coming here for weeks now at this time. This place knew so much of me, my tears, my self-talks, my self-coaxing. I wondered if I'd want some of my good moments with someone here. It was the first time since last summer that I was really thinking about the *possibility* of *someone* else. I didn't know if I wanted someone right now or not, but I was considering the idea of bringing him here and giving him another playlist to listen to.

I checked my phone screen. I was four minutes earlier than yesterday, cool. I sat on the low-walled periphery, the place which gave the view to the pretty streetlights. My breath was still heavy from all the jogging, I could feel the sweat evaporating from the back of my neck as I felt a cool brush of breeze against my skin.

I took a moment to myself before I clicked open the text, I didn't know what I was hoping for, maybe something like 'it was good', or 'they are nice', I didn't really know,

Damn, where the hell did you manage to scavenge that treasure from. I guess I gotta get into your mind and steal that little treasure. Lol.

I wasn't sure what I was expecting, but this was surely a bit over the top. Though I didn't know if he really meant it or was he just trying to be nice, but I guess I would give him extra points for trying to sound interested and decent. I wondered how many times he would have typed and backspaced the text before hitting the send button. I looked at the words, wanting any hint about the legitimacy of the emotions and reactions they were typed with. I looked at them expectantly, as if they'd dance out of the screen of my phone announcing the extent of their honesty. I didn't know why, but I really wanted him to mean what those words said, I just did. I wiped my phone screen with my thumbs where the mist had settled, my fingers typed away the words.

Smart people, smart choices, you see XOXOX

I didn't want to be too verbose like I usually was, I guess that was the basic etiquette. To not be too much before you even knew someone. And surely, I couldn't get all over with whatever words I wanted to pour out, with someone I was still getting acquainted with. I looked at the short text and thought of numerous other ways I could have possibly structured it in and the numerous ways those numerous ways would have resulted in. It was awkward and somehow different, I wondered what had changed so much to make me *care* about it. Because I hadn't, for a while now. But I did now, I guess.

I didn't know if I'd ever want to share the intimacy that I felt at this place with anyone. But right now, I wanted to. I imagined bringing him here and have him listen to another one of my favorites while we stared into the oblivion of those dark skies only lit up by human optimism that we tried to look for, in the celestial bodies. I didn't know why, but the sky had always been that one place where I could imagine floating away whenever nothing seemed to work out. I imagined sharing all of this with him. The sky, this place, the playlists. These were little secrets that always excited me. They were way more intimate. It was kind of funny though, how millions might have heard those songs and how millions of more would have liked it. Yet how they were so intimately personal. We shared this intimacy now, it was like I had trusted him with some kind of secret of mine, and I wanted to entrust him with more other secrets of mine. It had been a while since I really wanted to do it. But honestly, I had been thinking a lot about the idea of the ellipsis, just like Hella had said. I wanted to know all the possibilities they held, or maybe I just liked the *idea* of knowing those possibilities. I didn't really know if I was ready or not. It hadn't been easy, and it still wasn't, but I could feel myself breath now.

I imagined how it'd be, to have him here by my side and stare at those lights while the city slept in the darkness and we danced to our beats. I had always wanted it, like in the books. That perfect romance which usually ended with a full stop, but I didn't want mine to be like that. I didn't want a full stop. I wanted it to be open, even if it meant it wouldn't be complete, but I wanted it to have all those possibilities for which a full stop wouldn't leave a space.

I looked at my phone screen, it was time for me to get going. Just before descending, I took a long final look at the twinkling whites of the city as the cool air brushed my sweaty hair across my face. It was still a while before the sun would be up, but the darkness, it felt too calm to let go of, I couldn't help smiling, thinking how it was always the light that personified and symbolized hope, but how I didn't want someone to be my light. I wanted someone who could dance in the darkness that we all carried in ourselves, who could look past that blinding veil and see all that it hid, who could see the colors that darkness contained within it to look so opaque and dark. I knew it was aberrant, but who cared if I could have someone who looked at it the same way that I did.

I put in my earplugs and walked down slowly, the slope supported and saved my effort as I walked downhill.

This time it wasn't my usual jogging playlist that played in the background. I clicked into Spotify and scrolled through my playlists as I hit and played *Fomenta*. I liked it, but it had been a while since I heard it. I didn't know why but I suddenly wanted to cherish it a bit more, it had started to feel all the way more intimate and personal like a little secret long forgotten but resurfacing after a while. It might be so because now I shared this secret with someone else too. Maybe because now it wasn't just my secret. I walked down slowly, not timing myself for the first time since I had started coming here every morning. I just walked, trying to match my footsteps with the rhythm of the words, not music, but words. I had always belonged with them more, the words. It wasn't *Kelly Clarkson* this time though, it was *Snakehips and MØ and Birdy*. The songs I had always thought had so much more to them but didn't know if it was only me who thought so. I couldn't listen to them for long. I didn't know what changed today though, or maybe it wasn't *something* around me that had changed but *me* who was changing. I was just confused, but I didn't care, not now. Maybe those ellipses were what I unconsciously really cared about now.

I walked into the open curtains and lit up kitchen. The sun wasn't up yet but surprisingly, Hella was. It was so not like her. I walked into the kitchen, pulling my hair free from the messy ponytail which had been holding them back from coming all over my face. I could feel my body aching from lactic acid as my cells screamed and worked for respiring aerobically but of course, failing due to lack of oxygen. I kept my phone carelessly on the countertop as I filled myself a glass of water to hydrate and help my cells a bit by allowing better oxygen supply as water cooled my body down. Hella strolled into the kitchen just in time to take a seat at the countertop and carelessly peep into the screen of my phone to see another song from Fomenta playing.

"New playlist?"

"Nah, just haven't heard it in a while."

"I know, haven't seen you listening to it for a while."

"Yeah."

"Slow one huh? Not like your usuals." She said, looking at the cover of the paused song.

"Umhm, just felt like trying something different." I tried sounding casual, trying to hide the blush that had started to creep across my face at the thought of sharing this little secret with someone now.

"I see. Good." She said, giving me a sly smile.

"Forget it. How come, you're up this early?" I tried changing the topic, though I really did want to know about the reason behind this unusual event.

"I was just having a hangover, mild headache. Got up to take some Advil."

"You got drunk? Seriously Hella?"

"Not really, it was just one beer."

"You don't want to get into a problem with mumma, do you?"

"Oh c'mon, it isn't like am getting drunk every now and then, and my dear big sissy, just grow up. And get a..."

"Life, yeah I know. But getting drunk and then having to wake up mid-sleep to have an Advil is surely *not* the kind of life I'd ever want to get."

"Yeah, you'd wake up mid-sleep to run up to the hill to look into the darkness. Won't you?"

"I surely most happily would!"

"Damn, will you ever stop being so boring, who'd say you're the elder one when I've got the whole sense and fun too." She said giggling, like it was funny.

"Thank god I didn't get what *you* define as sense and fun."

"Hahaha."

"By the way, how was your first day?"

"What?" I got confused by the sudden change of topic as it dawned upon me what she was asking about, "It was cool. Why didn't you come? I thought you'd said we both were joining."

"Yeah, I just had to catch up with Jeane. I'll join from today; I'll be there before you hit the weights." She said, winking at me.

"Jeane? What for?"

"Nothing special, she knows the owner, so just wanted to know about the place some more, and build up some Indian acquaintances," she smiled at me coquettishly.

"Zayne? I mean she knows her?"

"No, the elder one, Zeeshan." I didn't know, maybe he wasn't there when I went. I smiled at Hella. Damn, she is smart. I knew it was silly of me to think so, but seeing her sitting there carelessly, dangling her feet, I couldn't help wondering when did my little sister grow up so much.

"I see." I moved to the cabinet and pulled out an Advil for her.

"Here, have this and no getting drunk from now on."

"What, are you going to ground me like a mumma now?"

"I won't, but just so you know, I very well can." I tried sounding authoritative, though, with that smile on her face, I knew I was failing miserably. And I couldn't help smiling at myself.

"I saw it."

"Saw what?"

"The text, last night." She said, playing with her glass of water, distracted, trying to avoid meeting my eyes which were fixed on her now.

"Which text?" I asked though I knew the answer even before she blurted it out.

"From him, I saw it. I was there, just to..." she let out a deep sigh, "...I wanted to see if you were okay. It just came in then." I looked at her blankly, not giving anything or any sign which she so desperately tried to gauge. When she couldn't make out anything from my face, she continued,

"I saw it, and I can't tell you how happy I was,"

"It's nothing like that, it was just the playlist that I shared."

"I know it might not be, I'm just happy. Am happy to see you coming out of it. Eea, I love you." She could leave me speechless sometimes, and I hated it when I didn't have words to back me up. But I loved her. And I didn't care if I failed with words for expressing it, because I knew she knew it.

"I love you too." I pulled her into a tight embrace before finally breaking away.

It was when I started for my room to get ready for work that she spoke softly,

"Fomenta." I turned, failing to make out what she had said,

"Sorry?"

"The playlist you shared with him." She looked me straight into the eyes, with all her warmth flowing through me, I could feel a blush rising to my face as I couldn't manage syllables out of my mouth. Instead, I just smiled, which was enough for her to understand.

#

"You look...different."

"What kind of different may I ask you mean?" I tried sounding naïve.

"I don't know, just more cheerful I guess," Eign said, not in an offensive manner though, just as a matter of fact. I knew it'd be hard to hide it from him for long. But making out something was different even before it really was, well, it was something I surely hadn't thought him being capable of.

"Oh, nothing much, trying to indulge into self-love I guess," I said punching him playfully in the arm, trying hard to avoid any further questions regarding something which I myself didn't know much about, "Now that you say I look different, I might as well believe all that shit in theory wasn't for nothin'. I guess it works."

"Um, guess so," he said, to my relief not pushing the topic further.

"So, how's your training program going?" he sounded pretty curious.

"It wasn't that bad, I guess it's okay."

"That's progress." He said, smirking.

"What do you mean by progress?" I turned to look at him from my computer screen, which I had been avoiding till now.

"Well, let's see, days ago you thought it was possibly the shittiest thing and was wondering why you agreed to it in the first place, right?"

"Kind of, yeah," I said flatly, knowing where this conversation was heading. It was heading to its factual conclusion of Eign being statistically right and me, refusing to back off, so for my contentment, being metaphorically correct.

"And now you think it wasn't *that* bad. So, I guess we both can see the spike in the rating graph, can't we?"

"Okay, fine!" I rolled my eyes at him.

"You know I'm happy for you, Eea." He said, sounding genuinely concerned, which I knew he was, but it kind of annoyed me too.

"God! Why can't you and Hella just not be so dumb and sentimental about everything that we talk about? It's so shitty you know. It doesn't make it better."

"Dumb?" he raised one eyebrow at me.

"Well okay, let's leave that dumb part, but the rest of it?"

"Yeah, sorry. It's just, we care about you and it's just we want to..."

"See? That's what I exactly mean, bringing it over, every time we talk, I know you care, but am very sorry it just makes it worse." I was surprised at my bare honesty, I hadn't talked like that to anyone, ever. And even if I had a lot bottled up inside me, I surely didn't want it to come out like this. Especially on him,

"Duh, I'm sorry. I didn't mean to..." I felt really bad, but not guilty. It wasn't all false.

"No, you're right. I'm sorry, we shouldn't do that, I just didn't know."

"No, it's okay."

"Wanna hang out? After work?" he said, trying to change the topic and drive out the tension that had built up between us.

"I don't see a reason to rather not. So yeah." I really wanted to make up for this one. It wasn't like we had a fight or anything. But I just felt bad about being too straightforward when all he really wanted was to make sure that I was fine.

"Cool then, seven?"

"Uh, eight maybe? I don't finish up until seven-thirty, so after that?"

"Oh, yeah, sure. I completely forgot. You've got his 'work-in-progress' board on you." He said, laughing at his own joke. Though I felt it was pretty lame, I didn't mind joining in. We were just trying to have one of our moments when my phone buzzed. I was expecting a text from him, and I was so surprised at my disappointment when it wasn't him. Mumma. Eign looked at the screen and gave me a smile as he shook his head.

"Aunty has such perfect timing." He said laughing out loud trying to hide his questioning look. Which I knew I'd have to face later. I knew he hadn't failed to notice that look of disappointment on my face. I gave him a dull smile as I pressed the answer button before the call went to voicemail,

"Mumma, hi. How're you. I was just about to call you, sorry, have been caught up in work."

"Tell me a time when you aren't," wow, being sarcastic was a talent that moms are born with, but then, you don't expect them to shoot it out straight when they've been hearing from their child who is miles away, after four days.

"Sorry," I couldn't think of anything else to reply with.

"How're you? How's Hella?"

"Am fine, and so is..."

"We've got your bookings done for Diwali, you're coming home." Now, I must say that though I knew this call was going to be somewhat of a hassle, I surely didn't see this coming.

"Mummy, why. You know I still haven't got my leave sanctioned," the fact was that I hadn't applied for it yet, "and I don't know if it even will. Plus, Hella's got assignments to finish, why can't we just see how it goes until we figure things out here. Why do you want to push things so fast?" I could sense irritation slipping out of my mouth even though I didn't want it to.

"Very well," she sounded pretty dismayed, "do as you like, you always have, so do it now."

"Maa," I sighed, I didn't like seeing her like this. I knew she missed us, but I just needed time, I couldn't tell her that it was me who didn't want to come, neither could I tell her that I wanted to stay away from that place for a while. I couldn't tell her that I didn't want to come back *home,* "I'll try, I promise. Just don't push it like this. I'll talk to Hella and see if we can make it, okay?"

She sighed, she wasn't the kind of woman who let her emotions show even if she might be breaking inside, she had always been strong, and though we knew how much she loved us, it wasn't often that we got to hear its honest manifestation aloud.

"We miss you, both of you." I could feel the tension in the air subsiding into something more somber.

"I know, am sorry. I love you, mumma." I thought she'd say something back, she just stayed silent, for a moment, a minute maybe, I don't know. But then she just hung up. I guess Eign must have seen my face which looked so terrible, that anyone would've told I had a tough talk because he nudged at my elbow like he did when I was upset or we were in a serious fight and weren't talking, and slid a chocolate milkshake towards me. He must have got it while I was talking with mom. Though I wasn't feeling up to it, he knew I couldn't say no to chocolate.

"Diwali?" he asked knowingly. We were so close that he had been closest to what I could call family here. He had even talked to my parents when I was new here and they were pretty glad that I had some good company in a completely foreign land.

"Yeah, the usual stuff," I said, taking a long sip of my milkshake.

"How long do you think you're going to avoid it like this. It isn't like it's their fault."

"I know it isn't, but it isn't mine either. I just..." my voice trailed off as I could feel a lump behind my throat.

"It's okay, I know it isn't. They just love you." He tried sounding casual, he didn't want to make me feel like he was intruding in my personal life.

"I know." I was just taking the last few sips of my milkshake and trying to pull myself out of the tense episode that had just happened when my phone chimed and to my surprise, I didn't even take a second to pick it up from where I had thrown it so carelessly just moments ago. It was him. I don't know why I had been waiting for his text so eagerly. I just knew something about it made me feel different. Different in a way that I hadn't felt in a while now.

"Wow," Eign exclaimed, trying to peep into the screen from behind my shoulder,

"That one must be really special to make your mood shift so fast like that." He said, giving me a playful look that he thought was sensuous enough to make any girl melt. Well, not me. Which he said was probably because:

1. He didn't mean for it to happen because we were just friends.
2. Or maybe because I wasn't a girl.

Both of which reasons I found extremely stupid.

"It's nothing like that," I said, trying to hide my excitement that was coursing through me at the idea of his recent text lying in my inbox.

"Surely it isn't, as that so shy smile on your face tells." He punched me playfully for one last time before he left my cabin to resume his work. Finally, I could see what was it that he had to say to the brief reply I had sent this morning. I took a deep breath like I was just about to see some kind of long-awaited result upon which life depended,

In that case, I guess I would like to know some more of those *smart* choices. And of course, the smart *person* too. If I may?

I didn't know how I was supposed to answer that question. I didn't know if it was even a question or not. Though I did know one thing, it wasn't just me who was pretty much trying to get this short random talk to turn into a conversation. Or so I thought, and God, only I knew how much I wanted for it to be true. I couldn't really make out what my answer should've been to that question, so I left it there, read, unanswered. I left it for the evening, to see what it might turn things into. It wasn't like I was expecting him to run up to me asking for a reply, but then how could I say that I completely wasn't expecting it either. When secretly, I knew I was. All of it was so tiring, but it felt nice, to have something, *someone* to think about like this. Though it had been a while now since I really thought I needed *someone*. But I had started to like the thought of it now. The thought of *someone*. And the idea that that someone might as well be him, kind of made me feel stupid because I practically barely knew him to think about it this way, or for that matter, any way. But then, sometimes, you don't want to give in to reason, even if you know that it's supposed to be that way, you just don't *want* to. And so didn't I. I didn't want to completely rule out the possibility of *something* might being there. Something, *anything*. Even if it was just an ellipsis, I just wanted something to look forward to, to my surprise I really did. So I thought to give this chance to myself, to *choose* it for myself. Because I guess I deserved it. And, because there wasn't a full stop, there was a possibility... an ellipsis.

#

Hella was already there, sweating her ass off when I reached the cardio section to start with my session.

"You're late," she said teasing me as she turned her wrist to look for the time in her imaginary wristwatch.

"Got more work than just goin' to college you know, kiddo." I teased her back.

"Yeah, whatever, I guess someone has been waiting for you quite eagerly," she said smirking and tipping her head slightly in the direction where he had been standing, talking to some other girl. I punched her in the shoulder playfully, trying to distract her from the topic. Only to fail miserably as he walked in our direction smiling once in Hella's direction while I tried hard to keep the color which had started to rise to my face, as minimal as I could. He completely forgot that she hadn't disappeared when he started to pick up on the topic of our texts.

"Hey," he said extending his hand for a shake, I took his hand hesitantly, not forgetting that Hella was still there,

"Evening, sir," I said, trying to sound formal, which was of course of no use as we exchanged a look that was far away from being anywhere near formal.

"Ahem ahem, I guess I gotta get going, I'm done with the cardio," Hella said, trying to break the awkward air that had started to build, "abs next?" she asked looking in his direction, "Sir, abs?" she said once again, with some emphasis this time, when he failed to acknowledge her for the first time.

"Oh, well, yeah, sorry, yes. Abs right." He said stumbling and jumbling all the words. Hella looked in our direction, shaking her head at me before she finally left, leaving us almost alone in the cardio room except for some other people who seemed least interested in what the trainer and a new client possibly had to talk about.

"Um, you can call me Zayne," he said, trying not to sound too embarrassed.

"Oh, yeah. Sure. I mean I can try." I smiled shyly. I knew that wasn't happening anytime soon because of my habit which I doubted would change anytime soon.

"I liked the playlist by the way," there it was. I had been thinking the whole day if he would try to bring up the topic to find a way to continue the conversation. And I wouldn't lie that secretly I had been hoping that he did. And he did, I didn't know whether I was supposed to feel anything different about it or not, but I did, I felt different. It felt nice. In a way that I hadn't felt since long.

"Thanks, I'm glad you did." I tried to sound polite and normal cause I surely didn't want to look like I had been hanging on to it too much.

"I wanted to ask something though,"

"Yeah, say," I guess I knew what it was,

"What's Fomenta?" I was kind of disappointed. Not because he was curious to know it and was really interested in my suggestions to try knowing more about them, but because I had expected him to ask about the last text, he had sent which I didn't reply to.

"Soothing, calming,"

"Oh, I didn't know that, sounds exotic," he said.

"Yeah, it's Latin," I said flatly, trying hard to hide my disappointment.

"You know Latin?" his eyes were wide out of genuine curiosity, which kind of made me smile,

"No, no. I just like the language, want to learn of course. Just a few words here and there, you know," I said, trying hard to suppress my smile.

"That's different"

"Different?" I asked shooting him a sharp look straight in the eyes, even though I didn't mean to.

"I mean not bad different, a good one, like different than common. You know what I mean, like different in..." he let out a deep sigh as he messed with the syllables, not knowing himself what he was really saying, "...sorry, I mean sorry for the mess."

I couldn't hold back my laughter this time, even though I didn't want to but I burst out into a full-fledged hearty laugh till my stomach hurt, he didn't feel too embarrassed about it though for which I was pretty much thankful.

"What do you like to hear? Like you must have personal favorites, right? Everybody does." I asked, trying not to sound too curious.

"Um, I doubt you'd like it. I mean I don't have as good taste in music as you." he said with genuine innocence which was kind of funny because of course, you don't expect six feet tall specimen of flawless muscular built to look that way, it's kind of ironic and judgmental but then that's how it usually is, so you can't blame someone who thinks conventionally.

"I'd love to hear your choice still," I didn't know where did it come from but I knew it was surely something he hadn't been expecting as a smile spread across his face and he looked straight into my eyes. I didn't know what we exchanged in that moment but it was surely something beyond casual. Though I didn't know if I was hallucinating or it was really there, but I felt like his eyes tried to reach out to me like mine had been, for a long time, trying to reach out to someone, only that nobody really saw it. But I guess he did, I guess he saw. And I was afraid of it. I wanted him to see it, but I didn't at the same time. I didn't know if I could let him in or not, if I was ready or not. But then, I had already started letting him in, be it unconsciously, but I had, and to be honest, it felt nice, I was glad about it.

"Really?" he asked, his voice soft, I could see the sweat rolling down on his temples, which made him look even more hot. And with that look in his eyes, I didn't know what I felt or did any more.

"Umhm, really," I said, biting my lower lip.

"I guess you'd be the first one to care about that though," he said, taking a step closer to me, "And the last one too, I guess." he smiled, trying to not make things awkward, but I didn't think they were awkward. They were being *normal* for the first time after a long while. I didn't know if they really were though, but it all *felt* better, right.

"In that case, I'd be honored," I said as color started to rise to my cheeks and a faint smile touched the corner of his lips.

"I... you're, you know..." I could see him blush too,

"I guess we should start," I said turning away from him, realizing how close we had been all this while, and that I had been holding my breath the entire time.

"Yeah," he said taking in a deep breath like he had been doing the same. I thought it'd be better to get to business before we both made it any more awkward. As I had thought, the idea was better because it tended to ease both of us out of the tense air that usually built whenever we tried talking. I guess it was because of our excessive cognizance, mostly mine though.

He smiled at me between the sets as he helped me with the weights and exercises.

"You aren't delicate," he said helping me with the leg press,

"Sorry?" I asked, questioningly.

"I mean, like at the first look, you don't look like a girl who'd lift one fifty kilos on the leg press,"

"That's quite stereotypical," I gave him a sarcastic look.

"No, I didn't mean it in that way, sorry." He whispered, lowering his head. I laughed at his chastity.

"It's okay, I was just messing with you,"

"Have you done such a physical workout before? I mean the gym and stuff?"

"Nope, I used to play, athlete body you know. Doesn't really give up on you easily." I said, smiling.

"Yeah, I get it."

"You used to play too?"

"Yeah, cricket, in high school. Until we shifted here."

"Why didn't you continue?"

"No time, and chance."

"You don't *get* chances, sir. You hunt for them" I said, feeling irritated at his resignation. Though I knew I didn't have any right to feel that way about his choices, but I couldn't help feeling the way I did.

"Sometimes you've got to give up things you love for things and people you love more." He said quietly. I could see there was a lot more to things than I knew, I had always known it and believed it. That people had stories, that nobody knew. I had and so did he. I felt stupid to have felt the way I did just moments before, for getting annoyed without knowing the entire story to it.

"Yeah, sorry. I shouldn't have said it the way..."

"No, it's okay. I know you didn't mean it that way."

"Yeah, still, I don't have any right to talk to you like this, I mean, to comment on your personal life,"

"Nah, there wasn't anything personal to it, plus I don't mind talking about it with you," he stopped suddenly as if he realized that he said something he shouldn't have had. Though to be bare honest, my heart skipped a beat when those last words left his mouth. It made me believe that it wasn't just me who had been thinking about the possibilities. And though I didn't want to raise my hopes, because I didn't know if I were ready for any such thing or not, I secretly had started to expect things to take the course which they had started taking. Or to be more precise and fairer, which I had *made* them take. It wasn't just natural right? I was the one who asked for his number. but then it wasn't quite unnatural too. Hadn't it been natural we wouldn't have been standing here in the first place.

"Sorry," he said trying to make up for his mistake. Only that he hadn't done any,

"No, it's completely fine," I said, as I stood up from the machine and picking up my stuff started to leave for the changing room. It was time, and I was already going to be late for the evening which I had planned with Eign. I could feel the heat of his gaze on my back as I started to leave. But I guess there was one thing I had to say because I meant it. I turned to face him, I could see Hella had come downstairs and was coming in my direction and I knew she could hear us just like the other people in the room, but I didn't care, for the first time, I really didn't because I wanted him to know this. I took few steps in his direction to make sure I was standing close enough to read his expressions when I said,

"You don't have to be sorry about things, okay." He just nodded, "And, I just want you to know that I'm here to talk about anything you want, anytime. I'm here, no matter what." I didn't know what I was expecting for his reaction to be, but his face went completely blank except just a faint smile that reached his eyes with such intensity that it made me shiver. I could see something in those dark eyes of his, I just didn't know what, or I'd rather say, I just didn't want to think it was something lest I might be wrong. I started to move when he held my hand to make me stop, and I could feel my heart racing inside my ribcage. He made me turn slowly to look him directly in the eyes and in that moment, seeing my reflection in his eyes, I felt like I was seeing through him, like he was trusting me with his vulnerability.

"That means a lot, thanks..." I just nodded, not wanting to break the spell of the moment even though I knew people were watching us now, "...Iana." He said after a brief pause. My name felt so familiar from his mouth, it felt like he had been saying it this way since forever. He let me go and I walked to the door as Hella joined me to get changed. We were just leaving when I heard him shout from behind,

"I meant that last thing," for a moment I thought he was talking about the last thing he had just said but no. when I paused to turn and look at him, he spoke,

"I'd want to know more about your *choices*," he smiled as he looked into my eyes, searching for an answer, permission. I just smiled and left. I didn't really know what I should've said, so I just left. Though I felt different, it was like the little goddess inside me was dancing to her own beats.

"You two are so cute," Hella said, pulling me out of my string of thoughts.

"It isn't like that. There's nothing," I said, trying to defy myself more than her.

"Yeah, I get it, I just said you two look cute." She said zipping up her duffel as she pulled her hair free from the messy bun, she had made to hold them back from falling on her face while she killed her workout.

"Whatever," I said, rolling my eyes, trying hard to push away the topic.

"Mom called," she said, not pestering me much about the topic,

"Yeah, me too."

"She said papa booked tickets for Diwali, what you think?" I couldn't help as all of the day's events wiped out and what took their place was a complete dark void, Hella saw me going completely silent,

"Hey, you okay?" she asked, rubbing my back,

"Yeah, I just need time, I don't want to go back there. I am not... I just don't know. I don't want to." I said, exasperated. Suddenly, I had started to feel exhausted.

"I get it, I'll talk her out of it. it's okay."

"Yeah, thanks," I said, not meeting her eyes

"Eea, you know he likes you," now that was something I hadn't seen coming.

"What?"

"Don't act stupid, I have seen the way he looks at you. And the way you look at him. Don't ruin this for all that you've been through, please give this a chance. You deserve it. Don't rob yourself of everything and much more that you deserve."

"I ain't robbing myself of anything, I just... I don't fucking know what I want anymore. And do you think it's fair to put it on anybody?" I was almost shouting now and I could feel tears pouring down my face from the corner of my eyes where I had been trying to hold them back since long,

"I know, and it's okay, it's just that please stop blaming yourself. You can't ruin your whole life thinking about it, you need to forgive yourself. You need to let it go. I know it isn't easy, but you being so hard on yourself isn't fair, is it? You can't be like this forever." I knew she was right, but it wasn't as easy as it sounded,

"I know it's tough, but you've got to forgive yourself, you've got to embrace it, and get over it." she pulled me into a tight hug as she said her last words, whispering in my ears,

"I love you Eea, and it hurts to see you like this." We pulled back looking into each other's eyes, she wasn't crying, but her eyes were solemn. I knew she was right, and I had to do it, I just had to, for her, for Eign, for my family, but more than anyone for myself.

I rubbed my nose with the back of my hand, knowing that it was only Hella who was there, and tried to gain my composure back, I didn't want to look like a cry baby being condoled by her younger sister, that'd be pretty embarrassing. I pulled her into a long tight embrace for one last time before we finally left the changing room,

"That wasn't the most perfect place for such an aphoristic talk," I said trying to shift the seriousness in the air to something light.

"Apho- what?" she asked confused,

"Nothing, leave it," I said, waving her question off.

"Damn, I guess I really should start carrying a dictionary while being with you,"

"I guess you should start working on your vocabulary in lieu," I winked and her while she made a disgusted face at my last word, before breaking into an insane laughter.

CHAPTER ELEVEN

ZEESHAN

I saw her descending the stairs, it wasn't like I had seen her before, but she and the other girl, who must've been the younger one, looked Indian. And it wasn't like there were many Indian clients. So, I just made a wild guess. She looked like she had been crying, her eyes were red and I knew it wasn't my place to judge but she looked pretty messed up. I had nothing to do with it though, I just wanted to get my job done. I knew Jeane would call again soon, to check if I did her work. So, I thought I'd get done with it. Plus, I didn't think there was any harm in getting acquainted with someone new. It wasn't like I was too much into knowing new people, but I was not too asocial either. I walked up to her slowly, trying not to be too abrupt with my introduction to them,

"Hey, this is Zeeshan, I own the place, it's nice meeting you," I extended my hand for a formal shake because that's what people here preferred. The younger one hopped in, taking my hand enthusiastically, she seemed to be the more active one,

"Hi, this is Hella," she shook my hand with childish vigor. I looked in the direction of the elder one while Hella chatted on.

"Iana, nice meeting you." Her words came out straight but soft. Like she knew the exact amount of force and emphasis she wanted to put on her words.

"Jeane told me about you being here and..." Hella, cut me in between,

"Oh, yeah. I told her about joining in and she told me she was friends with you. It's nice of her to help us out. She always does," she said the words at such pace that they sounded like an echo mixed with one another that they were almost incomprehensible rather than distinct syllables. The elder one, Iana, looked in her direction shaking her head disapprovingly like she knew her younger sister was messing things up perfectly. I'm glad though that she came to my rescue cause having to talk with a teenager who thought she knew very well what she was talking about when in reality she just made herself look like one of those kids who go blabbering about how much they know without really knowing anything.

"I'm sorry, she means it's nice of you to care about it. Thanks," Iana, tried to wipe up the mess that her younger sister was so keen on creating.

"It's my job, it'll be my pleasure to help you out anytime you need."

"Same here," she said with a polite smile. There was something about it, her smile. The way it reached her eyes sent a pang of hurt through me. They reminded me of something, someone, *her.*

"See you around," I didn't wait for any of them to say the last word. I just had to get done with my job. And that's what I did.

Though there was something about her that kept nibbling at the back of her mind, her dark hair, the way she smiled, it was too painful to know how much she resembled Easha. But what hurt more than that was that it was too difficult to ignore that fact. She was younger, of course, a lot younger than her, but the amount of resemblance in their features was unmistakable. Maybe it was just that I was being paranoid, but I swear it was something I couldn't get off my mind. She looked just like Easha. Like she did when she was probably her age, but no, she wasn't her. Nobody could be her, and even though it hurt, it was such a relief to know that I wasn't wrong.

CHAPTER TWELVE

ZAYNE

"I am here no matter what." Her words rang through my head like wailing sirens. Nobody had ever said that to me before, I mean it was kind of understood with your best friends and family, with Zeeshan. I knew he was there for me and so was I, but she had no reason to say that to me. But she did. I couldn't help wondering if it was the same way with her. If she felt something or anything like I did. Everything felt like it had been blurred out and the only thing that had my mind was her words that played on repeat over and over. I didn't know what she meant when she said that, but the way she said it and the intensity and weight that her words carried, it felt like she was calling out for me. Like she wanted to be reached out to. I knew I could be imagining things or maybe I'd suddenly turned schizophrenic, hearing voices and seeing stuff that wasn't there, but I swear I saw it. And honestly, if it were true, I really wanted to be the person to reach out to her.

"Hey, all good?" Zeeshan's hand landed on my shoulder, suddenly bringing me out of my head, where I had been spending too much time lately.

"Yeah, totally."

"You look distracted," he said, looking me directly in the eyes.

"What? I mean, no. I was just thinking'"

"About what?"

"Stuff."

"You've been thinking a lot lately, little brother, go slow."

"Yeah, you're early today? All fine?"

"Yeah, completely, just had to finish off Jeane's work,"

"What work?"

"Oh, nothing of significance. She wanted me to look after those new Indian girls."

"Look after?"

"Like just make sure they're fine, I know it's stupid and silly and whatever, but okay."

"Iana and Hella?"

"You know them?" he raised an eyebrow at me.

"I've been training them for a while now. Am I not supposed to, for that sake?"

"Wowoww, chill, I didn't mean to offend you." he held his hands up in surrender,

"You didn't."

"The younger one has a big mouth, though."

"Yeah, I know." I tried sounding disinterested.

"I think the elder one does have a way, she at least knows her way with words and etiquette. She looked pretty messed up, though." He had resigned to check out the entry register to see the latest enrollments, though he looked around once to see if I was listening, which I was. Particularly now, when he said Iana looked messed up. I didn't know what he meant by it.

"Messed up?" I tried keeping my voice as devoid of concern as I could. I didn't want him to pry on me for something which I myself hadn't figured out for now.

"Yeah, red eyes, messed up hair, wet face. Looked like she had been crying, God, why do girls have to cry all the time?" He tried to sound like he wanted to mean it, but his tone defied him. I didn't know why he had to be a complete badass all the time; he thought it looked cool, but it didn't. Especially when I knew it was forced and not like him at all.

"You never know the reason, big brother, let's not be too stereotypical." I didn't want to sound like I was defending her, which I kind of secretly was.

"Yeah, whatever." He waved me off. I was glad he didn't dwell on the topic; I knew it would have wandered off to somewhere I wasn't ready to go yet.

I couldn't help wondering about what it was that I saw in her eyes today, I didn't even know if it really meant anything, but I did know that her words caught a part of me that I wasn't sure was even there. Honestly, I had always thought that Jacey and I shared something that I had always ached to have with someone, but it all seemed so silly now when I knew this girl whom I didn't even know existed a few weeks ago. I didn't know if she felt the same way or not, but I wanted to know. I was pulling the leg press machine free of weights, which still had a hundred and fifty kilos on it, the way she had left it when my phone chimed. I barely ever cared to check my phone. I wasn't too tech-savvy. The gym was almost empty, the only few people left would leave soon, and anyway, Zeeshan was here to look after things and help Liz to close the place. Anyway, I wasn't able to concentrate; I needed fresh air. My head was buzzing with events of the day, it was heavy with her words, which refused to leave that space. Everything felt like it was floating away. I wanted to hold her, when she said that, to pull her closer and ask if she really meant what she had said, ask her why I felt so pulled towards her that I forgot about everything shitty that had been going on in my life. I pulled over my vest and stood under the cold shower, trying to wash away all the weight that I was carrying, hoping that it'd help me clear my head. I couldn't go on autopilot, resigning to think about something that I didn't know if it meant the same way to the one who had said it. I looked at my reflection in the mirror. I couldn't remember the last time when I really tried to *look* at myself, but I wanted to know what it was that made her say what she did. How did she read that I wanted to talk, that I wanted someone to hear, I wanted *her* to hear? My phone chimed again. It was for the second time in an hour, and even though checking upon who was remembering me was the last thing on Earth I wanted to do right now, I couldn't think about anything else to distract myself from my own thoughts. I switched the screen open and there lay two message notifications from the person I had been thinking about this entire time. Iana. I didn't know what I was expecting it to be. Maybe another playlist or something, though I badly wanted her to talk about what happened today, in the cardio room. I wanted to know if it was the same way on her head like it was on mine, or was it just another thing that, unlike for me, was pretty mundane for her; like what I thought and felt about Jacey, was of minimal significance to her.

You there?

This was the latest one that had landed in a few minutes ago. I scrolled down to find the one that she had sent an hour ago.

Wanted to know choices? Ready for some aesthetic?

Of all that I had expected, this was surely not on the list. The girl, who had been an enigma for me, or rather, I have been an enigma to myself lately. I didn't know where it was that things were going, but I liked it. It had been a long time since things felt like they were going right. I didn't even know if they were right. But they were *feeling* right.

Sure, place?

I hoped she would see my text and reply soon. I didn't want to lose this, or for that matter, any chance to get to know her better. I didn't want to look desperate, but then how could I not when the only thing that had been on my mind lately was her.

Her reply came after a few minutes when I was descending into the parking. I stopped for a moment to see the address. It looked familiar; I couldn't help smiling as the place in the text already sent through me a sense of relief. Familiarity.

I wasn't quite a believer, though, but now it felt like the universe had its way to make things happen. I was wondering how we were so analogous yet never really knew that somewhere in the corner of the world, away from our homelands, existed people whom had we met earlier, who knows where things would have been by now. But who cares, we met now. I didn't know if this was destiny or not, or whatever they might call it, like some kind of empyrean connection, but what I knew was that it was more than a mere coincidence that landed us in such a place.

"All good?" Liz almost bumped into me as I turned, stunned by her sudden emergence.

"Oh, yeah. You just, I thought I was alone." I said, taking in a deep breath, trying to calm my racing heartbeat.

"So you were, until now." She said, smiling and ruffling my hair like she did when she secretly knew I had been plaguing myself, thinking too deeply.

"Yeah, right." I tried returning her smile, still too occupied by my thoughts.

"Are you fine?" she asked, with a tinge of concern this time. I knew she could see right through me. There had been days when I myself didn't know what I was going through, but she could exactly put into words how I felt. I knew that could be creepy sometimes, but I'd never known a time when she hadn't been there when I needed her. Maybe she could possibly tell what was wrong with me and why I felt so confused, but then it wasn't her job to sort out my drama for me.

"Hey," she reached out for my hand and held it between both of hers. They weren't soft, like those ladies who they show on TV with perfect hair and neatly manicured hands. They were callused, but they were everything that I needed to calm me down, at least for the time being. Her engagement ring shone as it caught the light from the bulbs. I wondered how much she went through before she finally found the one she thought she wanted to live her whole life with. I didn't know how it was supposed to feel. I had only felt differently once, and that too for the wrong person. For someone who thought it was all too shitty to be cared about, that I was exaggerating. I couldn't help as Iana's name popped into my mind, and I wondered if what I felt for her right now, which I was too confused to process, was the way that you're supposed to feel for someone you know you'd want in your life forever. Someone you know you'd trust enough to show them your vulnerable side and trust them to not break you. Wasn't that what love was? I didn't know what love exactly was, but maybe Liz did. I wondered if she could help me out.

"I know you're having a tough time, but I know you're strong. You hear me? I know you'll be fine." I couldn't reply to her with what she wanted to hear, even though I wanted to. There was so much more I wanted to ask,

"How did you know?"

"Know what?" She looked confused, of course, she didn't know what I was talking about.

"That you love your fiancé?"

"You don't really know it, Zayne. You can never really know it."

"Then?" I didn't know what I expected her answer to be, but it surely wasn't this.

"You take your chances. It's more like taking a leap of faith. Trusting a person with your most vulnerable self, with your everything."

"What if they hurt you? I mean, there's a chance." She smiled at me like you do when a toddler asks questions that you know are too difficult to be answered theoretically, but you know eventually the child will grow on to find answers to them by himself. But for the time being, you know you've got to feed his curiosity with something.

"There's always a chance, but you'll never know until you do."

"But isn't that too high of a price to pay?"

"For love? No, it isn't."

"But there's got to be some way? Other than getting yourself ripped apart, you know what I mean?" She took a deep breath like she knew what I wanted to hear as an answer. I knew it myself, that I wanted to hear an easier way, which I myself knew wasn't there. There's no shortcut to life, to love.

"Zayne, I've said this earlier too, I don't know everything, and I don't have an answer to your every question." She let go of my hand,

"Sometimes you've got to take risks..." I saw her leaving as she patted me softly.

"...for what *feels* right." She didn't stop or turn around to look at me, but she had secretly answered me. I knew exactly what she meant, and what all of it meant. The only question was if I was willing to risk it for what *felt* right. For *who* felt right.

I'll be there in half an hour.

I texted her, watching my screen flash her name, I knew what I was risking, and I knew that I wanted to. This time I did. Her reply came within seconds,

Waiting.

She was waiting, I was too. I guess we both were, for something we ourselves didn't know, but surely wanted to find out.

CHAPTER THIRTEEN

IANA

"You look good," Eign shouted over my shoulder, the music was too loud to make out what he said, even when he was screaming at the top of his voice. Had he shouted even a note higher his voice would've cracked.

"Yeah, thanks." I smiled at him faintly. Sasha wasn't too cheesy but then sometimes she could be typical girlfriend type. I liked her though, for understanding Eign and my bond. She never, even for once questioned the level of intimacy that our bond carried and the closeness we had. She was pretty cooperative when I needed Eign, he was always there. Sometimes he couldn't even call her back for days, because I'd be so miserable to even be left alone. But she never made an issue out of it. I didn't know her much. Not more than you're supposed to know your friend's girlfriend. But she was a sweet girl, not at all cranky (to my relief). My phone buzzed in my back pocket and I wouldn't have heard its chime had it not been on vibrate. It was him; I was so desperately wanting to get out of here, all the *David Guetta* mixes and drinks were too loud for me, they made my head buzz. I hadn't wanted to be at a place like this lately, it was still too much to process. I knew Eign was just trying to get me out of my shell, but I didn't think I was pretty much ready for such party stuff right now. I kind of felt guilty for ditching him when all he wanted to do was to try help me feel better. But this wasn't working even remotely. *Asterix* was an amazing place to hang out when you felt up to it, but I was sure I wasn't in that mood, or for that matter even near that mood.

Though I couldn't fathom why would someone name an amazing club after a pathetic mathematical symbol or something, it sounded stupid to me honestly, but then people had their reasons, so I didn't care to dwell upon it much.

The lights and loud noises made my head spin, my pina colada was resting untouched on our table while Eign was about to shoot down his second round. Sasha was a bit tipsy too but she didn't fail in ruling the floor even then. She could be pretty badass when it came to clubbing.

"So, how's it going?" he said, looking at Sasha, who was completely hysterical but sexy and all over the blond DJ. Eign didn't care much though, he was pretty cool about it and knew Sasha well enough to not create an issue about such petty stuff. I wondered how he could be so calm about such stuff. Both of them. I guess I could never be. Or maybe I could, until it went to extreme. Humans have their limits, that's why we are what we are, humans. Though I wondered if I could have done things differently to not... land into situation I was now.

"Nothing much, just the usual stuff," I screamed loud enough to make sure he could hear me. I could feel myself going deaf and mute at the same time. My throat had already started to feel hoarse.

"No," he shook his head giving me a sly smile, I had no idea where he was going with this. But whatever it possibly was, with that reaction on his face, I knew it couldn't be too pleasant.

"I mean, with that guy," he tipped his head in the direction of my phone where my screen had come to life with his last text notification displayed on my main screen. Shit.

"It's nothing like that. He's just my trainer,"

"And friend," he smiled, "you always be there for friends." he bent close to me and tucked a strand of my hair which had been falling loose, behind my ear.

"Wait, what did you just say?" I could feel myself burning, I didn't know if it was all the crowd and suffocation and heat or was I really angry. I knew it was both but I was betting on the former one to be the major reason.

"I said, that you always listen to friends and be there when they want to talk." he said, still smiling, pretending not to notice my anger, or maybe he really didn't notice it. There wasn't a way I could've surely known.

I knew exactly, what he was talking about, and I just couldn't help as my fists clenched too hard that they almost went white.

"Who told you all of it?" I asked repulsively, though I knew the answer before he could've even uttered the other word,

"It doesn't matter Eea, it's that..." he trailed off as his eyes went wide, he was looking right behind me and it felt like something bad hit him straight in the gut. I was just about to turn when someone jumped over me, toppling our drinks over the table and almost bathing me in alcohol,

"Hey, big sister. I see you're getting a life," Hella hugged me tight and kissed me on my cheek before walking up to Eign and hugging him.

"I... um... Hella, hey." He looked at me over her shoulder. He must've seen color rising to my cheeks by then as he tried to pull her away and distract her so that she wouldn't see what was going on here. Though I knew he knew better that there wasn't a way this thing was getting done away with so easily,

"Having fun?" Hella smiled as she stood between both of us, none making eye contact with her as I looked at Eign, and he knew he was pretty dead. I finally took a last long glance at him before breaking my glower.

"What are you doing here?" I asked Hella in a sharp tone. Though she didn't quite react to it, I doubted that she even noticed it. But even if she did, she decided not to address the fact that there was something seriously wrong.

"Here to report the progress on your mission spying-Iana-and-what-goes-on-in-her-personal-life?" I stared at her, looking her dead in the eyes, only turning once to look at Eign who stood speechless, "or is it the other way round buddy?" I turned towards Eign, facing him completely now.

"Eea, it's nothing like that," Eign stuttered,

"What are you talking about? Will anybody tell me what's going on here? Did you tamper with her drink?" she punched Eign playfully on the shoulder, laughing. As if this was some kind of joke.

"You think this is funny?"

"What is funny?"

"You two, spying on me. Reporting each other stuff you see, as if this is some kind of mission you've got to accomplish, seriously? You find it funny?"

"Okay, now I want to know what this is about," Hella stared Eign square in his face.

"What did you tell him?"

"Eea, it isn't her fault, I just got intrigued when I saw the text on your phone this morning. You looked happy, it was different, so I just..."

"You got intrigued? Seriously. Okay, you got intrigued and decided to send my own younger sister spying on me? Is that what you're telling me?"

"No, it isn't like that, I just wanted to know,"

"It isn't his fault Eea, stop making an issue out of it. It's nothing." Hella, shouted. More at me than to make sure we heard her over the loud music.

"Oh, yes it isn't *only* his fault. I guess you go ranting about whatever you see? Or is it just me, who you like telling away things about?"

"Eea, you don't know what you're saying. We can talk it out." She came forward and put her hands lightly on my shoulders trying to shake me to reality. Like I was under some kind of simulation and shaking me would break me free from it.

"Really? I think I know exactly what I'm saying. And so do you. Don't you?" she looked taken aback. Hah. Hella zero. Iana one. For the first time, I had left her speechless.

"Listen, Iana. He's your best friend, and not to forget, the only person whom we can call family here, he has always been there for you. I thought he should know."

"You thought? Well, yeah. I understand that he has been there always and that you're concerned about me. But I'm sorry that doesn't give you two the right to have a round table conference about what's happening in my life." I could feel the acid in my words and was surprised at their intensity. I looked from over Hella to Eign, he was standing there looking like my words had pierced right through him.

"See, it's not her fault. I get it you're upset. It was me..."

"Do you even know that he was the person always having your back when you were too miserable to even comb your own fucking hair or get your shit together?" Hella spitted the words at me. I could feel she had unleashed her emotions which she had been holding back till now.

"Hella, no. Let it be." Eign sighed, as he tried to pull her away and break the two of us apart.

"No, let her hear it,"

"Yeah, I guess I better do." I refused to step back. Not this time. They couldn't present one ultimate excuse that they loved me, to justify everything they did. That fact didn't give them the right to intrude in my personal space. Even if they were everything that meant worth more than anything to me.

"All this while when you've been too busy to get yourself more miserable each and every day, God knows what we haven't done to keep you from jumping off the cliff."

"That's stupid. I'd never do that."

"Really?" she leaned in closer to me, I could feel her breath on my face, warm. I knew what she meant, and even though I didn't want to admit it, I knew she wasn't completely wrong. It wasn't false that I had considered that as an option. Only to fail. But I knew she knew me better than she let on.

"That's not the point..." I tried changing the subject, to the one which was more important than all this shit.

"That is the whole point. All this while when you've been pushing yourself astray, we have been trying to hold you back. Pull you back. Bring you back. Don't tell me you don't see it. He fucking cares about you, and that's the only reason he wanted to know."

"Yeah, Eea. I was happy when she told me about this guy. I thought it'd be better for you. You looked happy." he stepped closer, wiping away a tear that had rolled down my cheek. They might have started rolling down when I was trying to process what Hella had just made me face. The worst that we all avoided talking about, until now.

"Goddamit, why the hell do you guys always have to go there. For once can it just *not* be about guys and *love*?"

"Can it not? When it is all you long for? You think we don't see? Whom are you trying to deceive Eea, because it surely isn't us for a start." Her words were soft this time, she wasn't shouting. It had a tinge of maternal concern. This wasn't right. Any of it, I was supposed to be the elder one, and none of this was supposed to go this way. None of this had to happen for a start, it wasn't fair. They were my choices, and actions, which's consequences were too heavy to be borne by these people. They didn't have to. But I just didn't know how to make them understand that they couldn't just keep doing this to me, they couldn't just keep doing this *for* me.

"Why on earth..."

"Eea, you know we know you. You can't keep pushing it away forever. You've got to get out, see, feel." Eign pulled me into a hug despite me resisting. It was always like that, and it always worked, but not this time. Nothing seemed to work this time. Maybe because I feared they might be right. More so because I knew they were right. It was like I was trying to delay something which I knew was inevitable. Which I had myself set free, and I guess I was willing to risk it. or maybe not. I didn't know, I just knew how much I wanted them to be wrong. But more than that, how much I feared that they were right. I pulled away from his forced embrace even though that was the only place I wanted to be right now.

"Why, on Earth do you think loving again is the ultimate panacea? It fucking isn't some kind of magic potion. It asks for a lot more courage than I have, lot more things and people than I can ever sacrifice, lot more pain than I can ever take." I turned to leave, picking up my belongings, which meant mostly my cellphone as it chimed again. A text, from him.

You comin'?

"Okay, even though we're amidst a serious talk, more of a fight, I still can't fucking stop myself from smashing this glass at you. Can you fucking use normal language which we wouldn't have to browse through to make out what you're really trying to say? Especially in moments like these when we've got a lot more serious talk to do." She glared at me; her hands clenched into a fist.

"You know it better yourself Eea, tell me if you don't. It isn't the *ultimate* panacea, but you know it's what you crave." Eign spoke as I started towards the exit.

"I've got to go,"

"Of course, you have to. But you can't always just get away that easy. I hope you understand that soon enough." I didn't turn to address or contradict him.

"You know we love you Eea, but you've got to do this one thing by yourself, *for* yourself." Hella shouted as I almost quit the club, music fading slowly as I put as much distance as I could between me and that place. Of course, I knew they weren't wrong, I knew I had to do it for myself. I looked at my phone, his text still lay there, unread. I opened my phone and typed away my reply and pressed the send button before I could change my mind. I knew I had to do it for myself, and I knew I craved it. I just didn't know if I was ready. I needed time, for myself. I knew it wasn't fair for Hella, or Eign, or even *him*. But then, life's not always fair. I saw my screen going dark and took only a moment longer to stare at it before taking in a deep breath and walking down. I had to. Choose. For myself this time. I knew I had to, I didn't know if I was ready or not, but I knew that all of this that I was going through and where I was headed, it was inevitable. It was just a matter of time before it hit. And I guess it was time now.

EIGN

"Jesus, Hella, easy. It's okay,"

"No, it's not. It's not fucking okay Eign. She can't just keep getting away like this every time."

"I know Hella, and I know you're right. But she needs time. She'll be fine." I tried calming her down. Which I thought, after her third drink wouldn't be a much difficult task. But it just got worse. She was nowhere even near understanding, in fact, she was getting piqued. I knew I was getting myself into big trouble I couldn't measure the repercussions of letting her get drunk like this.

"When? Is there a deadline to her crybaby self or is it freaking eternal? Because I guess she knows the fact very well that we can't go on babysitting her forever."

I knew she was angry at her. And I totally understood it, but I could see it was consuming her slowly. It wasn't her fault, Iana was supposed to be the elder one, but it was her who had been acting that way for a long while now. But it wasn't Iana's fault either. I wish I could get both of them to understand that, but then no matter however much they considered me to be their family, I'd always have my limits to interfere in their personal affairs.

"I know Hella, but it isn't her fault, she's..." I let out a deep sigh, I knew I was delegating for someone who didn't even care to stop and clear things out. Honestly, even I was a bit annoyed, but then, I knew Iana, and that's what friends and family do, they have each other's back.

"... she's hurting Hella. She needs time."

"Really? That doesn't mean she's going to hurt all of us."

"She didn't,"

"Guess you wouldn't bet over that?" she shot the words so sharply at me that it almost felt like they'd have severed me into pieces had they been some physical object.

"Okay, I mean she didn't do it *intentionally*."

"For God's sake, she doesn't get to have it as a free pass for everything she does. You know that."

I knew it, I knew each and every word this young girl was saying wasn't devoid of even an ounce of truth and reality. But I couldn't just give up. Especially when I knew what Iana had been going through.

"I know Hella. Trust me it's going to be fine. I just think we should leave her alone for some time."

"Alone? I bet she has been that way since that thing with Arsh. Does she even let anybody in? That's just another pathetic way of being alone if you ask me. Being right there but shutting everyone out." I couldn't conceal my surprise at what she carried about her own sister. She was too young to know any of it. Knowing what she felt about Iana, kind of made me angry but I pitied her too. She wasn't completely wrong, in fact, even she was going through stuff which she shouldn't have to.

"You know," she let out a deep sigh as she moved into a corner where we wouldn't have to shout at the top of our voices to be heard, "There are times when I see her, sitting near the window, watching into the void. Crying to herself. She thinks I don't see."

"She doesn't *want* anyone to see." I added.

"Yeah, but she's a terrible liar you know," for the first time since she got here, she smiled. And the way that smile reached her eyes as she plunged into nostalgia, she looked like her younger self. The age she actually was, not the way she acted.

"I have seen her break, and I hate to see her that way. But she needs to know that being like this; she thinks she's in control but she's not. It's just a matter of time before she tips over the edge. And that's what I'm afraid of."

"I know, don't worry, she'll be fine. We'll get her to be fine."

"See? That's what I'm talking about." she pined one finger at my shoulder like she was making some kind of general and universal point that I was supposed to know without even being mentioned.

"*We* can't *get* her to be fine. No matter how hard we love her, how much we love her, we can't. She has to do it herself."

I knew she was right, but I couldn't get myself to tell her that I couldn't give up on Iana like that. No matter whatever happened.

"Yeah, I get it." I turned to leave; I didn't want to talk about it anymore. Maybe because I was afraid that she was right.

"You love her," she yelled from behind my back. It felt like someone had shot me dead right there, between that crowd.

"What?" I turned to face her, still trying to make out what she meant by that.

"You love her. Iana. Don't you?" she was looking right into my eyes like she could pull out the truth hidden behind the layers of lie. That would have been of use only if I would have been lying.

"Of course, I do, you know that. She knows that." She shook her head in disapproval and my heart raced as I could feel beads of sweat rolling down my neck. And it had nothing to do with the crowd because we were practically standing right under one of the air conditioning vents.

"Not like that. You *love* her. I see it, the way you're always there for her..."

"That's because she's my best friend." I cut her off before she could say something to make it any more awkward than it already was.

"Really? Whom are you trying to deceive? Cause it's certainly not me. I see the way you look at her."

"Hella, I have a girlfriend and I love my girlfriend." I was almost screaming at her now as if that'd change what there really was.

"Really? You don't leave your girlfriend behind to deal with someone's high-profile drama even if it means a lot of unease to you. You don't do it just for anyone. That's too much of trouble than the worth."

"You're right. You don't do it for anyone. But you definitely do it for your best friend. I don't know about you, but at least I do." I realized all I wanted in this world right now was for her to shut the fuck up. It was going way too far than I could handle.

"Best friend whom you love. See it's alright I get it. You can tell her and we can possibly together get her to see it, maybe she won't really need anybody..."

"Stop, Hella, listen to me..." I tried to calm her down. She was spitting out words like a video with playback speed at double.

"...there's nothing really with the trainer. She herself said. We can figure this out. She'll be so happy..."

Oh my God Hella just stop! Maybe she was right, you have to stop trying to get in control of her *life*. Do you hear me? Leave her alone. Please." I was yelling at her now.

"Now, if you would please excuse me, I have to go." I wanted to just get away from her. Out of here. I wanted to put as much distance between her and me as possible. This certainly was more than I had signed up for. I couldn't take to hear any more of it. At least not now. Or ever.

"Oh yes, you certainly have to. You can run however much you like from me, but you can't run from yourself. Can you?" she was laughing now, like a maniac. I couldn't leave her like this. I couldn't.

"Hella, you're too drunk. You don't know what you're saying. Let's get you home. We can talk about it sometime later." I moved to grab hold of her. She was almost fighting to keep her balance and from tripping over.

"I know exactly what I am saying Eign, I do. I just wish you knew yourself better to know what *you* want." I could feel the heat of her words. It was like she had caught me red-handed doing something I should have been ashamed of.

"For fucks sake will you shut up! Enough. Now I see exactly why Iana should be so wary of you. I get it. You've got this natural tendency to annoy even the calmest of being you know." I immediately regretted what I had said, as I saw her eyes getting wide as tears started to roll down her cheek and she wiped them with the back of her hand, not taking her eyes off me.

"Yeah, I have that tendency just because the only thing I have wanted ever so badly in my whole fucking life is to see my sister happy. To see her back like she was before that shitty Arsh appeared out of nowhere and then disappeared again leaving her broken beyond repair." She was calm, and even though I should have been liking it, I felt exactly the opposite.

"Look, Hella, I'm sorry. I shouldn't have said that."

"No, it's okay. I said what I saw. And you know I wasn't wrong. It isn't me whom you should be fighting right now. It's you yourself." I didn't like where she was going with this. I had to get out of here, it had already started to drive me crazy.

"I guess I should probably leave. That'd be best." I turned this time with finality, to leave. Though it didn't stop her from having the last word.

"How long do you think you can run like that, Eign? Is it really helping?"

"I am not running Hella. It's just you imagining stuff." I said, without turning to look back.

"Really? Say that to yourself. Now, can you?"

I just stopped for a while, only to keep going. I knew staying back would only make it worse.

"Let's just face it Eign, it isn't me or her you are running from. It's you. Hope you get knocked in with some sense soon to realize it. At least soon enough before it's too late."

She didn't say anything further. Or even if she did, I was out of earshot, too far to have heard it. I realized I had left Sasha behind, but I didn't want to go back in there, so I just kept moving forward. I didn't know where I was headed, I just needed to get out of here.

Pulling the seat belt, I revved up the engine. The sound wasn't enough to submerge her words which refused to leave my head even though alcohol had started to kick in. And I could feel the buzz in my head.

Maybe she was wrong, but then it wasn't helping either, because I *knew* she wasn't. I knew she was right.

I needed closure, I needed to see her. Now.

CHAPTER FIFTEEN

ZAYNE

It had almost been half an hour over since I had been sitting here, I should have left by now. But I just didn't know why I didn't even consider that as an option. Though it wasn't like I hadn't thought she might have forgotten, but then I didn't want to leave. One reason was yes, I didn't want to be gone when she came or *if* she came. But the bigger reason was I liked being here. Soon the sky would be dark and the lights would come to life, slowly, like a phoenix rising back from ashes. Just pretty. I didn't know if it was a complete coincidence that this was the place of her *choice*, unless she had probably been following me even before she knew me. That was an utter remote possibility plus I didn't want to bet on it because that'd be pretty creepy. *Angel's Top* had always kind of been my place of escape, away from the chaos of life, of people, of me, of... everything. I didn't freaking know how she had any idea about it or probably it was some kind of a cue. It would be crazy if she'd say she came here since always and we never even ran into each other. But then, anything that had been happening since the last few weeks, none of it was closely sane. So I wouldn't half doubt if it turned out to be that way. I could feel *Billie Eilish* singing softly in my ears, I had few more songs on *Fomenta* before I'd have had to put it on repeat. I felt different, like I was just there on edge, wanting to get hold of something but then not being able to. And after what she said today, I knew how would it feel to have exactly that. If I could have it. I heard the clicking of heels on the stones, the place was rough with rocks and sand. Not a perfect one to wear heels to. I was hoping it to be her, I just wanted to take my time before I finally saw her, for the first time, not as a trainer but someone else. I didn't know what this association that we shared right now was. But it surely wasn't on the line of formality. I took a long final look at the skyscrapers and the lights that were twinkling like those amazing celestials in the sky, just at a comparatively lower altitude. I took a deep breath as I turned to jump off the periphery where I had been sitting, thinking, listening.

"Hey, how're you..." what I saw was not anywhere near what I was expecting. But she did catch me by surprise. The black sequin dress stopped just an inch above her knees. For the first time, I noticed how perfectly her body was carved. She wasn't skinny, she knew how to carry her curves. And of all those girls I had seen till now, who were all over getting the perfect zero-figured body, she looked far more attractive than any of those girls ever could. Her hair was tucked at one side exposing the other side of her neck which sparkled as the silver chain on her neck caught the illumination of lights, though there weren't many here, and it was pretty dim. She tipped her hair back and squinted a bit to adjust to the dimness and in that very moment, her dark brown eyes caught a glint of light and sparkled to life like a firework. She looked taller, with three inches heel on her feet she came almost to my shoulder. I saw how beautiful she was, confident about her body, about herself. She wasn't too upfront, not like someone who'd just walk up to you if they liked how you *looked* and ask for a hookup or having a drink or catching up. She was the kind who would see right through the crowd if you were alone and needed someone when your friends failed to see that. That made her way more beautiful than any of her physical attributes.

"How am I...doin'? I guess that's what you intend to ask?" she pulled me out of my reverie. Damn, I've got to stop drifting every time I see her, but then I just couldn't help. She raised her head enough to let the streetlight cast a faint shadow over her face and I could see her eyes were red, cheeks stained with tear marks.

"You've been crying?" I couldn't help as it shot out of my mouth. I didn't want it to come out like this.

"What? No!" she turned away immediately and started wiping her face away with the back of her hands. I could hear faint sobs and her irregular breathing but I didn't want to make it uncomfortable for her, so I let her have it by herself. Though only I knew how bad I wanted to hold her face in my hands and wipe those tears away and let her know that what she said today evening wasn't just one-sided.

"I, um, I'm sorry I didn't mean to make you uncomfortable." I closed in on her, to see if she was fine. She turned to face me. Her eyes were still red and mascara had smeared to the corners which made her look messed up, but she looked just as beautiful as ever, even if it wasn't her best.

"No, it's fine. I just, I'm kind of having a rough night let's put it that way." she started walking towards the periphery, stumbling a bit, trying to keep her balance on such a rough surface with stilettos on.

"Maybe we could meet some other time if you want?" I tried to sound modest but deep down I hoped that she'd turn down the offer which I so stupidly made. I wanted to be here with her. I wanted to talk to her, about whatever she said this evening, about the songs she suggested to me. Because they seemed too much to just be songs. I wanted to ask her, how she knew the place which I always thought was my escape.

"No, it's fine. Anyway, I needed a break. I guess we both can consider this as one." She smiled a bit, though she didn't turn to look at me or face me. She looked straight to the stars.

"Do you come here often?" I asked, too curious to know,

"You mean this place? Yeah, I come here every morning. For a run. Or more like to get away from myself, before I get lost, God knows where." Her voice sounded solemn. Like it carried a thousand emotions weighed and held back with an utter tactic to not let them come rushing whenever they could find a way out.

"It is. This place has something that lets you feel tethered to yourself while you feel like you're floating away." I still couldn't take my eyes off her. How she looked so beautifully calm even while she was at battle with whatever plagued her inside.

"Right? But how do you know? You've been here before?" she looked at me for the first time, straight in the eyes. Though I knew it meant nothing, but it felt like she was letting me in.

"Almost every night," I muttered. Not wanting to break the serenity of the moment.

"Shut up, this is so funny, and crazy. I mean we've been coming to the same place for long enough but we never just really ran into each other, even by chance." She was laughing now, and I could feel her relax a bit as her muscles felt less tense than they were when she arrived here first.

"I know, maybe we were meant to meet the way we did. We never know what's meant to happen when." I closed in on her, taking few steps, trying to make sure that she didn't get uncomfortable. I could feel my heartbeat picking up with every inch that I closed in on us. She didn't move back, which I took as a signal that she wasn't really uncomfortable about it. I stopped at a safe distance to let her have her space and have mine too. I turned to look at the lights and then to her face again. She looked so young, but all that she carried, I didn't know what it was, but it seemed to make her age faster than she actually was.

"By meant to be you mean you catching me stalking you when I wasn't really stalking?" she smiled at me. I could see the color rise to her face as her pale cheeks turned red.

"What? No. When was it? You were looking at me? I thought you hardly even noticed me."

"Um yeah, I just saw you when that girl was giving you a near-murderous look,"

"Jacey, God! You saw that?"

"Of course I did."

That was the last thing in the world I would have wanted the girl I thought I was falling for, to have witnessed.

"Oh it was just a misunderstanding I mean not a misunderstanding but yeah like... okay, I'm sorry I don't know how to explain this," I could feel my speech faculty deciding to defy me at this very perfect moment. Wow.

"You don't have to be sorry. You don't owe me an explanation." She spoke softly as a matter of fact. I knew she was right, that I didn't need to explain myself to her. But I wanted to. I wanted her to know what it was with Jacey and me. I just didn't know why, because I hadn't wanted to clarify it to anyone. Not even Zeeshan, but I wanted to, to her.

"No. I mean just wanted to talk about it to someone, so..." I didn't know what I was saying, but I couldn't keep my diplomatic guard up forever, I needed to talk to her. At my bare honest. I knew that wasn't something you did with someone you barely knew, but then I wanted to know her and wanted her to know me.

"You know, I genuinely meant when I said am always here." She almost whispered. We were standing close enough to let our hands brush across each other's. The way she said it sent shivers down my spine. I had never, in a long time really talked. But now I wanted to. I realized how I was willing to expose my vulnerable self to her and wondered if this was what Liz was talking about. Because this surely wasn't the way I felt for Jacey.

"Yeah, I know. I mean thanks." I turned away. I didn't know if I could look into her eyes while I told her something I hadn't had the guts to figure out myself.

"So, you want to tell?" she said in a tone that was expecting but not demanding. I liked the way she could make things feel so easy. Like it wasn't a big deal. Not many could do that.

"Yeah, it was just we had an argument. Well, more than an argument." We both smiled.

"Why?" she asked with genuine curiosity. "Only if you want to tell. Completely your call." She added, trying not to sound like she was wanting to pry out a topic for gossip for her girls' club.

"Apparently, both of us took actions of one other for something that they weren't."

"Oh,"

"It was me mostly, who mistook. Thought she didn't feel the same way I did. My bad." I could feel my chest tighten as all the memories from that night came rushing like water from an inverted vessel.

"I get it. It's awful,"

"You know I never got into girl business. Like never. But then I always wanted to feel what they always romanticized in the serials. I used to watch them a lot with my sisters when I was young."

"You're still young." She said, smiling at me one of her full smiles that reached her eyes and they closed, almost disappearing. Like Asians.

"I know. But that's not the point. I just wanted to know how it really was to have someone whom you could go back to no matter what. For whom you could be there. I wondered if that love at first sight existed."

"You fell for Jacey the very first time you saw her?" she asked, with a tinge of a surprise to her voice. Like she didn't believe in love at first sight kind of stuff. But something in her eyes made me feel like she did, believe in love at first sight. Or at least something if not love, if that wasn't what she would want to call it.

"Nope. But over time, we hung out. Talked, spent time together, I did fall for her. I don't know if I can say it was love. Because I don't really know what love means. But whatever it was that I felt for her, I had never felt that way before. She understood me so well. Or at least she pretended to." I could feel the tension rising as vapors as it screamed to run out of me through tears. I was trying hard to not let my tears fall from the corner of my eyes where I had been holding them back for a while now.

"She didn't feel for you the same way."

"Nope. Evidently, not."

"But you can't blame her for that. Can you?"

"I don't want to. But I secretly do." I hadn't said it out loud to anyone, I didn't know why I was telling it to her. I didn't know why I was telling anything to her. It wasn't like I owed her anything. But maybe I wanted to be heard, which she was doing. Listening to me.

Not judging me for how I felt. Just listening. Maybe this was what I had been wanting since start.

I could hear her as she let out a deep sigh, her chest expanding, only to close the few centimeters between us and let her hands brush against mine only for a moment.

"You can't blame yourself for feeling the way you do. It isn't like you control how you feel. You don't get to choose whom you fall for. It just happens."

"Yeah, I know."

"Neither can you blame someone for not feeling for you the way you do. You're getting what I'm trying to say?"

"Yeah, I do." This surely wasn't what I was expecting. She wasn't trying to pity me or even sympathize. Which would have only made it worse. But the way she just pointed out such an irascible fact with such elegance made me see past through my irrational emotions which I had been holding on to till now.

"Look, I know it's difficult but it isn't her fault that she doesn't love you."

"I know."

"Hey, listen to me," she put her hands softly on my shoulders and made me face her. She was looking right into my eyes and might have noticed how hard I was trying to keep my tears back from falling.

"You feeling for her is not a bad thing. It tells how beautiful you are. Don't ruin it by turning bitter. Okay? You felt the way you did, it doesn't tell anything about them, but you. About how beautiful you are to have such pious feelings." I could feel the warmth of her hands on me, the tears finally started to roll down my cheeks. She didn't let go of me or react to them. She just wiped them off softly with her sweaty hands and let her hand rest on my face for a while before letting go of me.

"I know. I just. I don't Iana. Sometimes I just feel this strong urge to know for once how it feels to have someone who'd love you back just like you do. Who would fight by you. For you. I mean I know there isn't a shortcut to find that. But sometimes you just want that person. You just want to feel it. Especially when you haven't felt anything for long enough that you fear you might as well be devoid of any feelings." I knew what I was doing, and as much as I was scared of where this might be going, I wanted to do it. more than I wanted anything else. I just didn't know what she was thinking about it. Or if there was anything like that for her or not. Maybe I was just mistaking her concern for something more. But even if I was, I wasn't mistaking my feelings for her.

"You see those lights?" she pointed into the far darkness. At first, I thought she was pointing towards the highway lights, which created a perfect line like marching soldiers. But no. she was pointing behind them. There was a small light, twinkling. A star maybe, or a lighthouse. I wasn't sure. But I just nodded.

"I named it *Anai*, Iana spelled backward. My alter self." She was looking at the light, all the turmoil from earlier gone. Her features looked so calm as if her demons had suddenly fallen silent as a little girl spoke her secrets to someone whom she barely knew but trusted enough to show her vulnerable side. I wondered if she was that girl who made everybody fall for her the moment she entered the room. Not because she was beautiful, which she certainly was, but because the energy she carried made you feel loved, cared for. Seen.

"Whenever I felt like I had no one I could talk to about complicated feelings that I had, I used to run to the rooftop and talk to her. Tell her everything I felt."

"Did she answer?" I asked stupidly like I was expecting something I didn't already know.

"No, she didn't answer. But I did."

"I don't understand," I just couldn't help falling for her more and more as she let her little secrets slip away from the walls that she had made around herself. Even if they were as small as her playlist. Yet they felt like I shared an intimate relationship with her. Pious than anything else.

"Whenever I used to say all that I felt aloud, it was like I was hearing my words from the perspective of the person because of whom I might be feeling so."

"And that made you realize the rationality and limitations of that person as well."

"You can say that." She smiled at me as she slowly slipped her sweaty hand into mine.

"So did *Anai* give you some kind of advice or what?" I liked the feel of her soft hands in mine. They were small, chubby. It was like I was holding on to something I had always wanted.

"Nope, she ain't much of an advisor,"

"Then?" I felt like I was ten years old Zayne again, asking questions when *Ammi* told him that *Allah* was up there somewhere and was watching us all. I didn't know where that somewhere was, but I never failed to ask until either she got busy doing something else, or I found something else to busy myself with.

"She heard. What all of us want deep down. To be heard. She heard me."

"That sounds pretty amazing. Like you have someone who hears you no matter what."

"And who always will be there," she added, smiling.

"Always?" I asked, raising an eyebrow, though I was smiling too.

"You can't stop the night from happening. Can you? Like you'd have to stop Earth rotating, and I guess that isn't possibly happening. Not until I'm alive, I believe. So I can bet on this one at least." She said cockily.

"No, I meant you believe in always? Because apparently, many in this generation don't." I didn't know why I said that. But I realized how much I meant it.

"Let me tell you a secret," she leaned in closer to whisper in my ear. Like, there was someone else at this crazy hour who might overhear us. But her warm breath and the sense that we were so near made me shiver.

"Everybody wants a forever. It's just that everybody realizes it at different times." She pulled back a bit to look at me. But she was still too close. Close enough that if I leaned in right now, I could kiss her full-on lips, which had started to dry as the layer of red lipstick started to fade away, returning to the pale pink color of which her lips originally were.

"Everybody wants it. But does everybody *believe* in it?"

"I don't know about everybody. And as a matter of fact, nobody can know about everybody." She had a way with words. I wondered if that was what her job was. Because if it was, then she must be pretty good at it.

"But you know about yourself. Do you believe in forever?" I was surprised at my audacity. I never knew if I could even ask such a question to anyone. Let alone the girl I was falling for. But then, all of what I had been doing lately, I never thought I ever could, so this just added to the list.

"More than anything."

"Really?" I was pretty surprised by the shine she had in her eyes when she said it.

"You know, sir, I've always read about it so much and it's just like..."

"Sorry to cut you like this, but I guess sir isn't the best salutation for this time." I couldn't help as a shy smile spread across my face.

"Yeah, right, sorry. It's just the habit." She looked at our hands, which were still tangled together. I'm sure she must've felt them sweaty like I did. But it was like none of us really cared about it.

"So, with the forever thing, continue," I tried diverting our attention towards something less awkward and gross than the sweat that had been making our hands slippery, because I surely didn't want to let go of her hand to clean them. Maybe because I was scared that she wouldn't take mine back once she let go.

"Oh, yeah. You know, I've always read about forever, like in fairytales and then real-life novels, and I've seen it in movies, but somehow all of it seemed very superficial. Like how it always had to be happily ever after or a tragic end to have a forever."

"That sucks," I didn't want to sound skeptical but worse, I didn't want to sound afraid. Because I exactly understood what she was saying, and by seeing the depth with which she understood the idea of *forever*, it made me scared of believing that maybe that was something I subconsciously craved for, too.

"I don't want a forever like that."

"Good to know that even forevers have types." We both shared a small laugh before she started on from where she had left, taking me with her, to explore deeper sides and perspectives I was too afraid to do myself. Maybe I guess that's why I felt drawn towards her in the first place. She challenged the sides of you, deeper fears, but she stood there to explore them with you. She didn't make me feel weak for being vulnerable, instead, she was making me learn how to embrace it just like any other human emotion.

"For me, I guess they do," she looked to the star and then again in my direction, and as the faint moonlight lit up her features, she looked so pale and pretty.

"So, what is your type of forever then, may I know?"

"Honestly, I want to have a 'forever' that doesn't have to be perfect or tragic or even end. Like, I just want unconditional forever. Like forever for something, no matter how much it hurts. Forever, that doesn't have to be this impeccable, immaculate sentence with a neat full stop. Until I know it's always going to be there, no matter what, I guess that'll be when I know it's my forever. Like having an ellipsis. Never ending, always having room for something, for when you return."

"And what if you get someone who'd want to share that forever with you?" I was almost so close to her that I could feel her breath on my face, and I had never felt the way I did right now ever in my life. All I wanted right now was to tell her how beautiful she looked with her messy hair and mascara-smeared eyes.

"I don't know. I never talked about it to anyone. I just... You know, there's like this craving for an addiction. But then there's desire, like this fuming desire you so badly want to have satiated that sometimes you even feel like you're getting burned by its heat. I've craved it so bad."

"You have?" I could see that in her eyes when she talked about it. But something felt off. Like this hollow emptiness that eats away at the back of your head, even when you think you've got every possible thing in this world to make you happy.

"I always have. To know how it feels to be that way to someone. I just don't know. I wish I knew. But I don't know if I ever will. Sometimes it feels like I ain't in the right place. Like you know, I think all of this is too much to expect. But then I can't help. I don't crave some mystically mythological love story, I just want mine to be worth living for."

I could see the desperation as she spoke all of it; it was like she was screaming right to me, to be held and pulled out of whatever it was that she was trying to get away from. It was like she was trusting me with her bare side, warning me about the risks at the same time. She reminded me why Jacey had decided to back off in the first place. I remembered how she said I expected too much in this generation of transience and how I was silly to be so. But knowing that this girl whom I had been falling so hard for believed in the kind of love that I did, it made me want to pull her in and tell her straight away how I felt the same way, *for her.*

"Would you want that kind of story with me?" I spoke out loud before I could change my mind. I didn't know if this was the best idea. I saw her eyes go wide as she looked at me, completely spellbound. I hadn't seen her so quiet ever before. It was like even while she didn't really speak, her eyes always had something to say. But this time, they were completely dead. Though she didn't look away or pull back from me. I shook her a little to pull her back out of her reverie.

"Oh, I'm sorry, just. It was just pretty unexpected. I mean, I didn't see it coming. I'm sorry."

"No, you don't have to be, it's just that, I don't know what this feeling is... I just" I could see the puzzlement in her eyes as they shifted from mine to our tangled hands. She didn't pull away, she just let it in close as she rubbed my knuckles with her thumb. It felt completely insane. The way I felt for her, given the fact that we had known each other for just a few weeks. I didn't know if what I was doing was right, but I did know that I had chosen to take my chances and that there was no going back now. I liked her and wanted to have that forever that she so passionately talked about just a few moments ago, with her. I pulled back my one hand and carefully placed it on her waist to pull her close enough that we stood close enough to kiss, yet giving her a chance to pull away if she wanted to. She didn't. She stood there, looking right into my eyes as I leaned in and put my mouth on hers. I could feel her soft lips on mine as my tongue slowly found its way into her mouth, and my arms pulled her closer, wanting to close any distance between us. She tasted like a pina colada. No wonder she had been drinking, maybe to get through whatever made her look the way she did when she first showed up. I could feel her giving in to my arms as she leaned in further, deepening our kiss. She had her eyes closed, but I didn't close mine. I saw her, as she melted, all the worry from earlier, all solemnness gone. She looked so calm and young, and beautiful.

She opened her eyes suddenly and within that moment, I could see how much toll whatever she had been holding back and trying to fight had been taking on her. It was like something ate away at her as she tried to fight it away while crying for someone to reach out for her. But it was there only for a moment before she realized that I had been watching, and maybe that made her feel like she was standing naked, unguarded. Because in the very next second, with a flick of an eye, it was gone. She saw me dead in the eyes and stood still for a moment before pulling away suddenly, like she realized she had been doing something very wrong.

"I... I'm sorry. I didn't mean to, sorry." She looked intermittent. I didn't know what it was that made her look that way. But by that look in her eyes just before she became so, I could feel there was something wrong. Something very wrong.

"No, it's my fault. I shouldn't have." I tried to figure out what went wrong.

"Look, I... It's nothing about you. It's just me. I don't know what I want right now. I don't think it's a good idea for us, like this. I mean... everybody who comes close to me... I don't want to hurt you." She cupped my face with one hand as she rubbed my cheek softly, and her touch felt like something I had ached for always, but didn't exactly know what it was that I ached for. I opened my mouth to say something, but she didn't let me as she continued.

"I like you..." This, coming from her, made my heart race at the speed of Formula One cars. It felt like my arteries would burst from the pressure and force with which my heart pumped.

"...But I don't think it's the best thing for you to feel this way for me. I don't want you to get hurt. I just... I'm sorry. I just don't know what's wrong with me. I just can't. I'm sorry," She let her hand fall at her side as she turned to leave. She didn't stop to see if I had anything to say. I could barely make sense of what happened in the past few hours. I just knew they were the few hours that made me feel alive in a way I hadn't ever felt before. She turned and for once I hoped she'd come back and kiss me and it'd be me and her like they show in Disney movies,

"I'm sorry. But I want you to know that I'm here whenever you need me." I hoped that she'd say something else, but she didn't. She kept moving. I heard the engine rev somewhere nearby. But it was the last thing I cared about right now. All I could focus on was her silhouette as she walked away, straight.

I turned towards my phone and hit the play button as *Billie Eilish* picked up on *Everything I wanted*, from where I had paused the song. I didn't know what else to do, I didn't know what to think, what to feel.

CHAPTER SIXTEEN

IANA

I was still trying to get the hang of what happened back at the Angel's Top. As much as I should have been happy that there was something that he felt for me, I was afraid. I was afraid after what happened with Arsh, I might not be the person for whom he should be feeling this way. But somewhere deep down, I wanted it myself. I wanted to lean into him, give in to his arms and kiss him back. Tell him while we kissed that I'd want more than anything to have that forever with him. But I just wasn't sure. I wasn't sure about myself. I wasn't sure if I were ready. And I couldn't put him in a position from which he was already still trying to gather himself back. After he trusted me so much to tell whatever it was that happened with Jacey, and how he felt, I couldn't put him in a situation like that again. Because, of all that he deserved, being loved back like he did was surely on the top of that list. And though I knew I myself craved it, I didn't know if it'd be just to do that. He deserved nothing but best. I didn't want to be with him to just find an escape from my own hurt and failed love. I couldn't do that to him. But it was only so much that I could be sure of. I wanted to be there for him but I couldn't say to him things that he wanted to listen and wanted someone to feel, if I didn't really mean them. I didn't want him to feel the way I felt when Arsh did that. I knew those scars could last forever. But more than I was afraid of what Arsh made me face, I didn't want him to face what I did to him. I would never want it to happen to anyone. But it did. And all because of what I said in those last seven and a half minutes.

I walked into the hall, the door was unlocked, Hella must've been back and must've forgotten to lock it behind her. The place was dark since no lights were on, it looked like she might've been asleep. So much had happened today that everything seemed quite heavy to carry on till the next day. I wanted to see her, make sure that she was alright. I knew it wasn't her fault that she wanted to see me happy again like we used to be when we were kids. Like I used to play cards with her and steal a spoon of her ice cream when she would be fighting for an extra one. I missed all that myself too, and I knew she just wanted things to get normal, she just wanted me to get normal. And I didn't want to be tough on her but she didn't know that after what happened last summer, nothing could be normal, at least not the way she hoped it to be. It shouldn't be any of her concern, and I would have done just about anything to keep it that way. I wanted to tell her how sorry I was that I lashed out earlier today at the club. But I also wanted her to know that her pestering me to date new people and get to know new people wasn't a solution to all the problems I was facing. I wanted her to understand that turning away from them wasn't going to do any good like she thought it'd. I called for her once, to see if she was still awake but I could just hear my own footsteps against the floor wood. The lights to her room were off too. I raised my hand to knock but decided against it. I thought she'd be asleep and as much as I wanted to talk to her, I didn't want to disturb her. It was already so much that had happened today that I thought it'd be better if we talked about it with calm minds and clear heads. Still, I didn't move away immediately, I turned the doorknob to sneak in, just to have a look at my little baby sister who had grown up too early just to make sure that I was doing fine. The door opened with a creek as I peeped in to see if she was there in the bed, but the sight of the room made me barge in without even warning her as my reflexes kicked in. The room was completely turned upside down. Every single article fell out of place. The wardrobe mirror was smashed and all her clothes made this perfect carpet on the floor to not have one's soft feet touch the hard ground. At first, it felt like someone had a wrestling match in here but then as things started to fall in place, I could put all the pieces together. The room told the tale of Hella's temper itself. I could hear muffled whispers as I neared the balcony, she was on the phone probably talking to her best friend or maybe mine, I didn't know. But I could hear sobs between clenched teeth. She must've heard me coming in as she turned around to look at me before she hung up on whoever she was talking to.

"What is it," she sounded cold, distant. Like I was the last person she was willing to talk to right now.

"Look whatever happened back at the club, I shouldn't have reacted that way. I'm sorry."

"Yeah, you really shouldn't have. Especially knowing that you were doing that to only people who really care if you get your shit together in this unknown land."

"I know. I'm sorry. It's just that, you two discussing my personal life like it's some kind of experiment in progress which needs to be reported about every day..." I closed in a few steps to be just close enough to hold her at my arm's length, "...it doesn't make it any better, it just makes me feel like I am not normal."

"You haven't been acting that way, do you blame us for that?" she spoke that without tinge of any warmth like she had predetermined that she wouldn't let it be easy this time for me to get away with it.

"Look, I don't blame you for it. it's just that whatever happened with Arsh..."

"For god's sake, Eea do you want to go there? Again? Look, how many times have I told you that you can't just keep going there again and again and expect a different outcome. Like someday you'll wake up and boom, like some magic all if it will be gone like any of it never happened. You've got to fight through it, and locking people out who care about you, surely isn't on the manual for that." She held my hands which had been resting on her shoulders to support her, but it was more the other way round.

"I know, I'm sorry. I'm trying. I promise I won't lock you out ever again. I'll try better this time. I just don't like to see you this way, I'm sorry. You've just got to stop spying on me."

"Only if you mean it this time. I know I've told this to you millions of times but you somehow need a constant reminder that we love you, and seeing you like this, it hurts. That's the only reason we want you to be happy." She said smiling. Though the smile didn't quite reach her eyes.

"I know," I pulled her into a hug, closing my eyes to feel her chest rising and falling against mine. Feeling the warmth that her pale skin transferred to my cold and pale body.

"That and keeping you away from the cliffs." she added pulling away, smiling fully this time.

"Oh please," I rolled my eyes at her, tucking behind her ear a lock of her hair. She looked so much like me, just younger and stronger and more beautiful. I felt lucky to have her while I carried all that I did, even if she didn't know, she was the reason I felt like keep going. She was the reason who *made* me feel like keep going.

"Will you tell me now where you were?" she asked, picking up her favorite clothes which she had abandoned to the glory of the ground in a fit of angst.

"Just for a walk at the Angel's Top," I knew there wasn't a possibility that I'd get away without telling her but I wanted to see if there was a chance.

"And?" she asked, without bothering to look at me.

"Nothing, I just walked, looked at lights."

"You know I don't want to torture you for the details, so this is your cue. Guess you should've known that by yourself now." She punched me lightly in the shoulder while stuffing all her clothes in the wardrobe without folding them and falling onto the unmade bed like the labor made her run out of energy. I let out a deep sigh, it wasn't like I was hoping to get away with it so easily. I just didn't know how to explain to her what happened between me and him. Though I knew I had to tell her, so I did.

She didn't even blink while I spoke every detail of the night to her, it looked like she was in a theatre, watching a movie for which she had been waiting for months. Though I couldn't fathom the look on her face. I didn't know if she liked what she heard because she just looked so blank,

"Oh my God," she grabbed my shoulders as she took in all that I told her and twirled me around like a merry-go-round. She looked like she had received a piece of news she had been wanting to hear for ages and had started to give up on its arrival.

"What? You didn't just hear what I did? I pushed him away,"

"I know, I heard. But it's a start."

Seeing her so happy made me want to freeze the moment. It had been a while since she looked so happy because of me.

"Hella, don't get too excited. I don't know if I'm ready. Plus, I think he might be hurt. After how I turned away. I just wanted to tell you that don't get your hopes high. It's nothing like what you want there to be." I stood to leave. I paused there for a moment, taking in the smiling face of the little girl who was so grown up now before I crossed the room and held the door open to leave.

"Hey, Eea." She shouted for me just when I was about to leave. I turned to see her standing behind me while she hugged me tight, holding me completely off guard.

"Hey, what?"

"I just want you to know that you can't just be stuck forever and find a thousand reasons to run from what you feel." She held my right hand and placed it on the left side of my chest where I could feel my own heart beating as I fought millions of emotions that clouded my mind with only one face in focus. His.

"You can't run from it Eea. See it for yourself. You deserve this and all the other amazing chances in the world. Don't ruin it, for yourself, please. I love you." She kissed me softly on my cheek before I closed the door between us.

I knew she wanted me to be happy, and so did I. I just felt a bit lost. But I couldn't lie to myself that today after long, was the day when I had felt the most alive. Back on Angele's Top and then here, when I saw that smile on Hella's face after an eternity. And the reason behind both was the same. Him. I didn't know what I was going to do, but for now, I wanted to keep feeling alive. I fished out my phone as I searched for his number and typed out the text,

I'm sorry for walking away like that. Hope you'd understand. Want to hang out later?

I pressed the send button as I craved to steal moments of such life with him. I craved to feel alive like I did tonight. Because of him, *with* him.

#

That night seemed to evaporate in a mist of a longed dream as the reality swirled into its forces around me. Eign had started to act weird, nothing like he ever did. Even if we had worst fights like the one at the club a few weeks back. More than once he came and held on to me and looked straight into my eyes like he was expecting me to read his mind and know whatever that heavy thing was that he failed to get off his chest through his speech. It felt like he was expecting me to free him from some kind of burden without having to tell me what it was. But whatever it was that I saw in his eyes, it looked like it had always been there but it was ever more intense now. I wish I could be there for him, but he wouldn't let me. I tried asking if he was okay but it would always end in a void conversation. Every time he'd start to say something but end up changing his mind. Like he couldn't gather enough courage to face how whatever it was that he wanted to say would turn out.

Sir had been acting differently too. But I didn't blame him. After whatever happened at Angel's Top I won't be surprised if he's feeling... confused. But I just didn't know why I didn't want to let him be in it alone. Even though I was the one who pushed him when he tried opening up, I wanted to be with him, to talk things out. But it wasn't his fault that he'd want to avoid the girl to whom he confessed that he was falling for but she just walked away. I wish I could tell him my fears, that it was me with whom the problem was, it wasn't him. But it didn't feel right to burden with something that was mine to handle, that was my doing. I pulled out my phone and looked at the unread messages. They shouldn't have affected me the way they did. I had no right to feel pissed about it, but I did. It felt like someone who was bound to be by my side forever had turned his back to me, even though I was the one who walked out. Somehow, I felt that Hella was right, whatever I carried or felt wasn't an eternal free pass to the way I treated people who wanted nothing but to be there with me. But even though I wanted to go tell him that I wanted it and felt it as much as he did, I couldn't get myself to get over the thought that I might ruin it all, like I did with Arsh. And I wouldn't want that even for the worst of my enemies, let alone him. It was all just too much. I hoped that if I'd busy myself with work, probably more than enough work, it'd go away. The editor-in-chief made me in charge of the Founder's Day ceremony of Muses and Caerus. As much as I would've been obliged to do it, I thought it'd be a great escape to keep all the mess out of my mind, at least for a while. It was definitely a hell lot of work though. The job was something that seemed to require greater effort than I had thought. But it was good. I had already been engrossed in my personal life enough to forget why I was here in the first place. I didn't want to let it stray me away. This job was something I had wanted badly enough to go against my family. I couldn't lose it. It was the only thing that was keeping me from going insane. Like it was doing now. Thankfully, whatever it was that was up with Eign, it didn't stop him from being my partner while I took on the responsibility for the organising the golden jubilee anniversary of the firm. It could very well be my doorway to my dream position in the firm. And whatever mess was going on in my personal life, it could surely wait for this one.

"Hey, so coming to see the venue?" I asked Eign, he was working on the presentation for the event. I knew no one else could've been better for this job. He knew company better than I did and he had a way with technology. I scrolled through the slides as he grabbed his car keys and coat, getting ready to leave with me,

"Wait, what is this?" I saw a familiar title under the heading of planned launches of the year for the debut writers.

"What?" he leaned in over my shoulders, a bit closer than usual. I could feel his breath on my neck as he looked at the computer screen over my shoulder.

"This one," I selected the title with the cursor,

"even if it's not meant to be forever...?"

"Yeah. Isn't it the title I talked to you about? Like how it's so raw and..."

"Different. Just like something you'd want." he looked at me directly as his words came out more in a whisper.

"Yeah, but when did it get approved? Last time I checked the editor said he'd look into it. Nothing concrete."

"Well, let's just say I made a special request,"

"You did what?" I looked at him in disbelief as my eyes widened at what he spilled in,

"I read the manuscript. I could see why you liked it so much. So, I just put in a special request for its consideration."

"And the editor liked it?"

"He loved it." he smiled as I jumped on to him to hug him tightly, almost tripping him off and banging both of our heads to the tabletop.

"Oh my god thank you so much Eign. I just can't tell you how happy I am. I mean I really did want this piece of work to get out there, for everybody to read it, it was so nice. You made it happen, thank you so much."

"Look at you. You look happier than the author who got the publishing break." he laughed as he helped me to my feet, dusting off his clothes.

"I love you so much, Eign. I just don't know what in heaven did I do to get a friend like you." I picked up my bag as we left his cabin to leave for the venue.

"Yeah right, I love you too." he said, looking away to avoid looking at me than actually punching in the floor number in the elevator pad.

The place was beautiful, and I was glad that Jeane's father had trusted me enough to let me have charge of this event and do things my way. I was determined to make it nothing less than perfect. We went to the banquet area which seemed just large enough to accommodate all the guests, but it felt too conventional. For the success party of a firm whose achievements in such a small span was no less than a miracle, it had to be different, out of the box, amazing. I asked the manager if they had an open space, and he was more than happy to show it to us,

"What do you have on your mind, Eea?" Eign asked, confused.

"For an unusually successful firm, a usual banquet party seems a bit boring." I chuckled.

"Don't tell me you're trying to experiment with *Muses and Caerus'* success party,"

"I very well am." I turned abruptly to laugh right into his face as I patted his cheek as you do to a toddler to make him realize everything will be just fine.

"You must be kidding, you can try as much of your out-of-the-box ideas at your birthday party or mine for that matter but this is the firm's jubilee party, for fuck's sake no Eea. Don't act stupid." I liked seeing him turn red when he got nervous, he looked cute. But too bad that I was pretty keen on doing what I had in mind.

We walked through the backyard doors into an opening between lush green woods and lakeside, of course, it was a small artificial one, but it looked just so pretty. The lake had a platform right in the center to which stepping stones floated in the water just like in the fairytales.

"My goodness," he turned around to look at the place, I was happy that he was no less mesmerized than me.

"We're going to go for it" I looked over to the manager as he gave us a tour of the place.

"Do you like it?" I asked Eign, already knowing what his answer must be.

"This is surely something, Singh. You do have a taste, and knowledge of places I must say. How did you come to know about this place?" he asked, genuinely curious as we walked behind the manager to complete the formalities for reserving the place. It wasn't every day that you come across such beautiful places for such perfect occasions.

"I did my homework." I winked at him while he completed the papers that the lady at the reception had handed over to him.

"I must say you impress me out my wits sometimes. Roses?" he asked. I was taken back by the sudden question, I threw him a confused look as my brows furrowed while I tried to make sense of what he had just asked,

"I mean the floral decoration, it's here, they've more options if you'd like to have a look." he held the brochure out to me while he went on filling the other details,

"I guess let's play this one safe at least, roses shall be fine. Most people like them so shouldn't be a problem."

"You like them?" he asked, taking a moment to look up from the papers to me,

"Honestly, I don't. I like Lilies and Jasmines. Roses kind of seem, I don't know, overrated."

"Different, as you are," he gave a soft laugh.

The day was pretty long, but I was so glad that I had Eign by my side all the time. It wouldn't have been possible to go through all of it alone. It was more exhausting than I had thought, but it kind of made me happy, doing something that for once didn't confuse me or make me feel like I wasn't in control. Though I could sense something different about Eign all the while, but maybe I was just being paranoid. I was happy that he had forgiven me for that night at the club. And glad too, that he didn't bring up any of it while we wandered through the city to arrange for the perfect success party. I was going to make this one worth remembering, I pretty much was. It felt nice, to forget everything while I worked. But it was only temporary. Only a while before all of it came crashing. But for now, at least I had it, and I wanted to make it count.

#

"You've done an amazing job, Miss Singh," Mr. Schumer, Jeane's father raised his glass of champagne in my direction as Jeane walked away from his side towards me and pulled me into a long embrace.

"I love the party, Iana."

"Thanks," I said, pulling back, afraid I might be too sweaty. The place was nice and air-conditioned but it didn't do much to stop my anxiety which led to excessive sweating and ruining of my party-perfect look which Hella had so arduously worked upon.

"When dad told me that you were in charge of the event, I told him to rest assured that this one was going to be the best party of Muses and Caerus has ever had. Why dad?" she turned to look in the direction of her father who was taking a better look at the arrangements and making sure that a twenty-year-old employee didn't miss out on anything essential for a perfect success party.

"And you weren't wrong," he smiled at me, his eyes sending a wave of warmth through me. He was a generous and tacit man. But the aura he had never made me feel like I couldn't go to him if I ever had any problem. I was happy that he liked the evening. Muses and Caerus was like my abode of retreat, a dream come true. It was the reason I felt like keep going even when I felt like to giving up the most. Had I not come here, I would've driven myself back to that cliff. Even thinking about it makes me shudder.

"Hey, you look beautiful," Eign hugged me from behind, startling me. He looked handsome. Looking at him standing there as the bright lights cast shadows and illuminations across his sharp-featured face made him look handsome in the way they describe characters in novels. His hair was stuck in place completely by hair spray. I guess he had been working on pulling it off tonight. I realized how handsome he was. I had never noticed him like that before. The suit fit him just perfectly across his chest, his shirt creased when his chest rose and fell as he breathed. I realized how sturdy he was, he was lean but you could see ripples of muscles at slightest of flex.

"All good?" he shook me a little as I turned red. There wasn't anything good about being caught stalking your best friend.

"Yeah, thanks. You look hot," I coughed a bit as the words spill out of my mouth, unwelcomed.

"Sorry, I mean you look good too." He smiled an all-teeth grin, as I tried looking away from him, too embarrassed.

"Good job Miss Singh," he smirked at me, handing me a glass of red wine which he picked up from the waiter who served the guests, greeting them with a smile as warm as sunshine.

"I guess equal credit goes to my better half Eign, so it'd be better if you appreciated his work too, Sire." I smiled as I clinked my glass to his'.

"Better half?" his eyebrows shot in surprise as I thought I saw color rising to his cheeks while his ears turned red. It wasn't every day that you caught a person like him blushing. I punched him playfully in the shoulder to make it less awkward.

"Of course, you are my better half, I can never find a best friend, colleague, mentor like you, Eign. I love you." I gave him a side hug. He was completely red. I didn't know why, but he looked cute. Maybe I should embarrass him often.

"Yeah, of course, I am your best friend that's why you love me," he said with a tone I couldn't differentiate for happy or annoyed.

"Hey, I don't love you *because* you're my best friend. You're my best friend because I love you more than anything else." He looked at me with that look in his eyes which I had been trying to decipher since our night at the club. This time it felt like he was going to say something, he almost did. But then he just pulled me into a tight hug, deciding against it. Whatever it was that he was holding back, it seemed like he wanted to tell me so badly that had I pushed him a bit he would have. I opened my mouth to ask him but Jeane interrupted me,

"Hey, I hope I'm not disturbing you, Dad wanted to introduce you to some of his clients."

"Oh, I'm coming," she left to join some of the other girls from work whom she had known longer than she knew me.

"After the party, meet me at the terrace." Eign whispered just before disappearing into the crowd. I wondered what he'd want to do so late on the terrace, but I knew if he needed me, I'd be there. Like he had always been. I looked at him once as he looked in my direction and nodded. I didn't know what it was that was eating away at him, but I would find it tonight. But before that, I had a party to make a success. And so did he.

I let out a deep sigh and placing my half-drunk wine glass on the side table, with other empty glasses, I pulled my gown to gather its black frill to avoid people stepping over it, as I went down the crowd to look for Mr. Schumer.

I didn't see Eign for long after that. The party was quite a success. The board members were pretty impressed with the venue and arrangements. And I, for a while was happy that the one thing that kept me alive was something I was able to do justice to. My job, Muses and Caerus, my passion. It was midnight and the party was almost over. The last few guests bid farewell as the staff started to wind up and clean the place. I checked around the place for the last time to make sure I didn't forget anything there or if anybody else might've forgotten something. Maybe it wasn't really that, I was trying to push away the thought of having a really serious talk with Eign as much as I could. But I knew there was something up and I had to be there for him. Like he always had been there for me. I took in a deep breath and wiped my hands to the side of my dress to get rid of the sweat as I pushed in the button for the terrace on the elevator pad.

CHAPTER SEVENTEEN

EIGN

I was quite nervous about letting all that I had carried for so long out. I wasn't sure if it was a good idea but there was no going back now. The night when I saw her there at Angel's Top with that guy, I realized how badly I had wanted to be there instead of him. I wanted to be the guy to kiss her and tell her how beautiful she was and when I saw that guy doing it, it almost killed me. I thought I had lost Eea. Because the way they both were looking at each other, it felt like they had always been in love. I had almost left, but then I saw her pulling away, and saying that she couldn't, she couldn't because she was confused. And I didn't know and I might be expecting a lot for it to be even a wild possibility but maybe she couldn't because she was confused that she felt that way for someone else, not him. For someone who's always been there and who always will be, and it was only at that moment that she realized it. I guess Hella was right, I couldn't just keep lying to myself, and her. Pretend like I didn't notice her pulling her hair back into a messy bun when they fell in her eyes while she worked, didn't admire how beautiful she was even with her eyes all black with smeared mascara and face red with smudged lipstick. She was beautiful and I loved her. I guess I always had, from the moment I didn't remember and I always will, till the moment I won't remember. And of all that I wished for in this world, having her by my side always was at the top of the list. I looked at the table with freshly blooming white Lilies and the scented candles, not too strong, she didn't like strong scents, and then looked at the lights which twinkled in the background. Just the way she always talked about when we watched movies and some romantic scenes came in. She still had memories of her time with Arsh and didn't blame her for feeling the way she did because it wasn't her fault. She was too good and had given all that she had to that bastard. I understood it, and I wanted her to have all that she deserved and much more, I wanted her to know how pretty she was.

The elevator doors pinged open and I didn't care if it seemed dramatic but she looked like a princess walking down the aisle. The white Lilies complemented the black of her dress just perfectly to add to her beauty. Her makeup had faded and I noticed she had removed her jewelry which left her neck bare. It made her look so beautiful and exposed. I could see that she was surprised, her eyes widened as I pulled the chair for her before settling into mine.

"Wow, that's some surprise," she said, plucking one Lily from the bouquet in the center of the table and smelling it.

"As I intended it to be," I poured two glasses of bourbon and handed one to her.

"All good? Is there something special?" she asked taking the glass from me but not drinking from it.

"Not really, just wanted you to have some good time like you always talked about when such scene would come in a movie," she smiled and looked away at the lights,

"This is beautiful, thank you so much Eign. I just don't know what I'd do without you." She left the bourbon untouched as she stood up and went to the balcony side and looked at the lights. She always had something for lights and the only time when I saw her really peaceful was when she was watching them. It was like she understood their fragility and didn't want to affect their purity with her hustling demons which she fought inside.

"Hey, you like it?" I asked, not taking my eyes off her.

"I love it. I love you." She took my one hand in hers' and hugged me tightly. She smelt like lavender and body wash and sweat. Of course, she had been working too hard since the past week to make this event a success. And now that it was, she deserved a break. I hugged her back and held her for a little too long. I wanted to feel her there, in my arms completing me.

"Hey, is everything fine?" she asked while I still held her there, hugging. Not letting go.

"Yeah, it's just," I couldn't make words to come out as complete sentences. I was too nervous and happy and afraid. It was like I was feeling all the possible emotions one could feel at the same time. I pulled back from our embrace and let her go and before I could change my mind and say something to ruin this very special moment that we were sharing, I took in a deep breath and leaning in kissed her full on her lips softly. Her lips were dry with the lipstick fading away and all the drinking. But they felt like a breath of fresh air. I had been imagining it since forever and now that I was here and had her in my arms, I felt like I couldn't be any happier. I wished that I could make her understand how I felt about her without having to say it because I couldn't ever find the right words, and I doubted I ever would.

"Iana, I don't know how to tell you but trust me I'm being honest with you. I had always wanted to tell you how much I love you." Her eyes were wide as she looked at me in disbelief. It was like she had frozen.

"When? I mean how?" she stuttered as she tried to make sense of everything that happened so suddenly in the past few moments.

"I never had the guts to tell it to your face, but that night Hella and I had a talk and she told me that how she knew it. She made me realize something that I myself had been running from," she didn't say anything so I just continued,

"That night, I came behind you,"

"At Angele's Top?" she asked

"Yes, and I saw you with that guy, I guess he was your trainer, the guy who texted you,"

"Zayne," the name came out of her mouth like it was some kind of reflex fed in her system.

"I saw him kissing you and I thought I had lost you, I thought you wanted it. I was happy for you but I won't lie about how I wanted it to be me and not him." I moved in closer to her, as my hands closed on her waist and she fell so perfectly in my arms. It was like pieces of a jigsaw coming together, the way it felt to hold her.

"You saw us?" she asked credulously, surprised. Not angry.

"Yeah, I was about to leave when you pulled away and said that you didn't feel that way and I felt hope. I didn't know but I felt like it was maybe because you loved someone whom you knew loved you all along which you just couldn't see until then,"

"You thought I said that because I love you?" she asked stepping back, holding my hands off her and placing them at my sides.

"Don't you?" I asked as I could feel an unknown ache rise in my chest.

"I do, but not the way you think Eign. I love you and I always will but you're just my best friend. I'm sorry." I felt those words leave her mouth and hoped that I'd wake up with my hair tousled and me fallen from the bed on the floor. Only that it was no dream and I was here, with her and all that she said, all that I said was no less true than me and her standing here.

"But you said to him..."

"That wasn't because I loved you or had anyone else on my mind, I just needed time. I wanted to be sure about it, Eign. I'm sorry if you..."

"No, it's okay," I said as tears rolled down my cheek, I didn't want to but I didn't know what I was thinking when I involuntarily added, "You wanted to be sure that it was *him*?"

She didn't say anything, her dark brown eyes sparkled as tears from them caught the light and cast illumination across her face. I knew I didn't need her to say it aloud. I understood that silence of hers' like always had.

"I'm sorry," she turned to leave and I saw that those tears carried in them the weight I had just now put on her, I could see that she felt bad for me. She somehow thought it was her fault.

"Hey, don't be" I moved towards her and hugged her tightly, "I'll always be your best friend, no matter what." We pulled back and I could see there something that weighed her down, and I knew exactly what,

"I guess you should go and do it, you deserve it," I whispered in her ear, and she smiled at me that real-happy smile that was quite rare to see, just like some dinosaur's fossil.

"You really think that?"

"Totally. Now go," she started towards the elevator but stopped mid-way. She turned and ran towards me and kissed me on the cheek,

"Thank you so much Eign." She muttered and left almost running. Seeing her black frill drag behind and the elevator close on her I finally let my tears lose as they flowed down the cheek, I realized how much I loved her. I loved her too much to let her go like this, but then I loved her much more to make her stay when I knew what she wanted. I loved her, I couldn't help it like she couldn't help not loving me. I wanted her to stay but I loved her enough for it to be with someone she loved.

Letting out a deep sigh I turned to face the sparkling shards of light as the cool night breeze swept my tears away and new ones found their way down to take their place.

CHAPTER EIGHTEEN

IANA

He had been avoiding me since the night we last met, I didn't blame him. But I needed to talk to him this time, I had to. He wouldn't answer my text or calls so I just made a wild guess about his location. I wasn't sure but was hoping bad enough for him to be there, standing and watching the lights like we did that night. I parked the car at some distance and dumped my heels in the back seat. The night air felt cool as it carried away with it my sweat and tears. It felt like a perfect night to have a jog with Jassie Ware or Ruelle and Fleurie singing in the background but now was not the time. I had something more important to do right now than having a stroll. I walked slowly to the periphery wall of the empty parking, stopping momentarily to kick way stones and pebbles and wipe away the blood from the fresh-cut that I might have gotten when I landed my foot on a sharp stone while getting off from the car. The five minutes' walk seemed the longest walk of my life and those few meters felt more like miles. Though seeing his black-haired head, wind touseling his unkempt hair filled me with the kind of relief I hadn't really felt in a long time. He had his AirPods plugged in so he didn't quite react to my arrival, not immediately. And I didn't want to take it too fast, I wanted to slow down the time while I was here with him, at the most beautiful place. It felt so intimate that an anonymous kind of heat started to rise into my body as I closed upon him until I was standing beside him and he finally saw me, surprise filling those dark brown eyes.

"Hey, what are you doing here?" he asked pulling out his earplugs and stopping the music. While he pressed the pause I could see it was a song from my playlist and couldn't help as a smile spread across my face. He saw me looking at his screen and put it inside immediately,

"Oh, it's just, I liked the song,"

"Yeah, I like it too," I said shyly.

"What are you doing here at this hour in..." he had a look at my crippled dress and partially beautifully done hair, "...I guess this isn't the place where you're supposed to be."

"This is the exact place where I should've been long before." I closed in on him until we were standing close enough to feel each other's breath on our faces. I could feel his heart racing under his ribcage as I pulled back a strand of my hair and tucked it behind my ear.

"I... I don't understand what you're talking about," he fumbled.

"I had a date with my best friend," his eyes got wide as a look of confusion filled them. It was the last thing he would've been expecting at this hour of the night while he listened to music and watched stars in solitude.

"I...um," I held up a finger at his mouth stopping him from saying anything further,

"You know Eign, my best friend and I have known each other for long enough to tell everything. He has been by my side always and yet today looking at him there, I felt like I didn't know him at all. All that he carried within and didn't let out. I felt how much I have been avoiding anything that's got anything to do with love,"

"Happens, sometimes we choose to avoid things that we think are too difficult only not realizing that we can't avoid them forever. It's okay, you're a good friend." He took my hand in his' and rubbed its back slowly with his thumb.

"No, I'm not. How can I be, when I've been running away from something that has been there the whole time. When I've been running away from myself to avoid hurting,"

"It's okay, it isn't your fault. We all fear getting hurt. don't be too hard on yourself,"

"I hate it, feeling this way, I don't know why it isn't helping, I..." he wiped away a tear I didn't realize had fallen from the corner of my eye,

"I can't now,"

"You don't have to, it's okay. Calm down. Just breath." He pointed in the far direction where I did when we were here the last time, holding me closer with one arm wrapped around me. I smelt cologne and sweat. He must've come here straight from the gym. He lowered his head and whispered in my ear,

"Remember what you said that night? You talk to *Anai*," I looked at him smiling between my tears, looking a complete mess as I nodded,

"I guess we should give her a break, now that I'm here I guess you can share some of that heavy shit of yours with me," he smiled rubbing my shoulder, not leaving my side.

"Why weren't you replying me?" he went quiet for a second before opening his mouth to reply me like he was trying to channelize what he should say to not make this situation any more awkward than it already was. But to be honest, I felt something that I hadn't for a long time and had given up on feeling ever again.

"I wanted to, but..."

"What?"

"When I kissed you, I felt like I saw something in your eyes like you were calling to be reached out for like you wanted someone to rescue you from something that you were too afraid to let out, talk about loud." A gasp escaped my mouth as I felt him speaking out my thoughts, thoughts which I myself was too scared to say out loud, like talking about them would somehow make them worse.

"But then you pulled away and I saw something else. It felt like raw pain like it somehow hurt you enormously to be there, that you were fighting with every cell of your body to not be there, in that position. And I was scared, Iana. That pain looked like you could be dying carrying it yet it would refuse to go away. I was afraid that if I... we came close, you'd suffer. And I didn't want you to suffer. Not because of me," his words felt like some foreign language which didn't make sense to the cerebrum but they felt familiar to the heart like you get visions of prophecy in your dreams or kind of déjà vu. He was looking straight into my eyes and felt like he wasn't trying to turn down the noise inside me, instead, he tried to configure the melody in it.

"No, it's not like that. Another way round in fact," I held on to him so tight that I didn't realize I was digging my nails in his hand. Our hands were almost white where blood couldn't flow due to us holding each other too tightly,

"When Eign kissed me and said he loved me I realized how I did not not like that but how I wanted it to be someone else. I realized how all this while I had been wanting someone to pull me out, away from my demons even if I kept pushing them away. I realized how I wanted it to be..."

"Me." He didn't ask it as a question he said it in a tone that made me believe that I wasn't alone to fight my demons. The way he spoke made me break free from my worst fear of falling for someone again and getting myself into the cycle again. But I couldn't help. I could feel my rationality being side kicked by emotions. But I felt *alive*. For the first time, it felt like I wasn't running.

"Yes,"

He turned me swiftly as he pulled me closer until there wasn't any space left between us, I could feel the way our hearts beat in sync with each other in harmony. His hands felt strong and soft around my waist, holding me firmly in place. I realized how weak my legs felt. They would have given up and I would have crumpled on the ground had he not been holding me in place steadily. Wiping away my tear he softly moved away hair from my face which swept across my face as night air let them free from their bondage and they landed on my face creating a veil. His arms felt like an abode I had been searching for all along. He leaned in as I tilted my head backward and we kissed. His lips felt soft and warm on mine as he softly kissed me full on the mouth. Our tongues entwined as he kissed me deeper but not too hard. He held me delicately, like I was some kind of fragile figurine in a China shop or maybe even more delicate because he felt like any extra tension would force him back to reality and wake him up from his dream. Only that it wasn't a dream and we were really there, in the moment, together.

When he pulled back, I could see he was smiling as he let go of me, I could feel he was red and was blushing, my cheeks were full of color too as I couldn't stop smiling. None of us said anything, we just stood there, together, his arms around me and we just watched the sky, stars, and lights but more than that, each other. It all seemed too good to be real. But it was. And all I wanted was for it not to get ruined by anything, by me. After all this while, going through all that shit, carrying that heavy stuff around, I had almost forgotten that I was capable of something that he made me feel, or maybe I hadn't forgotten, I was just afraid. I was afraid that when he'd come to know what I had done, he'd hate me, Hella would hate me and Eign and that every person who said they loved me, they were there, they would hate me, see me for the person I am. I had thought that only if I kept to myself enough, I could void it, but Zayne, he saw it in my eyes. He saw that one thing that I was most afraid of but yet wanted to be rescued from. I wondered when did he see it, and was it the reason why he fell for me in the first place,

"When did you start liking me," I asked distractedly, or should I say I was more focused than ever, to not spoil this very moment that I had secretly been craving,

"I don't know, I mean I can't outline a specific timeline. I was about to leave that day when you came to Kratos'," he said in a voice loud only enough for me to hear,

"To avoid Jacey?" I almost whispered

"Yeah, but then you entered the room, just behind her and I couldn't help but notice you, I don't know why. It never happened before but at that moment I didn't care if I was standing there in front of Jacey, I just couldn't stop watching you,"

"Okay, you don't have to be so dramatic," I giggled.

"No, honestly. I ain't saying I fell in love with you at first sight or something like that because I know that'd be too unrealistic but yeah there was something that I felt when I saw you for the first time, I just don't know how to explain it..."

"*Koi no yokan*" I smiled to myself as words popped into my mind and out of my mouth.

"Sorry, what?" he asked, baffled

"It's Japanese for something you can say near to love at second sight. Like the feeling you have when you meet someone for the first time that you're going to fall for them," I smiled to myself feeling surprised at my relationship with words, I loved them because they never left my side but this was something I hadn't expected. It was like they were just waiting for the right moment to pop up and when they did find one, they came shooting out of my mouth,

"Yeah, precisely that. Sorry, I just don't do too well speaking my emotions out," he gave one of his innocent smiles, scratching the back of his head. He looked like his five years younger self and that made me want to take a picture of him like that.

"You know Japanese?" he asked genuinely curious,

"What, no. No, I just read it somewhere. It just popped up randomly,"

"You must read a lot then, because that isn't something you come across while reading just anything."

"Oh, it's nothing like that, it's just that my job demands that and I love reading so it's kind of bingo for me,"

"You do a job? I mean I did figure it out by the way you were dressed when you came in the first day but you're what, nineteen or twenty,"

"Twenty," I corrected him,

"Yeah, I mean isn't that too young. I mean it's amazing,"

"I know, it was of my dream job so I didn't want to let it go when I had the chance,"

"That's good. Since how long have been here?" he asked, I must've looked bewildered when he added, "I mean here, in States."

"A little over a year I guess,"

"That's a long time, do you visit your family?"

"I haven't till now,"

"Why? I mean you must miss them; I miss my family a lot,"

"No. I mean yeah, I miss them, but I didn't leave India in a very nice position let's put it that way. It's just too complicated. I... I don't know, I just don't feel like going there, at least not now." I wasn't looking at him, rather I was trying to find something to focus my gaze on, a star, something, anything. I just couldn't look into his eyes while all those memories rush to me like someone just opened the dam that had been holding them back. I could feel the heat of his gaze on me as the hair on the back of my neck rose.

"It's okay." He held my shoulders with both of his hands and made me turn to face him slowly and cupped my face in his rough but warm hands. He rubbed my cheek with his thumb and I didn't realize how cold I was until his warmth flowed through me and the difference in our temperatures hit me. He looked me straight in the eyes, and there was a look that I felt I knew, the same that I saw in my eyes sometimes when I was desperate enough to stand in the shower and cry looking at myself in the mirror. It was that look that called for someone, to look past the glamour and come for me even when I pushed them away at first. I could feel how he and I were singing to the same melodies just at different places until now when we were finally together, and there, to rescue each other or maybe fight all that ate away at us. There was so much that I wanted to say, but for the first time, I didn't want to use words, because whatever we shared at that moment was something that didn't need locution. He pulled me close enough to make sure that I wasn't cold anymore like I was before,

"I just want you to know that whatever it is, you can talk to me, I'll be here."

"You won't leave?" I felt stupid asking it, I didn't even know where did the words come from,

"Why would I?"

"I don't know, somehow in the end everybody does." He didn't look shocked or hurt like I had expected him to be at my audacity, instead, a look of understanding swept across his face. Like he understood every word and the weight it carried.

"I know. And I know it's hard. But maybe knowing it makes us value it even more," I didn't say anything, didn't want to. I just nodded instead. Not looking away or even blinking.

"Iana, I just want you to know that I'm here for you no matter what. I know things can hurt and there's nothing that we can possibly do to not get hurt at all, but I want you to know that you wouldn't have to deal with it alone, no matter how heavy it is," I wanted to tell him that there was a lot more than what he possibly understood or thought hurt to be. And that it wasn't as easy as he was signing up for. But then I remembered the look in his eyes when he held my face in his hands and wondered what if he possibly did know it better than me. There was a lot that we would have to figure out, but if I wanted him to heal me and if I wanted to heal him, I knew we'd have to let each other in. And even if it was difficult, it was something I knew I had to do this time, because I didn't want to be unfair to him, to myself. I could see our story unfold, it wasn't having any ugly commas or full stops, only ellipsis...possibilities.

I took a long look at him before leaning in to kiss him. He seemed shocked but in a good way. His hands were placed at the small of my back as he held me firmly while my hands played with his dark hair, tousled, while our lips pressed together like we both were waiting for this very moment. I closed my eyes to feel something I had been running from for long enough, I was opening to it, right now, right here while he kissed me and I kissed him back. The wind blew our hair and made the environment just perfect while lights scintillated and I could feel *Anai* smiling over us, just like others. And right now, in his arms, with him, I felt alive, happy.

HELLA

Eea looked happy after a long time. She smiled, of course, but I had never seen it reaching her eyes since she had that incident with Arsh. It annoyed me so much that how much he could suck out of my sister's life and still be happy while she cried herself to sleep. I just wanted her to be happy I didn't care if it was with Eign or Zayne. Though I could see the way they two looked at each other. I bet nobody in the gym would've failed to notice there was something going on between them. Even I was surprised at first when she told me, well, not really told me, when I caught her. The way she looked at him, I had never seen her this way, ever before. Even right now I could see, he couldn't take his eyes off her while she untied her hair and then rolled them up in a messy ponytail. It was kind of something any girl would ever want. Like the one they romanticized in all those romantic movies, to have someone who'd adore you even when you're a complete mess. I always found it kind of silly, I still did but seeing those two, I couldn't help *awwwwing* them.

"Is there something up?" Liz nudged me to have my attention as I adored my two little (not so little) love birds,

"Sorry, what?" I must've looked muddled because she had to tip her head in the direction where Zayne was helping someone out with the chest press while not failing to keep his gaze steady on Eea while she did hammer curls to make me understand what she was referring to,

"Oh, I don't know." She raised one eyebrow and I felt a pang of nervousness as I fumbled with words to add, "I mean no. Damn, freaking no."

"Wow, cool down. I was just asking. It's okay." She rubbed my back while shaking her head and then leaving with a faint smile on. I waited for long enough to make sure that she was perfectly out of sight and earshot, before leaping forward to reach to my sister.

"You know you two need to keep it a bit more low profile," I said it almost whispering. Hoping to avoid pulling attention to an already universally evident fact that something was up between the two of them.

"What?" she sounded as confused as I was when Liz asked me about them being a thing at first.

"I mean your personal life and the fact that you two are grossly into each other,"

"What the hell do you mean by grossly?" she shot a sharp look at me,

"Too cheesy, too cute. Typically couply." I couldn't help myself rolling eyes at her,

"That isn't gross" she sounded defensive,

"That my friend is the very definition of gross,"

"According to which dictionary? Because I'm afraid you aren't using a very accurate one in that case," she said sarcastically. However, she wasn't offended, I could tell that by her facial gestures,

"That's according to Hella dictionary. Now drop this and listen to me,"

"Yeah, shoot." She placed the dumbells on the rack and walked to the farther end of the room to pick up her towel, I continued while she wiped off the sweat which had started to drip on her sports bra and I could see its color going darker at places where sweat beads had landed.

"I guess you definitely don't want the whole planet to know that you and Zayne are something,"

"What are you talking about,"

"I'm talking about your little exchanged glances, only that they are a hell lot much more than little." I turned to point in the direction where Zayne was still helping the girl. Though as I had expected, his gaze had followed Iana to the corner of the room and he shot a guilty smile when we caught him stalking her. I couldn't help shaking my head, a gesture which very much should've conveyed how stupid he looked.

"Oh, yeah. I mean you're right. I'll talk to him about that." We picked up our stuff as we headed down to the changing room, we'd better be home for the conference video call with mom. She always freaked out whenever we missed one. We were just on the portal of the room when Zayne called from behind. As much as he tried to make it look like a complete coincidence, I could feel him trying hard to conceal his panting, giving away that he had run all the way to catch up with us. It freaked me out, I mean all of this cuteness and stuff. Yeah, I felt happy for her, for both of them but I wondered if I would ever be able to get used to all their cheesy stuff. Though it had been almost a month since they were together, still I needed time to get familiar with all this. Though I knew there was something that ate away at Eea at the back of her mind, but it was only few moments here and there now and then. It was like a flash of lightning, gone before you could tell if it was even there.

"Hey," Zayne said, trying to steady his breath, he nodded in my direction and I knew that it was my time to take off,

"What are you doing here?" Iana asked, failing to hide her smile that plastered her face whenever he was round.

"I...I was just going downstairs, had to talk with Liz. You going?"

"Yeah," I could tell without even looking that Iana glanced at her phone screen to look at the exact time. It had become her habit, to keep a tab of exact minutes, like it somehow made her feel in control of things.

"Uh, okay. See you later." He almost leaned in to hug her but then pulled back remembering where they were and that anyone could run into them while they hugged. Surely that wouldn't have been the best scenario. He smiled and held out his hand instead.

Iana took it hesitantly and I could see, feel, how he didn't want to let go of it, of her.

"Goodbye inamorato," I could hear Iana's giggle, she didn't giggle much but when she did she sounded just like an infant. I liked hearing her giggle.

"Damn, I guess I better carry a dictionary next time on," I heard Zayne laughing and I guess if he blushed too, embarrassed for not understanding what she said. I could feel it. However, unlike him I was too used to it to give a serious shit about it,

"Welcome to the club," I shouted over, just to make him feel better only remotely. I could hear them both laugh just before he let go of her hand and I could hear footsteps departing. After a while Iana entered the changing room, occupying the cabin next to me. She must've waited until he was completely out of sight to come inside.

"I am happy for you, Eea."

"For the first time, even I think I am too." It was the most shocking thing I had heard from her, it was like a drumroll with trumpets and an extra explosion of confetti. I possibly would have barged inside the cabin and hugged her, not caring if she was half-naked.

"I love you, Eea. I just want you to be happy. and am sorry for all those things but see, this how I always wanted to see you." I said over the sound of shower. I waited for her to say something but she didn't. Only after a long pause, I heard her words, so soft that they might've got lost in the noises had I not been deliberately focusing to catch them,

"I love you too, Hella,"

#

I fumbled for the light switch, the sun had set and it was almost dark outside. The room felt suddenly too alien, maybe it was the sudden splash of brightness that made it look so. The light was too much, so much so that it made my head buzz. I walked to the windows and peeled away the curtains and opened the glass windows and a splash of evening breeze swept across my face, filling the room swooping past me. I flung the duffel carelessly on the couch, too tired to put it at its respectable destination. The couch felt a little too soft as I collapsed on it like I was suddenly boneless, fluid. The relief of finally being able to stretch felt divine.

"Here," Iana kicked the duffel aside, handing me a glass of lemonade. One thing she did pretty well without needing babysitting was cooking. Thank God! The liquid felt like something that my body had been unconsciously craving for.

"Thanks," I said taking big gulps of my drink. I knew I was going to ask for a refill and also that she would've prepared it without having me to ask for it, maybe out of habit now I guess rather than to just be on the safe side.

"I'm going to take shower after a refill," I got up, prepared to make my way towards the kitchen before I left for the bathroom,

"No way I'm taking Mom's call alone," she spoke so abruptly that it made her lemonade tumble and spill a little on her leg.

"I'll be out in five. I'm sweating like shit,"

"Good for you that mom can't *smell* through the camera," she gave one of her lopsided smiles which made it pretty difficult for her to hide the mockery in her words.

"Lame." I threw a pillow at her; it caught her off guard but she successfully ducked anyway.

"I know how long your "five" lasts. So there's no chance in heaven and hell that I'm letting you go anywhere before we're done with it." she leaped from her seat and almost jumped on me as if I would somehow run away from there in front of her.

"Fine, go get the laptop, let's get this over with," I rolled my eyes at her while she hoisted her hands in the air in triumph, like she just won the battle of Waterloo, only that it was over with pretty much before we were even anywhere near atoms. Or maybe we might have fought in it as soldiers in our past lives, who knows. She picked up my duffel and disappeared into my room before going upstairs to get her laptop. I added some extra ice to my lemonade, I knew I was going to need it. Things could get pretty heated between Iana and mom and it was just barely that I could survive it with everybody blasting. Someone had to be cooled down, and by someone it always understandably meant me. Iana hopped down the stairs, skipping two at a time, and set up skype as the screen came to life instantly after the first ring. I let out a deep sigh and discarding my glass in the washbasin I staggered across the kitchen, into the living room to join our "family" call.

"Namastey, mumma, papa." I smiled at them my biggest possible smile which made my cheeks hurt. I didn't know what obsession Indian parents had with big-smiled greetings. I still remember how mumma used to poke or worse, taunt me whenever I would greet someone plainly without one of the most mandatory big smiles.

"Hella, namastey," she paused for a moment longer, taking her time to examine my discomposed appearance before continuing, "you look a bit...um, messy." I didn't think she could put it any more politely that I looked like complete shit as if I had been running to save my life from aliens or zombies,

"Yeah, just came from a workout,"

"You workout? Since when?" she asked with utter surprise crossing her otherwise taut features,

"Yeah, it's been a few months now," I said like it was no big deal. Which it wasn't.

"That's good,"

"Hmmm," I replied, waiting for the ultimate bomb to drop and cause catastrophe and finally get it over with,

"So, about *Diwali*," I could hear 'taaadaa' in my head. Like 'here's ladies and gentlemen what you'd been waiting for all this while.

"Did you apply for leaves?" mom asked with a tinge of optimism in her voice as she spoke. I opened my mouth to answer but Iana cut me off,

"I did, they rejected my application," I could see mumma opened her mouth to say something and knew that was it, here goes off the bomb, but she decided against it and closed it without saying anything, I thought that's what happened but then I realized Iana was speaking. I could see a smile spreading across mumma's face and realized that it was me that she was smiling at. I was kind of bewildered, astonished. It was only when I paid attention to what Eea was saying that I realized why.

"I talked to Hella's teachers, they agreed to give her three days off," she said as a matter of fact. Like it was something I was supposed to know,

"She did?" I couldn't hide the sharpness in my voice as I gave her a deadly look saying that she would be dead had they not been on a call with their parents,

"Is everything okay?" Mom's voice interrupted our secret telepathic conversation,

"Yeah, I mean they did. I mean yeah it is." I bit my tongue as I ate upon words being caught reparteed, I took in a deep breath before adding, "I mean yeah they accepted the request,"

"So you're coming," I could sense the joy and vivaciousness in mumma's voice,

"Yeah, I am." I looked in Iana's direction whose gaze was fixed on the screen, on our parents. I knew she was trying to avoid any kind of awkwardness in front of them.

"Happy?" she asked, trying to change the subject, I did believe that she knew she was in grave problem once this ended.

"Would've been more if you'd have cared to show up in person too," mumma shot, but she was smiling. She looked happy, for the first time it was them who weren't boiling but me. But looking at mumma, papa so happy, I couldn't help feeling a bit of that happiness too. But it didn't bail Eea out in any way.

"See you mom. Gotta cook dinner." I barged in happy family time, suddenly wanting to get over with it soon enough.

"You cook?" papa spoke for the first time during the entire conversation,

"I do help," I raised an eyebrow at him like he had hurt me by saying it. Everybody burst into a laugh, only, mine was half-hearted. We exchanged I love yous and soon as I saw the screen going static I pushed the screen shut almost shattering it, only that I hardly cared.

Iana looked at me wide-eyed,

"What the hell was that?"

"I'm sorry, I didn't want to fight with mumma and I was..."

"So you threw me as bait?" I was almost yelling at her, bet the neighbors must've heard even though the walls were soundproof.

"What? No, hell no. Not as bait. I just thought they'd be happy to have at least one of us,"

"So you bailed yourself out in my place," I could see she hadn't expected it. Her jaw twitched as she clenched teeth,

"It isn't like that Hella, it's just that..."

"Just what Iana? Go ahead, make one of your excuses about not being ready yet to be there, to face all of it. Go ahead, that's what you always do, don't you?" I had expected her to get mad at me for using such a tone with her, instead, she went still, something in her eyes changed and I could see sadness smear across them. Real sadness, the one that drags you down even on the happiest of days,

"I... yes that's the exact reason but I just can't explain it Hella, I just can't. I'm sorry. Sorry for being like that but I don't control it you see, it's just there. I'm trying. I'm sorry." I didn't know why but her words felt like a slap across my face. Even though they were as polite as they could be, soft as silk, somber. Yet something in them itched at me. I knew she didn't mean for them to make me feel guilty but they did. I could see how much she was suffering. What hurt me more was that it wasn't something external that was plaguing her. She was suffering from herself. And that made it worse. Suddenly I felt a strong urge to hug her. I leaped across to her, taking two short steps, and pulled her into a long embrace.

"I know, I just...you should've told me. It was too much and too sudden,"

"I'm sorry," she whispered in my hair, not letting me go.

"I know you're strong Eea, you'll fight it. whatever it is," I pulled away from her, just far enough to look straight into her eyes. They were dark, all emotions drifting somewhere into oblivion.

"I will." She murmured, almost a whisper in the ear of the air. She picked up the laptop, examining it for cracks. Fortunately, there weren't any. She turned around to leave and started ascending the stairs when just momentarily stopped and leaning back to look at me still standing in the living room spoke softly,

"I won't let you down Hella, just give me time," it was like she was apologizing for something which wasn't even her fault. I let out a sigh and nodded before finally managing the words to come out,

"I know you will, Eea. I love you,"

She didn't hear them though, by the time they could've made their way to her eardrum, she was already out of earshot. I waited for a while, letting the weight of words lay heavy. Finally breaking the calmness of the air, I let out a deep sigh and resigned for the shower which I suddenly felt like I needed more than ever now.

CHAPTER TWENTY

ZEESHAN

Something was up with Zayne, I could feel it. He seemed changed. In a good way though. It was like he was looking for that little extra sunshine in days and more stars on darker nights. It was unusual, in a good way for sure. Though I was pretty intrigued by what had caused such change in him, I decided not to push or intervene in his life. He looked happy, and that's what that mattered. And I haven't been much of an elder brother who asked about his girlfriends or invited mine over dinner to introduce them. Honestly, I haven't had any, at least not a serious one since... Easha. However much I tried to coax myself about her forgetfulness I would always come square with my feelings, they spat at my face. Even after all these years. She was the kind I would have wanted to introduce to my family, I wanted to, I would have if I could.

No matter how much we pretended that it was fine, we were better now than before, we were friends. Both of us knew better than that, only that none had the courage to speak it out loud.

I wouldn't care to poke Zayne about whatever it was that was up in his life like I didn't like being bothered myself. I wasn't that kind of 'big-old-brother'. I wouldn't have talked to that blonde girl either, but seeing Zayne passed on the bathroom floor, bloody, almost made me believe for a moment that I had lost him. Kind of fear I felt when I was fifteen or seventeen probably when they took her away. Similar to the fear I felt in my gut when I had finally woken up to realize that Easha was gone. It made me shiver to bones; I didn't want to feel it again. I *couldn't* feel it again. I had lost enough people whom I loved and I wasn't going to lose him too because of some girl whom he was too good for.

I could sense it was a girl this time too, but I knew it was different. The way he felt lively, was like I hadn't seen him ever before, and I was happy. It had to be someone very special to make him light up that way. I just hoped he stayed that happy.

I hoped they both stayed happy, I knew Easha would've wanted the same.

"Hey, junno," I hit him hard on the back as I jumped beside him on the couch and resumed our paused game. He had been typing away a text on his phone when I returned and suddenly pulled it shut when he realized I was just behind him.

"Who's the little secret?" I asked playfully, just wanting to tease him. I had no intention of prying for information about what was going on in his love life,

"What secret," I smirked a little as I nodded in the direction of his phone which lay lifeless between us.

"Oh nothing, just some friends," he tried to pretend like he was too focused on the game as his eyebrows knit together while he punched in the commands to kick my soldier on the screen. I knew it was all to make the topic die down, I liked seeing him like this. Uncomfortable.

"Does this friend have a name?" I hardly cared to look at the screen where I was being beaten to pulp. I was having a fairly good time reading his face to care about the dead entertainment on the screen,

"Uh...c'mon, go, yessssss!!!" he waved his hands in the air in triumph as the screen displayed 'player 1 wins'. I knew though, he was just trying to avoid the question and felt a bit guilty to find pleasure in his discomfort.

"Sorry what?" he asked innocently like he didn't really listen it at the first time,

"The name," I eyed in the direction of his phone which was bright now with a recent text, maybe this friend, "of the friend," I added to clarify any confusion he might pretend to have.

"Oh, that…uh… name…yeah," he stuttered and I swear I could see beads of sweat rolling down his temples as he tried to come up with the best possible answer,

"This special friend who apparently makes you so happy, tell her my thanks," I smiled as he gaped at me. Walking across the couch I ruffled his hair; I could feel his disbelief while he tried to snap out of his stagger.

"How do you know?"

"What?" I asked pulling out a can of soda from the deeper end of the refrigerator. It was one of the last and we would have to refill the supplies, maybe tomorrow or the day after.

"That we'd have to refill soon?" I spoke out loud, dumb.

"What? No. That it's a 'her'?" he asked, not pulling his eyes off me even for a second, like I'd give something away in that dark spot that'd be of great importance. I could see the tips of his ears turning red and knew he was embarrassed or reticent.

"Did you forget that I've walked this earth five years more than you," I threw the broken piece of the opening of the can at him jocularly.

"That gives you the superpower to identify genders without really knowing? I didn't know that." He almost yelled, throwing back the metal chunk in my direction. I ducked just in time to avoid it hitting my face.

"I wish it did. But being your elder brother does give the power to identify who can change your mood like that,"

"Creep!" he picked up the phone and left for his room, taking his eyes off to look at me just once. I winked at him and mumbled, only loud enough for him to hear,

"Keep her." He gave me an astounded look before smiling briefly and nodding,

"*Insha'Allah*," he spoke, words coming out only as a whisper.

I closed my eyes briefly just to let those words sink in.

CHAPTER TWENTY-ONE

ZAYNE

Sneaking out to text her felt like I was carrying a little secret around. My little secret. It wasn't as though I didn't want to tell Zeeshan all about it, but somehow, I couldn't bring myself to. Things had always been this way between us, like an invisible line we both knew better not to cross. It wasn't as if he'd get upset or judge my choice or ask me to not date a particular girl because he knew she had a reputation. But how was I supposed to know, I never dated before to have that kind of knowledge. Though something about the way he teased me today, told that he was fascinated, happy too. I so wanted to tell him, but I wanted it to be our thing, mine and her. Suddenly it dawned upon me how I haven't really ever met any of his girlfriends. I did have this vague memory of a girl whom he used to talk fondly of, with such certainty that he seemed almost convinced that she's the one. Like really *the one.* I couldn't help comparing if that was anywhere near how I felt about Iana. I was certain about her and as bad as I wanted her to be the one, it was still too early to tell that. I wondered where she was now, that girl, whom I was so convinced would be my near family. I wondered what went wrong. Zeeshan would never tell me, and honestly, I didn't know if I had the nerve to bear whatever the reason might be behind it.

Busy?

my phone buzzed, making me realize why I was back in my room in the first place,

Yeah, nope. Totally here.

Her reply came within seconds,

Up for fun?

I mentally went through the to-do list to see what else was there which could possibly hinder this awesome plan, which to my surprise was none. I guess it was so because I didn't really have a to-do list in the first place. Still, I just didn't want to sound too desperate, like my heart didn't just yelp a big BINGO!!! When she asked for it in the first place.

Cool, Be ready in ten.

I typed down looking at the time,

I'll be there in fifteen.

I looked at the text that landed in just as my last text read sent. I wondered if she was always like this, in control, or was it something that being with someone you never even considered even a wild possibility did to her. Anyway, I was just glad to really have some time with her. It had been over a month and a half and we hadn't been on a serious date unless you count the times when we hung out at Angel's Top. I started feeling uneasy when I suddenly realized that this was our first real date and it was her who asked me out. Shit. I was such a dumbass. Stupid. I threw on clothes, just making sure that I didn't look an utter mess. She did have an amazing styling code even for gym or office, and from what I had seen she slayed parties too I surely couldn't match that but I did my best to at least not look like her careless best friend who just trudged along, no offense to them though but still. I looked in the mirror to make sure my hair wasn't flying haywire like it usually did and sprayed myself with deo which I had almost go on a hunt for to retrieve it from my gym duffel.

I pulled out one of Zeeshan's sneakers and tightened them a bit while shouting over my shoulder to him

"I'm borrowing your white sneaks for the eve,"

"Don't ruin them," I didn't bother to call back while I walked to the cabinet over the fridge and popped in some mouth freshener, bad breath was the last thing I wanted to be worried about. It wasn't like we hadn't kissed before, or that somehow this time was going to be different but I was quite jittery. The idea of being on a serious *date* with her for the first time made me want to go sprinting all over until I was really back to my senses. I checked my phone I was ready seven minutes earlier, so I just poured myself some coke.

"Going somewhere?" I didn't notice Zeeshan entering the living area, apparently, I was too busy being nervous.

"Yeah, just hanging out, with friends," I looked away, not wanting to meet his eyes while I was so conscious already,

"Friends or the friend?" he smirked, not looking at me thankfully. I would've possibly evaporated by the heat I could feel rising to my face.

"Whatever," I crossed him to reach for the main door, there were still five minutes until she pulled over. But I'd rather be at the parking than facing Zeeshan. Not that he was the kind of brother who pestered you with questions until he got the answer he wanted to listen. But still, it was kind of awkward.

"Have fun, junno. And buy chocolates," he shouted over, to make sure I heard before the door shut with a final click. Damn, I never thought about it. Suddenly I felt too thankful to have a brother like him, and by like him, I meant a brother who could give you some serious helpful tips. Only problem was that there wasn't enough time to execute it. I let out a deep sigh, exasperated. Though I made a mental note about the chocolates, an idea popped into my head out of nowhere. I smiled to myself with pride as I gave myself a small pat on the shoulder. Then suddenly realizing that I wasn't alone, I flushed as she stared at me with those dark brown eyes looking amused. I could see she was trying to suppress a smile and act as though it was completely normal for guys to smile and give themselves a well-done pat on their back in public. I walked to the passenger's side slowly, she was watching me, I could feel the heat of her eyes on my back and suddenly it felt like I was too exposed.

"Hey," I said, pulling over the seat belt.

"So, ready?" she chuckled.

"I guess so, what's the plan?" I could feel a strange feeling of excitement as something tickled my stomach. It was like following someone into darkness, trusting that they won't let you stray away.

"You'll see," she pressed the gas and the engine made a little noise just before jerking us back into our seats as we rolled out of the parking on the streets. The streets looked comparatively calm, maybe the Sunday mood had made people want to stay home and have family time, play checkers, or tic-tac-toe while mothers cooked Sunday specials. I missed all such things with my family, it had been long since we even ate together. The young teenage boys rolled over at the sides with their skateboards, waiting to cross the traffic. I wondered if they were planning to paint some corner of the city with one of their badass graffitis. I loved this place, it was beautiful, but not beautiful like the Amazon or the sunset near Goa or Ladakh. It was beautiful like a synthetic and artificially modified barbie doll placed with utmost care behind the display to lure you. Sometimes it was too hard to make out if the lights high up were stars or just illumination from someone's room living on the top floor.

"Why do you like going to Angel's Top?" I asked her, wanting to know if even she felt clamped sometimes between this artificial marvel of humankind and felt that urge of being somewhere where she can really breathe and not wonder if the lights were celestial or artificial for once.

"To know that I'm here, not slipping," she kept her eyes at the road, "it's like this calm escape of mine, it feels real. I don't know why but everything else doesn't." she turned her head to look into my eyes, maybe to see if I was following. But it was only for a moment, she suddenly pulled away as someone honked behind us.

"Not even us?" the words spilled out before I could ponder upon them,

"What?" she asked perplexed,

"I mean, even this doesn't feel real?" I asked gesturing towards the fact that not a few weeks ago we were complete strangers and now I was sitting there beside her, not having a hint about where we're headed but just satiated by the fact that I was with her.

"I...um, well," she let out a deep sigh as if trying to rule out the volume of the world and her own thoughts and tune in with the ether which might carry an answer to my question that somehow seemed too difficult to answer.

"It feels so much like a fairytale, I mean sometimes all of it feels too good to be real that I can't help being anxious about the possibility that someday I will wake up and all of it will be gone,"

There was something in her voice that made it clearly visible how vulnerable she felt. Though it wasn't like she was sharing something that could be classified as top secret. But it was something more important. I realized she just admitted her insecurities, and somehow that made me feel happy. Not about her being insecure, but about her trusting me enough to share it with me on the face. I would have hugged her had it been possible,

"This," I pointed towards her and then me, creating an invisible thread that bind us, "Is not going anywhere," I reached to hold her hand which was resting on the gearstick and squeezed it gently. She gave one of those smiles which completely lit up her dark brown eyes and made them small as her cheek fat pushed upwards while her lips part to form a perfect specimen of what might be awarded as a life-giving smile. I could see her like that forever, and I mean *forever.* Though she tapped at my knee to drag my attention to the exquisite building which could take every ounce of your willpower to not stop and look through its displays. The fabric fitted the curves of mannequins like it had been carefully stitched to caress them while they flaunted and lured people. I was so engrossed in admiring the sheer artistry that I didn't realize we had parked and Iana was holding the door open for me to hop down, I looked at her, confused. But I stepped out finally, too excited to know what she was up to.

"*Manyawar?*" she nodded with such enthusiasm and energy that it felt like her head might bob out and fall on the floor, disintegrating from her body. And there was nothing pleasing about the idea of a headless girlfriend (literally).

"I don't think so it's a destination for a first date?" I asked too curious now,

"Not for a *normal* first date," she smiled as she dragged me along toward the door, the guard gave us a warm smile ignoring the fact that I looked like complete shit as I gawked around while being dragged by my girlfriend, "but perfect for a Diwali shopping date." She finally let go of me and we stood there in the store, surrounded by crisply dressed mannequins in traditional Indian outfits. I couldn't believe she planned *this*,

"Diwali shopping?" I asked trying to hide how pleased I felt about her idea, and about the fact that this was the girl I fell for and was still falling for.

"Yeah, it's Diwali next week. So that calls for mandatory Diwali shopping," she giggled like a toddler,

"They don't celebrate Diwali here, I hope you know that," I asked, thrilled.

"Don't be too quick to judge. But that's for later. First, let's get you something to make you look human," she gave me a side smile as if she was mocking me,

"Human," I raised one eyebrow at her, and she giggled again. She skimmed through the enormous displays and racks, brows furrowed like she was trying to concentrate picking out the best outfit for his guy and all this while I couldn't help but stare at her and feel thankful about having her. I couldn't take my eyes off her, I bet someone who'd have cared to notice might've thought me to be a jerk, stalking a girl at a public place but I didn't care. The mere idea of the fact that she was mine gave me goosebumps, even now when we'd been dating almost for two months. I crossed over to the other side of the shelf where she was comparing between a golden and a black kurta and slipped my arm around her waist, pulling her closer into me, and kissed her full on the mouth. I could see her eyebrows raised in shock as she pulled away just for a moment to see my face. I smiled at her and she leaned in again, kissing me fervently as her hands curled in my hair and my grip tightened around her waist. I could feel her lips curl into a smile as we kissed like we weren't between a gigantic store and there weren't about a dozen people around.

After a moment she pulled away, not taking her eyes off me, and threw a black kurta at my face shoving me in the direction of the trial room.

"Here, go and try this one," she almost pushed and dragged me to the trial room like I was putting on much of a struggle to resist her which she'd have to rule out by putting in extra force.

"I already like it," I smirked at her without even seeing what she had picked for me. She punched me in the chest lightly and I collapsed on the floor pretending like it broke my heart literally, and there it was, that three-year-old giggle that made me fall for her a bit more.

"You're so..." she stopped mid sentences and turned away smiling pushing me into the trial room with the apparel.

"I'm so...?" I shouted over the closed door, pulling off my rugged tee and opening the neck buttons of the kurta. It had been a while since I wore Indian attire, it seemed out of place here, alien.

"Corny," she shouted back and I could picture a faint smile as she looked through the perfect piece of clothing for me.

"Does that have something to do with corn, because I hate it," I replied, though my voice got a bit muffled as I tried to pull down the kurta over my head and I doubt whether she heard it. The fabric felt so soft and adjusted just to my size that it felt like an extension of my skin. The fact that the size was just perfect surprised me at the fact that how much she knew about me, how much she remembered. I opened the door and walked to the aisle where she was picking out some other colors to try on and stood there posing like a model. I could see her expression shift from utter concentration to that of relief and happiness as brows relaxed and she leaped towards me, turning me swiftly to the life-size mirror. The fabric fitted on my muscles just perfectly to highlight curves whenever my arms flexed. The buttons on the chest felt perfectly plastered as my chest rose in full capacity to inhale. Only one person had such a beautiful choice and the perfect idea about what'd suit me, *Ammi*.

"You don't like it? I'm sorry. Let's try something else..." words came out of her mouth in such a hurry, as she saw the change in my features from jolly to that of something more solemn.

"Yeah, I mean no. I totally like it," I pulled her towards me. Her hands rested on my chest as she traced the delicate golden embroidery by the neckline,

"You just, I thought you didn't because," she gently pushed aside my hair from my forehead and touched my creased forehead, I hadn't realized I was frowning. I relaxed a bit under her touch, her eyes locked with mine all the while.

"No, I like it. I love it. I just got a bit..." I couldn't find words to explain, I didn't know if this was the right time to talk about it,

"Nostalgic" she whispered softly, trying to keep it between us. I nodded,

"Only *Ammi* could choose so perfectly for me, better than I ever could," I tried a to smile but it ended up in my lips being curved awkwardly so I gave up on fake attempts. And something about her made me not want to regret being so vulnerable and real with her, I trusted her,

"You bet," she smiled, and then added, "Maybe I can get some tips about your choices when I meet her," she said with such enthusiasm that it made my stomach churn,

"Hmm," I couldn't manage syllables. I didn't want to drift, not now. It was like she was the thread holding me here, at bay from straying away into oblivion, into my own thoughts. Maybe this what I had been longing for all along, unconsciously, someone to hold on to. She wasn't looking at me now and for a moment I felt relaxed but then I realized she had been looking, not at me but my reflection in the mirror. At *our* reflection. And I realized how much I had been craving it, how much I've been getting used to her. I was drifting, but no, she was here, holding me. And with her head on my chest and my arm around her waist and the subtle faces staring back at us from the mirror with a tinge of a smile at the corner of their lips I knew this was what perfection meant. This was what *my* perfect was. And suddenly it hit me, maybe this was what Liz meant when she said it'll feel right. Because this felt like the very definition of right. *She* felt right. *This* felt right. *We* felt right.

#

The spices made the place smell so much like home. It wasn't usual to have an olfactory feast of aniseeds, fennel seeds, basil seeds, sweet basil, and their whole fraternity.

"How come I did not know about this place?" I asked with a curiosity of a ten-year-old. She tipped her head back like the question in itself was some kind of compliment on her choosing skills.

"Talent," she smirked, "not your fault, ain't everybody blessed with it," she smiled and ducked the bunch of tissues that I threw at her playfully as if trying to defend my respect against her impudent remark.

"I used to miss Indian food when I came here first," she said straightening the pleats of her skirt,

"You don't know how to cook?" I wondered how she might look between all those instruments of taste, an alien figurine, exotic. I wasn't stereotyping but she seemed to be one of those women carrying crisp immaculate business-type aura. I couldn't help imaging her picking up the fresh vegetables to cook special dinners and delicately bring up the spoon to her soft lips, to make sure all the spices were in proportion,

"I do, but not everything." She stared at me with a questioning look, as if asking if I was following. I nodded as she continued, "I love south Indian. But that's out of my league to cook. So, I found out *Ammaa's.*" she unfolded her hands and spread them to gesture at the place. The excitement on her face was no less than on someone who might've found Eldorado. The waitress came in to take our orders and I could see her features brighten up as she saw Iana. Of course, she knew her, because even before Iana could order she spoke her choice aloud like she had it embossed in her mind by now.

"So, what will you have?" the lady, maybe in her mid-forties asked me giving a polite smile,

"Biryani" Iana gleamed before I could even manage to get the words out of my mouth. I had lost count by now how many times I felt thankful for having this girl in my life. I just smiled and nodded as the waitress still eyed me for my last word.

"You two look so adorable," she gave us a broad smile before leaving, I could see Iana blush and couldn't hide the flush of the color on my cheeks too.

"You know how to cook?" Iana asked, trying to push away the awkwardness that had build up.

"I do. I learned it when I was twelve" I nodded biting the corner of my lip.

"Wow! That's so damn cool. I mean my mom still yells at me sometimes for not knowing enough, I don't even want to imagine how'd she react if she knew a *guy* knows more than me about *cooking* and that too since he was *twelve*!"

"That's sexist,"

"Impressive," she gave me a side smirk as she lifted her apple juice glass to her lips to take a sip like she was drinking wine at some sophisticatedly pretentious high-class party to add some drama,

I bowed my head a little as if I had just finished a laudable performance and was happy to be able to please my lady.

"I can swear on my life your Mom is one of the happiest and lucky women, I mean not every woman gets the luxury of having a culinary expert heir," she said with utter sincerity.

It was the second time that it had come up and I couldn't help as I deflated a bit and my features drooped. I didn't show, ever, but it mattered. I missed her and no matter how much I pretended I could push it away, it was always there, that emptiness, the place I wished where she was. Iana saw my features changing and started apologizing, like any of it was her fault,

"I'm sorry... I didn't mean it in a bad way. I didn't want to offend you,"

"Was..." I whispered, my voice seemed so unfamiliar as it trembled, I could feel a pang in my chest, dread. The words hung there on my tongue as I feared that somehow saying them aloud would make the facts definite as if they weren't already. Seeing Iana's features turned in worry and her eyes looking at me with affection and genuine concern I knew I trusted her. And if I was taking this leap of faith then why not completely let go. I took a deep breath and locking my eyes with hers I pulled her hands into mine as I let go of my guard and gave in to her,

"I was ten or maybe eleven when she..." I let out a deep sigh, there was no going back. I looked into her eyes from where a stream had started to pour down, but she didn't pull away, she was looking right into me. There wasn't sympathy, for which I was thankful, I hated when someone sympathized not even knowing a fraction of how it really felt. There was something in her eyes that said 'I am here' and that was enough. This girl, whom I had not known by this time last year, I wondered how it was possible that she meant so much to me that with her I didn't care thinking twice before letting go of things that I held within for so long that they almost felt like an extension of myself.

"I..."

"No, it's okay. You don't have to be sorry. I've made peace with it," she looked unconvinced and I broke away my gaze to stare into nothingness behind her.

"You know," she leaned in closer; I could feel her scent and warmth as she spoke softly, "you don't have to pretend that it's okay if it isn't. I won't say I understand because honestly, how can I when I haven't been there in your place, I can't. But I'm here, no matter what," I pulled back to look at her, her chubby hands fit in mine like a key in its lock. I wondered how could someone be so capable of soothing your gravest scars and hurt without even sugarcoating things because that's what exactly she did. She didn't say something which I was *supposed* to believe. Like it'll be fine, or God did it for a reason, or anything like that. But I guess that's what made her different, she *connected* with me.

"I still miss her, every day," I whispered. For the first time, I didn't care if someone saw my tears and how much I missed her or how behind this muscular body carved by weights and hits I was still a boy who missed his *Ammi* who was taken from him even before he could remember her face clearly. She didn't hush me or try to wipe my tears, instead, she stood up and walked across the table to my side and pulled me in a tight hug, and let me cry. Her hand rubbed my back slowly as my face buried in the curve of her neck and my tears wet her shoulder.

"It's okay to not feel okay all the time," she whispered in my ears softly, and the tone with which she said it, made me believe it. After a while I pulled away, wiping my face with the back of my hand, not taking my eyes off her face even once. She gave me a calm sad smile as she passed me a glass of water. I set it aside as I craned my neck to be just near enough her ear and spoke softly,

"Of everything and everyone, I'm glad I got to love you," she didn't speak anything for a while, and I didn't know why but I felt relieved and was thankful that she didn't. I was hoping though, that she'd whisper back that she loved me or something like that but she didn't. Pulling back I could see she had something in her mind, that look which I saw the first time when we kissed, for a moment I thought it was there. This time stronger and clearer than before, like it was engulfing her as she tried to wrestle her way out,

"Hey, are you fine?" I gave her a light shake to bring her back, and just in that moment everything weary in her eyes evaporated and she looked back at me with clear eyes, her eyes. But something had changed in her features, and I could feel something was up. But I didn't want to force it, she didn't, so how could I. But whatever it was that plagued her like that, I wished I could just jump into that darkness and pull her out of it.

"What? Yeah, completely. Sorry, I just, I'm sorry." She looked away as if trying to clear her head and avoid me having to see whatever it was that she was trying to conceal so earnestly.

"It's okay," I squeezed her hand gently, and she smiled faintly,

"Um hey, I just wanted to...um. Just one thing," I looked away from her, suddenly it felt like I couldn't manage to see her directly, not now at least. Her hand caressed my palm while the other one rested carelessly on my thigh. I wanted to touch her, hold her and pull into me and kiss her and tell her how much she meant. I took her free hand in mine and kissed its back gently. I didn't wait for her to react or say anything and continued,

"I was very young when it all happened, and I did miss her terribly." She was looking at me and by now I could see she was really going through all of it with me, not sympathizing, but understanding, "though I was the youngest, but after Maa, I didn't want to be a burden or concern for my family. Papa was going through a lot, we all were, so I never really showed whatever or however much it hurt. I didn't want to be looked at like a pathetic unlucky boy. I didn't want sympathy. That's why I didn't share how I felt until I did, with you." I could feel her grip tightening reassuringly, "I never let anybody act like something is wrong in my life or I am different. So I don't want you to treat me any different than you would if it wasn't like it is either,"

She pulled her one hand free from mine and cupped my face with it, I could feel the warmth of her hand passing through me, the hair at the back of my neck rose as a strange sensation passed through me with her touch. She rubbed my cheek with her thumb, tracing the structure of my face,

"You aren't some pathetic unlucky person and you dare say that again. You Mr. Zayne are one of the strongest and purest people I've ever come across. You deserve the best," the seriousness and sincerity with which she said those words left me speechless. I was anything but utterly awestruck, "I have the best," I mumbled. A bright smile lit up her face and I could see her chubby cheekbone rise as her lips parted and she shied away.

We were startled as the waitress cleared her throat a bit loudly to indicate our not-so-loneliness at the place. We pulled away, a bit embarrassed and I could see Iana turning red as the color rose to her face while my face burned with the heat that had risen to it.

"Sorry to disturb you guys." She said, trying to suppress a smile as the corners of her lips curled upwards, indicating a failed attempt at hiding her smile. She placed our order on the table and asking if we needed anything else which we didn't, gave us an understanding smile like it was nothing new for her to see couples cuddling up in the corner booths, she left. The tension had built up so much that none of us realized that we were sitting almost on the edge of our seats and even an inch forward and one of us would have tumbled down.

"Okay, that was a bit, embarrassing I guess," Iana finally broke the silence, releasing the tension like releasing a deflating balloon,

"A bit?" I raised an eyebrow and both of us burst into a fit of laughter.

"Sorry if this might sound unsophisticated but I can hear the giants in my belly playing orchestra now, I guess you wouldn't want to witness that. And the food doesn't taste good cold anyway so shall we?" she asked eyeing at the food with her spoon ready to declare war over it,

"Sure," I mimicked her as we both jumped on our platter. I hadn't realized until now how hungry I was. I dug my spoon in my plate and the first bite sent a sense of familiarity and nostalgia as the taste hit full-on and I felt grateful for it. It felt like ages since I had such home-like food.

CHAPTER TWENTY-TWO

HELLA

I liked seeing Iana like this, she was brighter and happier. Happiest I had ever seen her. Though she wasn't getting away with setting me up for this trip so easily but I could take a break. And whatever it was that she was trying to avoid, she'd get around it eventually. She was stronger than she thought,

"Ready for some fun, kiddo," she threw my bags in the backseat with little effort,

"Wow, how much you've been lifting? Those things were pretty heavy," she was taking her workouts seriously, and for one good thing, it was because she had grown to like them, not because of her hot trainer turned boyfriend. Or even if it had some credit to be given it was minor.

"Not much," she winked at me sheepishly, I rolled my eyes at her,

"You're turning into lady hulk you know," I said shaking my head,

"Hulk you like flaunting about," she kicked me with her crocs lightly, I wondered how on earth was she going to turn up to places, it shuddered me. I liked dressing her up, like a doll, and without me, I was afraid if she would show up dressed like someone just out of their sleep just the hair made, or maybe not even that.

"Who said,"

"You don't just go around people's shoulders highlighting the weight plates," I knew my play wasn't up for long, she had seen me talking to Jacey or rather messing with her while she looked at her doing the squats with sixty-fucking-kilos on her back.

"Her eyes were literally popping out, she was counting the weight plates herself, I just helped her by giving a perfect figure." We both giggled and she didn't chide me,

"That's not something you flaunt, Hella," she said shaking her head as one strand of her messy hair escaped her braid and fell on her face,

"You don't until someone acts bitchy," though I knew her to be better than that, I knew even she could feel the fuming dislike that girl radiated. It wasn't until she had crossed her line. It was a week ago, or maybe two. I was just about to rush into the room when I saw her stomping towards the place where I knew Iana and Zayne would be, I thought she was just messing around, instead, she walked straight up to them and mocked Zayne saying, "Finally you found someone for your 'typical Indian' love," she was trying to act cool but I could feel the acid in her voice. Even though the remark wasn't for me but I felt like someone had punched me in the face. I was ready to charge at her and break her ever so pretty face, but am glad I didn't, Iana's reply did more than any blow could've ever done. She just walked close to her, so close that from where I was standing it looked like they were almost kissing, which was kind of funny. Her voice was so soft that I had to press myself to the door to hear what she was saying, "If that's what you say, Miss, then shall I know what 'normal' love is like?" though she said it with such sophistication, you couldn't miss out that sharp sarcasm which hit just the nail head. Jacey opened her mouth to say something but I saw Zayne stepping forward and pulling Iana closer to him he just raised one eyebrow at Jacey and didn't speak but I could see he mouthed "don't" and before words could leave her mouth she just froze there wide eyed. I couldn't help laughing at her dumbness if she had really thought Zayne would be taking that kind of shit, because he didn't seem that kind of a guy.

Iana had told me that she had adored Jacey so much the day we first went to Kratos' though I'm glad Iana's on my page after that incident.

"You'll be fine?" I asked, suddenly feeling more concerned.

"Of course, I will be." She didn't react much, pulling into the parking of the airport. Then she stopped as if something crossed her mind demanding to be expressed instantly, "I know Maa papa miss me but I can't. Not now. I hope you understand," I nodded even when I didn't really understand what it was that she wasn't ready for. She looked at me once and added, "Tell them I'll be home for a holiday soon,"

"Your 'soon' hasn't come across for one year though," I couldn't help as words shot out of my mouth unguarded, she didn't flinch or react,

"I know, I'm sorry." She took my hand and squeezed it gently, something in it made me calm down and I could see that whatever it was that she was fighting it wasn't easy. I just wished she'd let me in, let anybody in, and not just fight it alone. But I knew her, she wouldn't. she would be there for people, trying to pull them out even when she knew she couldn't do much, but she'd be there. But she won't let anyone fight for her, I knew I got my stubbornness from her. I couldn't think of anything to say to her so I just pulled her into a long embrace and whispered,

"It's okay."

The speakers chattered as the announcements added of the bustle of the airport, thankfully, two sisters having their moment wasn't much of a show so we didn't acquire any more stares than we had could've bet for. The speakers came to life once again and a sweet but mechanical voice announced in a banal tone,

"It's boarding time," Iana helped me with the luggage,

"Yeah, see you soon," I muttered, suddenly feeling too tired.

"Soon, kiddo." She ruffled my hair before finally breaking away. I could feel the heat of her gaze on my back until I walked to the farther side of the door, turning only to have one last look at her. She was there, but she wasn't looking at me, her eyes were fixed on a plane that just took off, and I could see she ached to be home, but I just couldn't fathom why she wouldn't be. I took a long look at her and turned to leave.

It wasn't on my list, but now I had one important task at hand and I was very much sure to make this one trip ack home count. I fished out my phone and typed to the only person whom I thought could help me,

"Ma'am, your passport," the lady at the counter asked, her voice a bit louder this time. Her eyes narrowed and I could sense a tinge of irritation in her aura as I was clearly slowing her fantastically mechanized speed down,

"Yeah, sorry." I fished out my passport and visa and the tickets and handed them over to her not taking my eyes off my phone screen which showed three dots, I was surprised by the instant reply.

"Here," the lady handed me my stuff without a nod or not even a complimentary 'have a safe journey' smile. I didn't care much though, I was too busy typing back lest she might just go off-hook. But she was there still typing. After a while, my phone chimed and the screen came to life with a notification from Anayaa,

I don't think it's a good idea.

I wasn't quite sure about it myself, but I knew it was the only way.

I know you care about Eea, and that's the only reason why I reached out to you for this. I need your help.

The message displayed read instantly but then there was nothing. I waited for a few minutes but there was nothing. I could feel my stomach go in knots, I lost her, my only chance to figure things out, I lost it. The speakers were rattling to life as the stewardess outlined the basic instructions for the zillionth time in her life. The robotic motion of the hostess who converted the syllables into signs was so precise that it felt like she had it embossed in her subconscious.

"Passengers are requested to put their phone and electronics on flight mode," the lady said in her monotonous voice. I looked at my blank screen as despair loomed over me. I was just scrolling over settings to put my phone on flight mode when the notification popped. I exited the setting bar to directly read her message, nervousness making my heart race as I looked at the screen through half-closed eyes, wanting desperately to not be disappointed but somewhere also expecting the answer to be upsetting.

Tomorrow at 5. I'll pick you up from your place.

I finally opened my eyes completely to check if it was really true. She had agreed to it, I felt a deep desire to jump and do my hallelujah dance but I decided better against it. I finally took a deep breath as relief passed through me, and realized I had been holding my breath all this while. The knots in my stomach eased and I could feel myself relaxing.

"Ma'am, please put your phone on airplane mode," a dark-skinned stewardess spoke softly, only loud enough for me to hear as she nodded in the direction of my phone,

"Oh, yes, sorry," I couldn't reply to Anayaa as the attendant stood there watching as if she didn't trust me with it. She gave me a warm smile seeing the slider to the flight mode going yellow, indicating my phone was surely on airplane mode.

I tossed the phone into the handbag and eased into my seat, looking out at the darkness of the sky, feeling anxious but excited. The sky was clear of disturbance and the idea that within the next twenty hours I'd be hunting down my sister's trouble forever and for good gave me a sense of satiation that no college adventure ever could. It felt like being on my own secret mission to rescue my sister from the villain who haunted her even at such a faraway place and after so long. I wouldn't let him eat away my sister's world piece by piece while he built his own. It was going to be dead and buried for and for all. I could feel a wave of relief sweep over me at the thought of Eea being free from that bastard forever. I didn't know what I was going to do. I didn't have step by step plan, in fact, I didn't have a plan at all. The sudden realization made my heart pound, but I was so much into it that I knew I was going to close this matter for once and for all. I didn't know how, maybe I'd make him apologize to her, him and the girl he cheated on Eea with both, maybe, or I'd make him accept that what an asshole he is and record it and send it to Iana. Anything. But one thing which was sure was that this was going to be buried dead forever, I won't let him haunt my sister anymore.

My head felt heavy like it'd burst with these million thoughts oozing out of it. But the mere idea of seeing Eea free from the weight she carried, which wasn't even hers' made all of it seem worth it. This was my chance, but right now I needed sleep. I could feel my head go light as I slipped into darkness, floating.

CHAPTER TWENTY-THREE

IANA

"One more," I said after Zeeshan had put on seven twenty-kilos plates on the leg press machine, his eyes shot up in surprise, he bent down and pulled out another twenty-kilo plate from the steel bar holding the weights and slid the plate into the weight holder of the machine. The plate hadn't hit the base when I said, counting the total weight,

"One more," I pulled over the headphones, pausing the upbeat music and walked to the sideboard of switches, and turned the fan over the machine off.

"How much in all?" he turned to look at me,

"Two-twenty," he shook his head with a faint smile curling his lips, "you're insane, this is insane," he added, putting on all the weights and bringing over extra weights to mark the scale at two-twenty kilos.

"I know," I said, lying down. My back scraped against the rugged surface of the cushioning of the machine and adjusted my feet at an angle that would allow my body to have just the perfect position as the exertion of weight would tone my muscles, only the ones which were supposed to.

"Keep your knees a bit bent," Zeeshan said, taking his place beside me, holding the pressing plate in a steady position to support me, in case I would need it.

"Don't support until I need it. And then too not too much," I said without looking at him, he nodded but I could see his expressions go grave as he stood there, not willing to take any risks. I pushed the plate with my feet and the feeling of exertion kicked in as I opened the support bars which had been holding the weight, which now was on my legs. I pushed the plate with full force letting out a loud cry as it took every ounce of my energy. People there couldn't help gaping at the weight holder while they counted the plates on it and counted and recounted it mentally in disbelief. I could hear Zeeshan's voice as he shouted to cheer me, more out of habit than need. I completed the last set with four extra repetitions and pulled in the support bars. My legs fell limp as soon as the weight rested on the bars setting my muscles free.

"That was something," Zeeshan stood there, looking at me, with a look in his eyes which said 'you're crazy-but-amazing'.

"I pretty much intended it to be," I lay there, not moving, trying to regain my strength and feel my legs which felt like they weren't there.

"You've got an audience," he spoke, scanning the room, looking at the guys who had been gawking and only just a while ago snapped out to go back to working out.

"Have I? good then,"

"How many guys here have tried to hit on you by now?" he smirked. He wasn't flirting, just messing,

"None," thought of Zayne popped in my mind who was just a floor above, toning his flawlessly carved muscles and my cheeks started to heat up, "girls out of the league are supposed to be watched, not hit on," I winked at him, sitting up now. I could feel beads of sweat trickling down my spine and my tee was already wet from sweat,

"over-confidence?"

"Not really, sir. It's just knowing self-worth," he was staring at me side-eyed walking to the side station where he usually stationed himself,

"that's different," he was idling with his phone, not stopping to look at me for a reply.

"Different than girls you've usually come across," I said holding my water bottle just mid-air, my voice flat,

"Which are many. So practically, I've come across almost all types of girls," he was looking at me now, his phone lying ignored on the table,

"Yeah, I know. But there's always an *almost*. So I'm that exception, you see?" my eyes lingered on the display screen which showed the camera recordings from around the building. I looked idly at the random screen and just like that my eyes landed on the rightmost corner which displayed a tall lean figure and I could feel the color rising to my cheeks by just the thought of him,

"How do you know?" Zeeshan asked, snapping me out from my personal moment. I must've looked confused for a moment because he raised his eyebrows in question as he waved one hand in the air to have my attention back,

"What?" I asked, finally gulping down water from the tumbler which I didn't realize I had been holding mid-air for a while now.

"That I come across a lot of girls,"

"You give playboy vibes," I shot back, and suddenly regretted my outright answer. It was more straightforward even on the lines of straightforwardness. He looked astounded and pulled back a bit like I had slapped him hard across the face. I opened my mouth to apologize but then a wide grin spread across his face, not like he was trying to hide his shock but something about it told that he didn't take it offensively,

"I take it as a compliment,"

"I didn't mean it like an offense so I guess you can," I bit my lips lest I might have said something silly,

"You notice me a lot," he said, and I suddenly I felt like I was caught red-handed doing something wrong,

"I just notice a lot," I pretended to ignore his earlier statement,

"Notice to pick out best out of choices?" he asked, retiring back to his phone, typing, and scrolling, stopping just momentarily to look that if I was still there,

"I don't need that really,"

"Maybe yes, you don't have to be that cautious, have *fun*," he lay an awkward emphasis on the word 'fun' that couldn't skip the innuendo even if I it intended to,

"Am not much of that 'fun' girl," his smile faded and he bit a corner of his lips thinking what to add which wouldn't make this already awkward conversation more awkward,

"Oh, I didn't mean it that way," he sounded like he was trying to cover up for his careless remarks.

"Oh no, it's just fine. I don't think there's anything wrong with having fun, I just ain't the one to have it myself. So you don't need to really cover up for it, thinking what I might make out of it, it's cool," I smiled at him and I could feel the tense air around him ease.

"You believe in lifelong love I guess," he said distractedly, trying hard not to sound sarcastic.

"I believe in true connections, don't you?" his eyes darted to mine and I could see a flicker of hurt sparking through them. But it disappeared before I could make out what it was,

"No!" he was almost yelling, like raising his voice would somehow prove his point to be correct, "it's just fad," I could see his fists clenched so hard that they were almost white at the knuckles.

"Is it?" I asked questioningly, trying to break that ice that had built around his eyes, making it tough to read what it was that I had seen, grief? Sadness? Or maybe hurt?

"Yes," he was nodding his head vigorously, trying to persuade himself more than me, "it's just illusion, idea everybody likes to believe in. Nothing much. Childish whims," he rolled his eyes, trying not to sound too desperate,

"Okay, suit yourself with it." I held up my phone and started for the flight stairs to complete my workout day, he stepped aside to make way for me, avoiding to look me directly into the eyes and for a moment my heart went out to him. I wished I could make him see that it wasn't bad to suffer, we all do. But I knew he wouldn't like it, and even I didn't really know if it was really what I thought it was. So I thought it to be better to let go. I walked past him, only to have a last look at him. I knew he wasn't convinced, not by my argument, but by his own.

I was just settling in the extension machine to get done with my workout when Zayne tapped on my shoulder, startling me,

"Hey," he took a step back when I almost jumped out of shock, "easy, it's just me," he said holding his hands up in surrender like I would just attack him.

"Yeah, sorry," I said, shaking my head, trying to clear the haziness of my thoughts.

"How much today?" he asked, bending to pick up his protein shaker. The pink liquid smelt bad enough to make me want to throw up. He sat on haunches to gulp down a bit of the liquid but stopped the bottle mid-air to raise one eyebrow at me in question. I realized I had been staring at him and being caught like that made me turn red,

"Uh, oh... yeah, not much."

"How much?" he put down the shaker and was looking fully at me now, I could feel the heat of his eyes on me,

"Two-twenty," his eyes went wide as the words escaped my mouth,

"You mean two hundred and twenty fucking kilos?" I nodded, setting my feet in the holder as I leaned back a bit to extend my arm to adjust the weight plates on the extension machine. My arm brushed across his thigh slightly and I could feel the hair on my hand stand up as a current shot through me. He smiled a bit but then returned to the topic, I knew what was coming,

"You know that's too much. Why do you like taking such risks?"

"Because I know I can do that, I know my limits," I made sure to not sound too annoyed which I always did whenever this topic came up,

"You do, but that's way too much."

"I had Zeeshan sir supporting me," he opened his mouth to say something but I knew this was the last argument he couldn't think anything against. He let out a deep sigh as if deciding to let go of it for better and I could feel a gush of relief pass through me. I was in no mood to argue over such a petty issue, especially amidst a room full of dozens of people,

"Fine, just promise me you'll be careful, please."

"umhm, I will." He was about to say something but stopped and scanned the room to see if anyone was hearing us, once he made sure that no one was interested in eavesdropping he dropped near me casually and whispered,

"You still haven't told me about your plan for tomorrow, it's Diwali" he was smiling. Looking at him so closely with that innocent smile on made my heart leap. I bet he didn't know how he could light up someone by that look on his face. I leaned in just close enough so my lips were almost brushing his ear,

"You'll get to know when it's time." I pulled back and started to leave, giggling to myself,

"When?" he shouted and all the heads jerked to turn at us, to look what was going on. I could feel dozens of pairs of eyes staring at me as I crossed the room to take the stairs. I let out a deep sigh once I was far out of the grazing gazes and realized my face was burning and I was almost red. Though I couldn't wipe out the stupid smile which had been pasted to my face all this while. Before I could change my mind, I was walking back in the direction I had come from. I stood at the threshold and craned my neck and shouted,

"Soon," I could see faces jumping, startled. It was for the second time and I could see some felt annoyed while others smirked at Zayne like they'd decoded a mystery that something was up.

It was my turn to make him blush and I think I did a pretty well job. I could see him turn red as he bit his lower lip and scratched his head, trying to hide a smile. I raced out before he could make another comment, smiling like an idiot.

CHAPTER TWENTY-FOUR

HELLA

Mumma was pretty pissed at my expedition just within few hours of my arrival. But luckily, it was easy to coax mom, though it meant being stuck at home for the next three days and torturous visits to relatives I hadn't even heard of before, I guessed it would be worth it. My back was stiff from eighteen hours in the air and my head was throbbing with pain which had started to claim the better part of my rationality. The first thing that my body longed for was the bed. I raced to Iana's room, I used to love her bed and had taken over it after she left. The familiarity of the place hit me so hard in the chest that it made me sick. The place still felt like us. I was afraid that it'd feel anonymous and awkward, like being a guest in your own home, but I hadn't imagined that the already knowingness of place would hurt more. My eyes felt heavy though I had almost slept for the whole journey, which was long. It was just minutes after my head hit the pillow that I could feel myself drifting away.

It felt like minutes had passed when mom was shaking me, telling me Anayaa was waiting for me. I rubbed my eyes and stretched out for my phone to check what time was. Five twenty-three. I was already late. Though I knew it wasn't much like Anayaa to get pissed about timings because it was always Iana who worked by the clock and we always thought it was funny. Still, I didn't want to keep her waiting, especially because this was solely my business and she was already being generous enough by accompanying me. I didn't want to push it any further, making it more inconvenient for her than I had to. I pulled out the first pair of clothes I could get my hands on but I had to stop for a while to fish out another one. It clicked that I was back home and it was the festive season, not the best time to go out in my casual shorts and Sando or crop tees. I pulled sober jeans, examining it to make sure it wasn't distressed more than necessary because un-distressed jeans were out of service at the moment, and matched it with a dull pale-yellow kurta which Iana had so thankfully tucked into my stuff at the last moment. She knew better about dresses for the place than me. I suddenly felt so grateful for this humble garment that I'd have hugged her had she been here. I jumped out of the bathroom in two minutes, still getting used to my new attire. Although I made sure I didn't delay our departure, I was still tying my hair on the way outside when mom prompted,

"Where are you off to?" I didn't turn to look at her as I was trying to slip into my sandals while my hands were still trying to coax my hair into a presentable position.

"I told you, I am going to visit some of my old friends and then some of Iana's too. She asked me to wish them from her side," I nodded in Anayaa's direction explaining her presence though mom didn't question it.

"She should've done that herself; it isn't your job. She's supposed to be the elder one," she almost snapped. I could sense that she wasn't completely okay with the fact that Iana hadn't been able to make it.

"It's okay mom, will you please stop making a mountain of a molehill," I said defensively.

"Whatever," she snapped again and a wave of fear crossed over me briefly as I thought she'd not let me go. But she came out of the room holding a pair of earrings and slid one each in my ear delicately, making sure not to hurt me, "at least you should look presentable. No way in hell you're running so carelessly here," she turned me towards her, with her both hands resting on my shoulders, a soft smile lingered on her lips. I could see how much she'd aged, worn out. But yet she looked so beautiful. She turned me and untying my messy ponytail, started to braid them into a fishtail.

I was about to protest that we're getting late but even before I could get jittery which I have an amazing talent for; getting restless pretty quickly, she was done with it as she patted my shoulder lightly, indicating me to turn around.

"Here, go now." She gave a little smile that reached her eyes and I suddenly felt a pang of something in my chest. I halted for a moment longer to hug her before I left to get the work done.

"I love you mumma, bye." I started, without waiting for her but she whispered back what I thought was, "Love you too. Take care." I shook my head at her last words and smiled as the door clicked shut behind us. It was always like that, us before her. And even after all that nastiness and short-temper and sharp remarks it was always that one thing which was layered beneath, care.

I settled in the passenger seat in Anayaa's car. She gave me a hug, at least much like it which you could give sitting there in a crammed-up car. I could sense from her vibe that she wasn't too convinced that it was a good idea.

"You sure?" she asked, eyeing me optimistically like there was a chance I'd back out.

"Pretty much sure," her grip around the gearstick tightened and a nervous look swept across his face. I sighed and unbuckling my seat belt turned to face her,

"Look, you don't have to do it. It's just that I've had enough of his shit." when she didn't speak anything I continued, "Anayaa, you're the only one here who knows things how they were. I see my sister hurting. Even now when she has this amazing guy who finds his world in her and is ready to get the world for her it's like still his shadow keeps looming over her. Threatening her, reminding her of all those terrible things. I see her hurting, and I can't anymore. She deserves to be happy, that guy deserves to get to love whole of Iana and not just parts. Especially not because of some shitbag." She didn't flinch at my language but was looking at me and nodding like she understood, "I just want to be done away with this forever now." I wasn't expecting a reply for what I'd just confessed so I buckled my seat be and looked straight ahead. I waited but she didn't start the engine, not immediately. Instead, she spoke, her words came out more of a whisper and I had to lean in closer to hear her clearly.

"She was my best friend and whatever you're saying, I saw her changing. I know how much she was hurting," I didn't realize until then the tense air that had built up inside the car. Something on her face told that she understood exactly how I was feeling and why I wanted to do what I wanted to do. I hadn't said a word, I was expecting her to make up for my failing words, and she did,

"It's as important for me as it is for you. Even I want to see Eea happy."

"Thank you," I managed to bring the words out though I doubted they were barely comprehendible,

"You don't have to thank me. It's fine," she reached out for my hand which I hadn't realized I had been holding in a knot and clenching hard, they had turned white. I unclenched them and could feel Anayaa's sweaty palm squeezing mine gently.

"No, I mean really, thank you. Even after all these years, you're helping me so much. I mean you don't have to do it now but still, here you are. It means a lot. Thanks," I said feeling too grateful to this girl whom I hadn't even talked to for almost a year. Yet here she was, helping me.

She shook her head smiling what felt like at my naiveness. Though I didn't know what I had said which she found so amusing.

"Friendships don't have a shelf life, Hella. It's like an unsigned bond. You enter into it willingly but you don't get to get out of it. Eea'll always be my best friend and I'll always be here for her. Which I'm sure she'd do the same" she was smiling fully now. I couldn't help feeling a bit jealous by the fact that how blessed my sister was. But then she served it, I knew she was the one who'd go beyond limits to be there for her friends. So seeing that she had people who'd do the same for her made me feel happy. I gritted to make my sister see what she deserved what she had, but before that, I had some work to take care of. I was going to free her, from the douchepants and from all of his' that hurt her.

"Let's get this done," I looked in Anayaa's direction who had started the engine and was already hitting the gas. She gave a small smile as she pressed the race to its full limit and shouted over the revving engine with the strong wind gushing through windows,

"Yeah, so let's fucking get this over with,"

CHAPTER TWENTY-FIVE

IANA

It's kind of funny, how some days can be completely normal yet special. The city was still sleeping under the quilt of darkness and the lights were blinking like usual, yet something about them seemed different now. Angel's Top seemed different now. Like an integral part of my memories. It was Diwali, not that it mattered here, but I couldn't help imagining how happening it'd be back home. A wave of nostalgia hit me and suddenly I felt too euphoric, longing to be back home. I still remembered how I used to hop around the home and always nudge mumma about helping her over making rangoli. I missed days when my biggest concern was to not let lehenga catch fire while lighting *diyas*, when fights were over who gets to burn more crackers. It felt like I aged forward years together when none of such things were capable of filling the void that fed inside of me constantly. I smiled like an idiot wondering how I had never thought this is how growing up would feel like. It felt ironic, how petty things held all that power to change our mood when we were younger yet as we grew up and ran behind other things more, they didn't matter. What mattered was people. Maybe this was what growing up meant, knowing that you don't control people and you don't own them yet you can't help how much they matter to you, how much their actions affect you. How much *they* affect you. There was something different though, I felt happy and sad at the same time. I had Zayne, my present, the person I had so randomly made so important part of my life that it felt like it was never that he wasn't a part of my life. Yet a part of me was thinking about Arsh. It wasn't as random as this one, maybe not natural too, yet I was here, looking at lights and thinking about him, even though it had been years but I couldn't really say he wasn't there, that I didn't care, that I was done with it forever. How could I? When I knew it'd always haunt me no matter if I moved on or not. But today wasn't about this, it was about us. About me and Zayne and it'd be that way. I wasn't going to be unfair to him, neither to me. I was suffering what I deserved yet I had him with me, and I wouldn't make him suffer too. I fished out my phone and typed down,

Twelve today, be ready.

Happy Diwali

I wasn't expecting a reply so I almost jumped and dropped my phone when it buzzed,

What's the plan?

I could feel his excitement and confusion of lack of knowledge of fact but I wanted it to be a surprise so I just left him hanging,

You'll know when the time comes.

I giggled and started down. All the while I kept wondering different scenarios which could happen today as the soft voice of *Andy Grammer* played in the background. It's funny, how your playlist could change from hardcore motivational to sweet love songs and all of it just within months and because of that one person you never thought it possibly to be, even in your wildest dreams.

Walking into the room and pulling away the curtains I opened my mouth to call for Hella only realizing she wasn't here, I suddenly missed her. How much I'd underestimated her presence, nothing specific, just her constant presence. The confirmation of her being here. The perfectly made place tended to remind me that she wasn't here. I was surprised how much I missed the chirpiness and her constant complaints about being woke up early. The crispness of the sophistication of the place irritated me now when she wasn't here to mess it all up.

I opened the jewelry boxes and lay them on the bed, trying to figure out a perfect match to suit the kurta. it was after so long that I was really putting effort to plan my outfit. It was Hella's job, but today was too intimate that I was happy I had the chance to do it by myself. Though, I hadn't expected it to be so tiring. I kept on trying stuff and throwing it away somehow not convinced by their perfection. At last, I settled for large golden *jhumkis* which dangled and brushed by the side of my neck when I moved. I took a bit longer to caress myself as the warm water sprayed away the sweat and soil of the morning work. The bubbles from the body wash swam in the mild and damp air from the steam of the water. One of it rested swiftly on my skin briefly before bursting and disappearing, taking away with it the spectrum which had covered it. Everything felt a bit more colorful. I didn't know if it really was like that or was it just because I was looking at it that way. I bet it was the latter. It was amazing, this feeling. The fact that one person could change so much. Walking out of the shower I wiped myself dry and slipped into the black kurta with the golden thread dancing, woven in an ethnic pattern all across it. I had paired it to twin with Zayne's black kurta. my ears started to go red as his face appeared in front of my eyes while I imagined his eyes going wide seeing me twining with him. I knew it was so stupid, but I loved it, it felt like I was finally doing all that I longed to with someone I loved. Best if it was the requited love. I slipped the *jhumkis* slowly, carefully putting them into the piercing of my ear. I didn't want to add too much volume to the makeup, so I dabbed my lashes with mascara and put on a layer of matte lipstick, and took one long last look at my reflection. I knew Hella's hand would've itched to add a little more drama but I liked this simple look, in fact, I felt proud of myself. I put all the stuff in the bag carefully, it took more than some effort to arrange all this stuff here. In India, it was kind of omnipresent, but here it took almost five hours of driving across the city to find all of it. Checking that I had everything I needed I locked the door and slid into the drivers' seat, pulling the seat belt and buckling it, adjusting the mirror once, I took my time to stare at the happy and gleaming girl there in the mirror, she returned my gaze with one of her bright smiles and I felt happy for her, for me.

CHAPTER TWENTY-SIX

ZAYNE

People had only started to turn around to have a better look at me when she pulled into the parking. It wasn't Diwali for people here, so evidently, some random person standing in completely different and foreign traditional attire was no less than an exhibit. I could feel the heat of stares all over me, and as much as I loved Iana's choice of apparel, I still wanted to vanish into thin air. I wasn't quite so attention-friendly. She was rolling down her window glass when I didn't wait but jumped right into the passenger seat beside her.

"Wow, easy," she looked at me shaking her head, "looks like someone's getting his fair part of attention," she said, brushing away a strand of hair that had fallen on her smooth face.

"Quite much. But I guess someone else deserves the better part," I turned to have a better look at her. He looked beautiful. She always did, but there was something different about girls in traditional. I realized she was wearing the same color and patterned kurta as mine,

"Is it on purpose or is it just utter coincidence that we are kind of twining?" I asked, not taking my eyes off her. I swear I could see her blush and at that moment I fell for her even more.

"I'd love for it to be a coincidence but I bet it's the former one," she said, giving a shy smile, biting her lower lip just a bit to expose her perfect lip line.

"You look beautiful. Damn, can I just ask you something?" she raised her eyebrows with a soft smile, not speaking anything, answering with those dark brown eyes of hers'.

"Will you marry me?" she went blank for just a moment but that silence and look on her face terrified me to the bones. I hate myself for ruining just perfect moments. I opened my mouth to apologize but was cut short by her loud laughter. The knot that had formed inside my stomach loosened as I relaxed. I realized I had never seen her laughing fully like this. God! She was just perfect, her smile, the way she laughed, not caring how she looked but just enjoyed the moment. I reached out to her and cupped her face with my hands, she had stopped laughing but her lips were curled up into a small smile and her eyes were lit up. I wanted her to say something, anything but she didn't. Instead, she leaned into me and I could feel her soft lips on mine, briefly at first, soon I could feel her body pressed against mine as she let go of herself into me and we were kissing fervently now. She smelled like lavender and her lipgloss tasted sweet in my mouth. I pulled her closer and soon she was sitting in my lap, closing the distance between us. Her lips were parted just enough to let our tongues intertwine with passion which literally translated into passionate claims which I couldn't make verbally because words would always fail me. But now I wanted to kiss her deep, hard, I wanted all of her. Her eyes were wild and bright when she pulled away and settled back into her seat. She brushed away the hair from her face in a swift move and without giving me another look pulled out of my parking onto the road.

"May I know where are we going?"

"You'll know" she smiled meeting my eyes in the mirror.

I wasn't quite used to surprise and stuff and honestly, there was something about the sense of knowledge and certainty. It was like having assurance. But it wasn't like that with Iana. With her, every moment was something I wouldn't know about, but surprisingly I liked it, I liked every bit of it and didn't care about the uncertainty of time until it meant being with her. There wasn't anything unusual about the day, it was the same sun, same roads, same city, yet it was different, all of it. It was special, I didn't care looking at the sprinting trees and skyscrapers, I couldn't take my eyes off her. She must've noticed but she didn't turn to even glance at me,

"You've been staring at me for the past thirty minutes. How much longer do you plan to do that?" she asked, taking a sharp left turn, the inertia pushed me in her direction, I didn't fail to take the advantage of the motion just to brush her shoulder with mine.

"I would've said forever but addressing the fact that it'd be too cheesy, I'd settle for let's say however long this drive is," she punched my bicep playfully, and shook her head.

After what seemed like an eternity she pulled into the parking of a quiet neighborhood. The place looked deserted but I could hear chirps and commotion from somewhere not too far away. I unbuckled my seat belt and hopped out to see what the place was. I'd never been to this part of the city. I was trying to figure out my surroundings when she fell in beside me with a large ashet decorated with flowers containing garlands, dry coconut, and vermilion. I couldn't contain my surprise, I could see her watching me and she must've noticed my bewilderment because she spoke without having me to ask,

"It's what you're thinking," she didn't stop so I followed her.

"How?" I was looking at her and trying to keep up with her but I was too surprised, "How did you come to find this place? I mean it's amazing I just..." she stopped so suddenly that I almost bumped into her. I turned to look at what made her steps halt. I almost gasped at the sight of a grand tomb with a saffron flag waving at its top. The temple was so brightly decorated and lightened, just like at home. All of it was so grandiose that I suddenly longed to be back home. To visit places and streets I was familiar with, to celebrate the festivals with my friends like I used to. Suddenly I was missing all those things and looking at her standing beside me I felt like that gap which felt so empty since I had come here, filled up. I felt like I'd burst. I followed her to the corner stall where we discarded our footwear and mounted the marble stairs to the main porch. The feel of cold stone was so soothing that I took a bit longer to let my skin savor the brush, every touch of this pious place. For a moment I completely forgot where I was and all I wanted to do was to sit there and feel the familiarity of this place, which was kind of funny because I'd never even heard about this place, yet it made me feel so close to home. Iana stepped beside me and balancing the worship plate in one hand she slipped the other hand into mine and took me inside the worship hall where the grand deities were placed. The priest was performing the festivities. I stood there, awestruck, overwhelmed, and even grateful. She pulled me with her and we walked to the front handing over the offerings to the priest as he performed the *pooja*. Iana was pressed against me and I could feel her heat as her arm pressed against mine, hands clasped together, head bowed down and eyes shut. She looked so serene that I took a moment longer to cherish this holy and intimate moment with her before mimicking her. I didn't know what she was asking for but I could only thank for everything that I'd now. I never felt so whole so right in my life. Maybe this was it, this was what right felt like. The priest sprinkled some holy water on us and I could feel his hand on my head while he gave me the blessings saying,

"May *Laxmi* fulfill all your wishes,"

I could feel my lips spread into a faint smile, he gave me his blessings but standing there with my hands clasped, feeling so grateful I didn't really need anything else. Yet I did make a wish, I did ask for something. After few moments we opened our eyes and taking the *prasad* we walked slowly, stopping once to ring the temple bell. We were sitting at the back porch of the temple looking at the brightly lit structure when she asked,

"Did you like it?"

"Thank you," I couldn't think of anything else because no matter what said I wouldn't have been enough.

"It isn't over, there's another surprise,"

"One more?" I asked, suddenly feeling quite excited.

"Umhm, let's go," she was already standing and pulling me to my feet. I could feel my legs twitching restlessly. I'd almost forgotten what it felt like to be excited, until now, with her, when every coming moment was filled with this once bygone feeling of me. She suddenly stopped and pulling me to fall in beside her she asked,

"First tell me what you asked for," she wasn't smiling.

"What? When?" I asked incredulously,

"Back inside, I've never seen you so engrossed. What were you asking for so earnestly?"

"Just something," I teased her,

"What something," she was looking more seriously now, all humor from before gone,

"Something too precious to tell,"

"Fine! Don't then," she turned to leave.

"I asked for..." I grasped her hand and pulled her close, I might've pulled harder than I meant to because she swung into me almost bumping her head into my chest. I bent down just enough so that my lips were aligned with her ear so she could hear me whisper,

"*You,*"

We stood there like that for minutes, seconds, years, I don't know but it felt like none of us wanted to break that perfect moment. I wanted to be here, with her. She broke free from me and started walking slowly towards the car holding my hand, pulling me lightly behind her. We didn't speak for what seemed long enough until I broke the silence,

"Where are we going now, ma'am?"

"You'll see, sir," she gave me a wink before we set off and got lost in the running highways of the city end.

#

I couldn't believe what I heard. I looked at her with astonishment to confirm that I wasn't hallucinating or rather I hadn't suddenly turned schizophrenic, hearing sounds in my own head. She reached out for my hand and gave it a little squeeze nodding in my direction, approving what I was thinking to be no imagination. Her face was calm but I could see her eyes bright with happiness and so were mine. The distant hums were closing in on us as we drove closer to their source and could feel myself already jumping out of the car even before she had pulled into the driveway. The golden tomb and serene white of the place, the divine notes of *qawwali*, the scent of *itra* and roses, and the holy shrine covered with bright green *chaddar*. It felt like was lost till now but she held me tight and brought me back to where I belonged. I hadn't realized that tears had started to tumble down my cheeks until she softly brushed one away from my cheek. I didn't realize she was even there until now, I felt so lost. So full. She was holding a green *chaddar* with beautiful golden embroidery, the roses over it were so fresh that I could see the mist over them as their scent med with her lavender spread across me. I held the *chaddar* with her with one hand and slipped the other one into hers as we started to walk inside. We were just about to enter when she stopped me abruptly and handing me over the *chaddar* delicately, she wrapped her dupatta around her head making a perfect *hijab*. The border of the dupatta made her round face look even more beautiful, I could see her small bright dark brown eyes without her hair obstructing and veiling them. She looked chubby, cute.

"You look cute, beautiful," I said, taking her hand into mine.

"Thanks," I could see her flush as her face was more exposed now. I could feel myself blush too, seeing her like this, it felt like I had seen her naked. Without her hair to hide her expressions which she may not like to show, it felt intrusive. Yet I couldn't help staring at her.

The *sajjadanashin* took the *Chaddar* and spread it across the shrine, while I went down on my knees, bowing down to touch my forehead to the shrine, I took moments longer than usual to take every moment of now, just before breaking away I kissed the shrine softly. My hands cupped together eyes closed I could feel myself breathing, and suddenly, I felt close to her, to *Ammi*. This felt like the closest I could ever get to her living. I didn't know how long I had been like that and I could feel my eyes soar and cheek wet with running tears which I realized hadn't stopped since I'd been here. I opened my eyes and Iana was there, sitting content, calmly beside me, her eyes closed and hands clasped as she prayed. I hadn't been sad, not really. But for some reason it felt like today, after long, I was really happy. She waved a hand in the air to get my attention and I realized I'd been gawking at her, but rather than speaking something she stood up and walked to the opposite side of the shrine into an open porch. She didn't stop to see if I followed, but I took the cue and fell in behind her. And there she stood, with the carved wall's falling shadows falling over her face while the lights from the background illuminated her features. A scene that any painter would want to paint, any singer would want to sing about, any writer would want to write, but I wasn't any so I just stood there awestruck. After what seemed like forever, she looked at me and with one finger gestured for me to come and follow her. I crossed the porch, closing the distance between us, and picking up one thread, tied it into clean knots beside the one on which she had been working so meticulously. She stood there, looking intently at me, waiting. When I was done, she slipped her hand into mine, knitting her fingers with mine we walked and sat beside the small pond. It was dusk and the sky was flaring its colors ranging from orange to pink to blue to a hint of black that had started to creep in from the corners. After a while, we stood to leave, yet our every step was slow like it hurt to part from this place. She was too quiet, but her eyes were everywhere like she was trying to have enough of his place to have for a lifetime.

"What *mannat* did you make?" I asked, nodding in the direction of the wall where threads were tied, knotted with it a part of themselves.

"It's a secret," she smiled and ran, the sudden change from calmness to such action confused me a bit. But not enough to let her get away with it so simply. I chased her for a while before finally catching up with her and pulling her to a halt.

"That's not fair, I told you mine. Now you've got to tell me," I intended it to be serious but with such a huge grin pasted to my face, I could barely manage to babble out the words, let alone make them sound serious.

"Okay," she stretched to stand on her toes to reach to my head and then leaning in just enough so that I could feel her breath warm against my neck, she whispered,

"I asked for..."

A shiver went down my spine and I could feel the hair at the back of my neck rise as I could feel the heat rising to my face as the mere idea of her being so close to me made me go red. The sky was almost dark now but there weren't many stars. There was one though, in the far corner, *Anai*. And I swear I saw it twinkled twice when she finally whispered in my ear,

"*...you*"

IANA

"I guess that's enough surprises for a day," I could feel him getting jittery in the seat beside me. He had been scratching his palm and cracking his knuckles and fiddling with the tissue box in the holder.

"Last one I promise," no way I was going to let this one get spoiled, I had been waiting for this for the whole day.

"You know I feel like a rag doll being dragged around,"

"Too big to be dragged around, aren't you?" I suppressed a giggle; I knew he had exhausted his move-around-without-being-informed quota for the day and I didn't want to push it harder.

"Haha very funny,"

"I bet,"

"Okay, stop it. Tell me now," I could sense the aura of annoyance catch up on him.

"Few minutes, and we'll be there,"

"You've been saying this for the last twenty-five minutes. I handled the steering with one hand to reach out for my phone. 7:52 p.m. we were running late, I'd to speed up to be there within the next five minutes.

"What is it?" he asked, scrutinizing my face for some clue.

"What?"

"What?" he mimicked me,

"Stop staring at me like that. I ain't telling you anything and you know that." He opened his mouth to speak something but I hit the gas to the fullest and he was pushed back in his seat by the inertia of motion.

Pulling into the driveway of the huge open place, I could see people had already gathered around and taken their places, I fished out my phone to see the time, 7:58 p.m. okay. We still had two minutes. I ran towards his side of the car and wrapped my hands around his eyes just in time to not let the surprise blow off. I had to stretch on my toes to reach up to his height which was quite awful in the fancy sandals I was wearing. I missed my shoes more than ever as my feet ached with the labor of the long expedition of the day.

Leading him to the curbed side I took the middle spot for which I had to nudge a few people aside which was quite a task, given that my both hands were securing Zayne's vision. Thankfully he didn't bother me much with questions. We had just taken our perfect place behind the iron railings when I let go of my hold of him. The wind wasn't too fast but it had enough velocity to shower us with sprinkles of water from the artificial lake.

"What the..." but he the words hung there mid-air. From the middle of the lake, there went a trail of light and in the next moment, the sky above us was full of sparkles and colors. It felt no different than the 4th of July. The fireworks were so simply elysian. I was feeling euphoric as a pang of nostalgia hit me.

"This is beautiful," he didn't take his eyes off the sky which was now pink with sprinkles of golden glitter in between. He slipped his arms around my waist, pulling me closer to him and I felt so grateful. My legs felt like they'd give up any moment, sending me crashing to the floor only if it hadn't been Zayne holding me upright. I gave in to the exhaustion and leaned further into him, letting my body weight press against his side. The lights, the fireworks were mesmerizing even more with him by my side. After a while when the sky was dark again only illuminated by the streetlights and half the crowd had dispersed, we walked slowly back to the car and sat there, without speaking. All of it felt too delicate that none of us dared to break its spell by the slightest of noise. I didn't know how long we sat like this. Might've been minutes, seconds, days, years. But after what seemed like forever he reached out for my hand and taking it in his he lifted it to his lips and planted a soft kiss on its back. I could feel my cheek wet where the tears had started to pour uninvited. Suddenly I felt too overwhelmed. He didn't say anything or let go of my hand. With his free hand, he reached out to wipe away my tears. He let it rest on my cheek, cupping my half face, not looking away while he did that I could feel his skin warm against mine and I craved for him. He was here, right in front of me, holding me yet every inch of space between us made me ache for him to be closer. I wanted to close every bit of space between us. I wanted the whole of him, the whole of him as well as the part of me which he had.

"*Qubool hai...*" I whispered in a muffled voice that I thought he didn't or even if he did he didn't understand because he looked at me stupefied. But that was for a moment before he realized what I was saying. And soon as he did, a broad smile spread across his face and I could see tears spilling down from the corner of his eyes too. I reached out to wipe it away without stopping,

"*Qubool hai, qubool hai,*" even after wiping each-others' tears we could see it was of no use as new ones took their place, flowing unguarded. So we let go of it and let them flow, smiling at each other stupidly. I could feel his gaze hot on me and realizing that this was the man I got to love, I felt eternally grateful. After a long pause, he pulled me into an embrace and murmured,

"*Insha'Allah,*"

We sat like that for few more moments, smiling and crying at the same time, before I finally pulled away,

"I guess we should head home,"

"Yeah," we were still speaking softly, too enchanted by the spell that was cast upon us.

'Want to come over to my place?" his eyes went wide like he was trying to figure out if I'd really asked him to come over to my place or had he just imagined it,

"You sure? Hella?" he asked dubiously.

"Hella's back home, remember? And yes I'm pretty sure. What do you say? Comin'?" I could still see he was in a dilemma,

"It's okay if you don't want to. I'll drop you..."

"Yes," he almost jumped, cutting me mid-sentence, "I mean yes I'd love to come over," I tried to suppress a smile but he must've seen the hint of it because I could see the tips of his ears go red. Like he was embarrassed to sound too excited.

"Let's go then," I looked at him for one last time to see if he might change his mind but he just nodded his cheeks bright red. I drove out of the driveway, to home, with my one hand still glued to his', smiling at the road in front of me.

He didn't speak much on the way back home. He was radiating nervousness like a human anxiety bomb ready to explode.

"I'm pure vegetarian," I said trying to fiddle with the buttons the elevator pad distractedly,

"So?" he wasn't pretty much questioning, his hand, other than the one slipped into mine, clenched and unclenched restlessly.

"So, I won't eat you. And the biggest proof is you still have all four limbs attached despite spending your whole day with me. Convincing enough?" I asked, trying to lower my laughter sound lest the whole floor might know I was up to something.

"Oh please, such a bad joke? Seriously?" he narrowed his eyes at me. The elevator door opened with a ping and he followed me to the door and stood there, jittery, behind me while I fumbled with the keys. The place was pretty dark and the curtains were drawn which left the whole place into shadows and darkness. Stretching out for the switchboard I lit the softest light. The pale shade of yellow took over the shadows and illuminated the place with just the right amount to not make us squint. I crossed the room slowly, discarding my bag on the floor near the coffee table, and told him to make himself comfortable without looking back at him. Walking slowly to the windows, I peeled away the curtains and the city came into sharp focus with all its illuminations cast and scattered like diamond stones. For a moment the place was so quiet that it almost felt divine, I could hear the faint bustles of the activeness of the life below even from so far beyond. I reached for the rubber band securing my braid and pulled it away and slipped it on my wrist, freeing my hair into a mess. I wasn't paying attention to anything but the lights and motion happening down there. Somehow it felt like I was part of it without being part of it. The room went dark behind me, engulfed by the shadows again. The only light illuminating the place was the faint light coming in from the window. I turned to look what had happened when Zayne, moving swiftly in shadows crossed the room in two long steps stood so close to me that he almost knocked me off. Only his hands reached for me in time and held me arching mid-air before I could hit the ground. He pulled me to my feet and when I was about to pull away, he turned me around in quick motion. My back banged with his stomach lightly. I could feel his one hand slipping around my waist until he was having a complete hold of me and his other one traced upward to my arm, then shoulder, and then softly, he brushed my hair, which was flailing in a frenzy to one side, leaving my neck fully exposed. I was too awestruck and blissful to let words out. I opened my mouth but could only manage a moan. I could feel his calloused hands marking the curves of my body and was surprised by the sudden desire that had started to take over me. I never imagined I could crave someone so much because right now, all I could think of and want was him. With the hand which was wrapped around my waist, he pulled me closer and closer until there was no space for air between us. A shiver went down my spine and I could feel the hair on the back of my neck rising as my arms gave in to the sensation and I could feel the goosebumps on them. My head felt light and all I could think of was to let go of myself into him. His soft lips touched my skin and the desire grew stronger. It was taking all of me to not jerk and turn around and crash into him, kissing like there won't be any tomorrow. I could feel his breath on my neck as his lips grazed at the nape of my neck. He started from my shoulder and planted soft kisses all over until he was whispering in my ear,

"I love you, Iana. God! I love you so much." I could feel the fireworks going off inside me as he spoke those words into my ears. It felt like a thousand butterflies fluttered their wings and took off at the same time while I stood there dumbstruck.

"Did you hear me?" he said, his voice muffled between the kisses, "I love you, Iana Singh."

I turned so suddenly that he almost tipped off, only, I held him there firm, or maybe the other way round. His eyes were wild and he was biting his lower lip in that way you do while seducing someone, it was taking every ounce of my energy to not push him on the couch and kiss him to the core. He raised his eyebrows with a cocky smile like he had somehow read my mind or worst, I had spoken my thoughts aloud. The feeling had just started to sink me when I realized nothing like that had happened, I was hallucinating, imagining.

"Stop," I said, with too much emphasis that he stepped back,

"Sorry, I didn't want to overstep. I'm so sorry," fear and something else crossed his face and I realized he thought said stop because I wasn't comfortable. Yeah, I wasn't comfortable, but not with him, with the space between us. I wasn't comfortable with the idea of him being away when I ached for him so much. I wasn't comfortable with the discovery of the fact that I could long for someone so much, that I longed for *him* so much. I was shaking my head, trying to clear my hazy thoughts.

"No," a look of confusion took over fear and I could see his partially illuminated face tense, with his brows knitted together, I was still shaking my head, "I'm saying stop messing up with my head," he relaxed and his face went back to its calm beauty as his brows relaxed.

"I'm messing with your head?" he asked making a fake innocent face. I could see him smiling and God! He was so handsome. I nodded like a kid and he laughed more fully now,

"How?" the fact that he stood there, so far away, not closing in towards me, annoyed me. So I leaped to cross the distance between us in one step and wrapping my arms around his neck kissed him hard. I pulled back to see only a moment of surprise on his face as he was taken back by my audacity. I wasn't like this usually, or even unusually. This girl surprised even me. But maybe that's what happens when you find the one you thought you never would. His eyes were resting on my face, searching mine. I gave him a long look, hoping he could read all that I was too afraid to say out loud, but then I let it go and leaned in to kiss him full on lips. His lips parted and I could feel his smile while we kissed and collided with each other,

"I love you too, Zayne." I guess my voice would've sounded more like a moan than understandable syllables but then he pulled back to look at me briefly, smiling, before resuming our kiss and I knew he heard it.

#

I could hear my heart beating steadily while my head rested on his bare chest, all the nervousness from earlier melting away as our bodies gave in to each other, following their rhythm. Something crossed my mind and I turned and reached out for my phone pulling the duvet to the side. I'd almost fallen face-first on the ground when Zayne pulled me towards him and my head bumped with his nose. It must've hurt because I could see his nose go red even in the dark folds of the room. He rubbed it gently for a while before returning his gaze to me, shaking his head he guffawed and after making sure that he was okay I joined him. He was pretty relaxed, I hadn't seen him like this before, putting his guard completely down. But then maybe that's what it costed to have responsibilities at such young age, you couldn't show your lows even when they were eating you away, at least not in front of people. He shook me a little and I realized that I'd been staring at him, stupid me. I shook my head to show that it wasn't anything, but more than that to clear my head. Something about him made me steer away so often that it could be so hard sometimes to focus with him lingering around.

I clicked into Spotify and tapped on *Photograph, Ed Sheeren*.

"Hear this," I held the phone a little closer in the air so he could listen it clearly. As I tapped the play button, the baritone filled the room with life. The song was the definition of perfect,

"Our song," I was looking straight into his eyes and even he was smiling fully at me now, his nose still red by the bump we had earlier. He laced his fingers with mine and raising our hands to his mouth, kissed it softly. I could feel myself floating, head clouding. It felt like getting drunk, only, I didn't lose track of my senses, instead, I felt alive, awake. I heard *Ed* singing fantastically the lyrics which felt like they said everything I'd ever want to say to him. I jumped on Zayne horizontally and reached for his phone which he had discarded carelessly on the side table when we'd entered the room in a complete wild frenzy. He gasped by the sudden trauma, his eyes wide, following my every action with question in them. I handed the phone to him and he unlocked it and handed it to me back. I opened the camera and sliding nestling closer to him clicked some weird pictures of us. He looked confused for a while but then seeming to understand, gave me a tough competition in making the weirdly-funniest-face ever. Clicking the pictures, I heard the most apt lyrics for the moment. I turned towards him and sang along, not taking my eyes off him,

"*We keep this love in a photograph, we make these memories for ourselves*

Where our eyes are never closing, hearts are never broken,

Times forever frozen, still." His eyes were twinkling and were wide now, his cheeks stretched with a full grin pasted on it.

"I love you, Eea. I do." I swear I could feel myself turn into a living red fireball. Suddenly, I felt grateful for the darkness in the room.

"Hey," he said again when I didn't reply for a while. I was too tired and excited and overwhelmed at the same time to be able to manage words, so I just settled for a muffled sound,

"Hm," his hands, still laced with mine were warm and sweaty now. His thumb grazed at the back of my hand.

"I'm leaving for India," my eyes widened as I turned to look at him to see if he was kidding. But the fact that there was no humor in them made my throat go tight.

"When?" I managed in a small voice,

"January, first week," I knew he could feel the uneasiness that had started to build around me because he straightened and pulled me into a full hug and was rubbing my shoulders to calm me down,

"Okay," I was trying to relax but the tension wouldn't leave my body. Suddenly I felt the need to say something more,

"You need this, the time with your family. It's nice that you're going. I'll miss you though," I tried to accompany it with a weak smile.

"Yeah, about that part," he was looking straight into the darkness, his hands still resting on my shoulders,

"Which part?"

"The missing part," while he brought those words out, I could feel my stomach go in knots and it felt like I might've thrown up anytime, "I was thinking it'd be amazing if you came,"

"Came as in to drop you? Like at the airport?" I could feel my heartbeat racing inside my ribcage.

"No, I mean to India," he said those words with such ease but my heart was pounding, ready to burst out in a complete bloody mess.

"You're kidding. Tell me you aren't serious," I was looking at him with a ray of optimism. Like I was so badly wanting it to be some kind of joke, even if it was a pathetic one.

"No, I'm not," he was holding me more closely now and could feel him squeezing my hand in a meek assurance, "See, I know you didn't leave India on very good terms. But you can't run from it forever. You've got to face it someday, Eea. And I want you to know that you aren't alone, whatever it is, I want to be there for you. Please," his words were fast but calm, but something about them irritated me. The fear I had been feeling suddenly turned into rage,

"I appreciate that. But you can't do this." I was pulling away from his embrace, trying to put distance between us,

"Why can't I? Or rather I should say why *you* don't *want* to?" he wasn't shouting, but something in his voice was alarming. I knew where this conversation was heading and was already dreading it. *Photograph* was still playing in the background, botherless of the aura of the place.

"You don't get to say this when you don't know the reason behind that, so please."

"Then tell me, Eea."

"I can't," I could feel my cheeks burning with heat and anger. Anger at his stubbornness.

"Try, please." He sighed, and for a moment I thought he'd finally gave up. But no, he was just trying to take it slow, "You don't know how I feel to see you suffer like this. To see you smiling one moment and then drifting away to some distant place where I can't reach you the other. You're strong I know, but I see that pain, Eea, and it hurts to see you like this. I feel helpless for not being able to be there for you," his head was hanging low, and seeing him like this hit me so hard in the chest that it hurt.

"It isn't your fault, it's just me..." he didn't let me finish

"I know it's your battle and you've got to fight it and I respect that. But please see around that it's hurting everybody in your vicinity, it's hurting them to see you hurt and suffer like this. And it hurts more when you push them away and don't let them help you. Please don't do this. I can't see you like this; they can't see you like this."

I wasn't feeling annoyed anymore, I was feeling tired. Tired of carrying all of it around not let it affect people around me but now when he had so bravely told the truth which I was too coward to accept, it was laughing at my face, bare and shameless. He didn't say anything that I didn't already know, but somehow, I was just trying to delay the inevitable. And I knew I couldn't avoid it anymore. I knew I'd have to do it someday. Now, when he was with me, wanting to fight it with me, I knew I couldn't be unjust to him or for that matter to me, anymore. I knew I'd have to let it go someday, and it was today.

I crossed the room slowly, taking my time, and bent down to pause the song. I could feel the warmth of his eyes on my back and despite the normal room temperature I was shivering. I turned to pull the duvet and wrap it around myself for some warmth but I just fell there in his arms as my legs gave up under me, crumpling me like a skeleton on the bed near him. Thankfully, he was there, holding me firm while I waited for the wave and exhaustion to pass. It was tiring, to part from something you've been holding on to for so long, but I knew it was time. So, taking in a deep breath and nestling closer in his arms, I finally let go.

CHAPTER TWENTY-EIGHT

HELLA

I could feel Anayaa's discomfort, her hands tightly knotted, resting in her lap. She was scratching the corner of her pinkie so hard that I could see a red patch starting to grow over it.

"Are you sure about it?" she said so consciously that it started to bother me even.

"Don't you think we are far past the situation for that question?" I said nodding in the direction of the dimly lit room. The fact that the place wasn't decorated or lit up was kind of awkward and absurd, given the grandeur of the festival here. It could have been anything, personal reasons may be, I didn't want to dive into the fact. I just wanted to get the job for which I was here done and be back home, celebrating Diwali.

"Did you find any other way to contact him? DM? message? Calls?" I had the prescience of what her answer would be, but I needed to see her confirm it. She did, with that sorrowful shake of his head.

"Then this is our last straw. And as much as I'm pretty clear about it, I'm not letting this one thing go undone while I can take care of it. So yes, I'm pretty sure." I wasn't looking in her direction but I could feel the tension in the air turn into something else, determination maybe?

The old lady placed the cheap chinaware in front of us with snacks unpacked from the 'for-guest-containers'. Everybody here had those. It was something of a standard ritual to have those. Like not having them would somehow make you less Indian. When she bent to put the heavy tray on the coffee table in front of us, the light fell sharp on her face, illuminating her features perfectly for me to have a better look at them. She wasn't as old as I'd first thought her to be. She might've been somewhat my mother's age, but the lines and sacs under her eyes made her look aged. Her hair showed hints of gray between crisp black strands. Eyes heavy, like she'd been going to sleep crying. I suddenly felt pity for her, for whatever it was that'd turned her like this. The sudden dawn of fact that I was here to burst upon who might be her son made me feel ashamed. But it was wiped away soon enough at the thought of what he'd done with Eea. Yet I somehow wanted to reach out to her, console her in any way possible. I decided I wouldn't bother her with the deeds of her son. Apparently, she was already suffering enough, the least could do was to spare her the embarrassment of the younger sister of his son's ex chiding him. I wondered if she knew what her son had done, that he'd been the reason, my sister doesn't want to come back home, I didn't think she did.

She looked at me and Anayaa without a hint of recognition, not that we'd expected any anyway. Her gaze, steady on us was filled with questions which she was trying not to bombard us with out of sheer courtesy.

"Namastey Aunty," I clasped hands to greet and she just gave me a small nod. Like even the slightest of movement hurt her. I realized how weak she was, fragile. Like slightest of tension would shatter her like a glass doll. When she didn't say anything, I took it as a sign to continue,

"Can we have a quick meet with Arsh?" her eyes went wide at the mention of his name, "We're his friends," I looked at Anayaa who was nodding so hard that it felt like her head would bob out any time, "We wanted to surprise him. Wish him Diwali." She wasn't saying anything. Just a look of pain smeared her features and blurred the lines of her face as tears started to roll down her face.

"I...um...I'm sorry aunty. I didn't mean to...what happened? Did we say or do something wrong?" the confidence I had when I'd entered this place had all evaporated and all I could feel now was tension and confusion. I tried to replay the words in my head to find the flaw but couldn't come out with any in those humble combinations of the word. I looked at Anayaa who was sitting dumb folded, a look of bafflement and fear pasted onto her features. She looked at me with a 'told-you-it-wasn't-a-good-idea' look. I took a moment to clear my head and let out the next syllables with utter care.

"I'm so sorry aunty. I didn't mean to..." before I could manage anything any further, she stood up and walked to the door at the other end of the room from where were sitting. I thought she was leaving and that was our cue to leave too. But no, she stood at the threshold of the door and looked at us and I realized she wasn't asking us to go, instead, she wanted us to follow her. I stood up meekly, all my courage and grit melting into something remorseful, dread maybe. I looked once in the direction of Anayaa if she was following and seeing her behind me gave a little relief.

We walked through a short dark corridor and after few steps entered into a huge room that seemed more like a hall. The room was grandiose, like those which they show on TLC under the tag of most amazing rooms. The walls were full of band covers and signed posters. The bed wasn't made, it was messy. Like someone had just slept in it and left it that way, not bothering to make it. The room was clean and messy at the same time; if something like that could be possible. My eyes wandered to the room, to its details. The curtains were drawn, corners were full of unwashed clothes thrown to be taken care of later. I ran my fingers across the tennis racket that'd been lying on the study table distractedly. This must be Arsh's room. I wondered if he was out and would be back in some time and her mom wanted us to wait in here. But that didn't seem right. She could've made us wait out in the guest room, why bother to bring us in here. I was trying to process and ponder over the facts when she slowly walked past us and towards the one corner of the room. I followed her to the place because the way she moved told that she was expecting us to follow her. She didn't turn to look at us but when we both were standing behind her, not knowing what to expect, she took a small step aside and pushed herself into the corner to let us have a clear look at what lay there ahead of us. Seeing it there I could feel my legs go numb and my throat constrict. Near me, I could feel Anayaa go completely still. Of all the possibilities I'd imagined in my head, I hadn't thought about this one to be even wildly possible. Hadn't even considered it to be a possibility. I could hear the muffled sobs of his mother from the corner where she had crumpled onto the floor. I wanted to comfort her, but all of it would've been too superficial, and even if I'd want to, my legs wouldn't move. I suddenly felt ashamed, all the anger from earlier turning into something I couldn't clearly point out. The image of the young boy, smiling fully at the lens, eyes crinkled at sides felt like he was laughing right at me. Arsh. It was him. My body was too shocked to process the garland around his photograph. However much I might've wanted him to pay, this wasn't something I would've ever wanted for him. Suddenly, the tears I hadn't realized I had been biting away, started to flow unrestricted. It was him, his photo secured by a fresh garland. Too beautiful yet reminding something so dreadful.

Arsh...

he was dead.

CHAPTER TWENTY-NINE

ZAYNE

I could feel her go limp in my arms. There was a long pause before she finally broke the silence. I feel could the enormous amount of hurt it inflicted on her to get off something that she'd been trying to bury away for so long. But I couldn't let her face it alone. Especially after seeing what it was doing to her. She let out a deep sigh and I could feel the warmth of her breath on my neck where she had nestled her head.

"Arsh and I were together since grade nine." Her words felt like a burden which she was finally getting done with. Each word pulling away some weight with it, weight which she'd been carrying alone, for so long, "he proposed me a year after we met and the connection, it felt so real that I couldn't think it to be any better. Silly me," she scoffed at the memory.

"We were young, silly but the fact that it all felt so good was real. We were kind of that popular high-school couple, even though we weren't in the same school. Things were pretty cool but then the summer before last year my parents caught us together..." for a moment I thought I missed what she said, but no, she was quiet,

"And they didn't like it," she shook her head,

"They didn't. Arsh's mom came to my place, he hadn't been doing well at school,"

"And she thought it was because of you?"

"Pretty much so. My parents did what they thought was right for me,"

"Made you break up with him?"

"I wish. No. They grounded me. No phone, no contacts, twenty-four-hour-surveillance,"

"That suck,"

"It does. But stubborn as I was, I managed to find a way to keep in touch with him, to let things cool down and things pass. For a month it seemed fine but then he started to grow distant, didn't reply to my weekly texts, texts of my friends. I knew things were changing so I just asked him to talk it out for once and for all. As much as I wanted for it to work, I'm not the kind person to force someone for something which I know is beyond control." I could feel her emotions fuming. After all those years of repression, they were blasting out with more vigor. I rubbed her shoulders gently to calm her a bit but didn't interrupt her narration.

"He didn't conform to it. So, I left it for good, tried to bury it away, forever."

"That's why you didn't want to date ever again? I know he hurt you..." she shook her head and that left me too confused to continue. Seeing that I struggled to put together what she meant, she continued. Something about the look on her face told me there was something more it, something more dreadful.

"A month after my birthday he texted saying that he thought it was better if we broke up. Which was kind of funny because I'd already accepted before he had even said that. I didn't say anything, just wished him luck for the future but then what he said next was like someone pierced the knife through me without any sedation." Fresh tears had started to pour down her cheek but for some reason, I couldn't reach out to wipe them, I let her shed them, shed their weight which she'd suppressed for long enough, she needed to let them out.

"He said there wasn't any sense of having a trophy girlfriend if he couldn't flaunt it, that I was just a burden now with orthodox parents and that he would rather be fine with someone else. He'd found someone while I suffered all that just because *he* wasn't doing well in his academics."

"Found someone while you were together?" the words were out before I could've stopped them. She didn't say anything but the way her head fell answered my question.

"I don't know but it seemed like he *wanted* me to hear all of it. Like somehow, me not begging for him to stay hurt his ego. It was like he was angry at me for not asking him to stay even when he'd already made his mind to leave."

"Freaking chauvinist," I could feel myself fuming, but I knew it wasn't my story to tell, so I apologized immediately though she waved it off like it didn't matter.

"it was terrible, every bit of it. And what was more terrible was that I felt so much for him that I couldn't let anybody in,"

"I know," suddenly Jacey's texts from that night flashed in front of me and it was like while I was here with her trusting me with a part of her, I could feel that night replay in my head over and over. I understood exactly how she must've felt even though I didn't know how worse it'd have been with even her parents blaming her. The mere thought of it made me shiver at the coldness of her situation.

"Last summer, when I got my appointment letter from Muses And Caerus I was so happy to think about any of it. I'd almost pushed Arsh into a dark corner of my mind which I never visited. But then, things you love and hate the most don't leave you so easily, do they?" her voice was flat but I could see her eyes shimmer with tears.

"a week before I was to leave for America, he called me, said he wanted to meet once. To apologize for everything." She turned to look at me, "I had forgiven him long before that but I'm no sage Zayne. You can't expect to almost kill me with your words and then victimize yourself, and then show up out of sheer dust and expect to see me and apologize in person? I'm human, I couldn't do it."

"It isn't your fault, Eea" I could barely manage the words out in a whisper, her head was pressed hard against my chest and I could feel her sobbing hard now,

"Only, that it was. It was my fault, Zayne." She wiped her face with the back of her hand only to make way for new tears to replace old ones,

"The day I was leaving for the States, he called me. I was at the airport. He said he was coming there, he wanted to see me for one last time, tell me how sorry he was."

"That shitbag doesn't get to do that," such venom in my words for someone I didn't even know surprised me,

"Neither do I get to say what I said," her voice cracked,

"What do you mean?"

"He called me, and I lost it. On the phone, with him. I told him I didn't want to see his face ever again and that I wouldn't care less if he was dead," my eyes went wide at thought of those words coming from the mouth of someone I had always seen being there for everyone. Everything about them seemed so wrong. Even the thought of it seemed wrong.

"I hung up on him, only, he called again, seven and a half minutes later. I declined his call but it wouldn't stop until I finally picked up to lash out at him, only, it wasn't him on the phone,"

"Wasn't him?" she nodded so slowly like the slightest of movement hurt her.

"It was someone from the scene,"

"Scene?" everything she said sounded like some kind of foreign language I tried to make sense of, only to fail miserably.

"Arsh had been in an accident on his way to the airport. Apparently, the last and the most dialed number was mine. He died on the spot, broke his neck. They said the last word he spoke was Eea. He was dead before they could take him to the hospital." A fresh stream of tears had started to flow down from her eyes and she was crying, not muffled sobs but louder weeps.

It hit me, the hurt I'd seen in hers for the first time when our eyes met at the Angel's Top, the connection I'd felt back at Amaa's, it wasn't imaginary or just because she empathized with me. It was because she was carrying the guilt of something so heavy with her. She knew every inch of that pain of losing someone you loved so ardently, but she knew the worst of it. She was carrying with her the pain of being the reason for the death of that loved one, at least that what she thought to be her fault. I pulled her closer to me, she didn't protest and fell weakly into my arms, she looked so small and worn out. Seeing her like that made my heart hurt, I felt annoyed at the fact that she, of all people, had to go through all of it. If anyone didn't deserve to carry such a burden, it was her. I tightened my embrace and rubbed her back gently, too afraid to let go of her, and what it felt like, even she tightened her arms around me while she cried fully now,

"It wasn't your fault Eea. You can't blame yourself for any of it. You couldn't have changed any of it,"

"I could've changed my words, how do you know that only if I hadn't said any of it he might still have been alive,"

"No, I don't know. Neither do you that not saying them would've saved his life. The truth is none of us will ever know." She didn't say anything, just continued to cry, "Eea, I know it's tough, but one person whom I know to have a heart who wouldn't ever want to hurt anyone, it's you. And I know that even you know that you never wanted anything bad to happen to him," she nodded a short nod in my chest.

"It was meant to happen, you couldn't have possibly changed it even if you hadn't said any of it,"

"Can you love me the same despite knowing that I might be the reason someone is dead?" her voice almost broke at the last word,

"Knowing that my girlfriend has been so strong to face all of it alone and still hasn't turned bitter when life gave you every reason to be so, God! I love you even more Eea. You just have to stop blaming yourself and see that you've got people who want to be there for you. Just don't push them away, Hella, I, Eign, we all love you." Her eyes went wide at the mention of his best friend but she let it go and didn't question me about how I knew about him.

"I love you, Zayne." She said, her voice hoarse from crying.

"I love you too, Iana. I always will."

Seeing her so vulnerable, I knew she trusted me, even loved me. But what she had told me today, all of it felt so much more intimate than any physical engagement ever could. It was something I couldn't describe. It was probably more intimate than any physical contact. I wasn't surprised by the intensity of what I felt when she was here in my arms. What I was surprised by was how much she'd started to mean to me. I loved her. God! I loved her with all her flaws and perfections and scars and adorations. I loved each part of her, the whole of her, her.

CHAPTER THIRTY

IANA

There was something off about Hella since she'd returned. I couldn't just point out what, but there was something off. She wasn't her nosy self anymore. And though she was more careful around me about picking up topics and arguments I missed her carelessness. I could feel her tensing up whenever I asked about her time back home, her answers couldn't be anymore vague. It was kind of annoying.

"You should come," she said, trying on the dresses for the party for New Year's Eve,

"I'm helping Zayne packing up. He's leaving day after,"

"Umhm, join in after that," she wasn't looking at me,

"What is it?" the words popped out of my mouth out of the blue, though I didn't specify what it was that I was talking about, she knew. I could feel her tensing up,

"What is what?" she tried ducking the question, useless.

"How long do you think you can continue acting weird without talking about whatever it is that is bothering you?" her eyes widened, "what? Do you think I can't see how changed you've been since the past month since you've returned?"

"When you were planning to tell me?" out of all the possible answers to my questions, this wasn't the one I'd even imagined,

"About what?" I didn't quite make out where this conversation was headed,

"I went to Arsh's place, wanted to talk about something," it was my turn to get shocked. I could feel my body go stiff as words held caught up at the back of my throat, refusing to back me up.

"When were you planning to tell me that he was dead? I don't think so it'd have been anytime soon because from what I got to know you already had ample time since last year," she wasn't shouting, but that calmness in her voice made it worse. It wouldn't have been much of a problem had she been yelling at me, it was her standard response to such issues. But something about the way she was talking right now, with calmness and subtlety in her voice but a storm in her eyes, my throat went dry.

"I... I'm sorry," the words were a bare whisper and when her expressions didn't change, I wondered for a moment if she'd even heard me,

"That's all that you've got to say?" she started towards me; her hands folded tightly in front of her chest. How much I'd underestimated her desperation to get the old me back. Of everything, I'd never imagined she'd do something like that. I felt angry and proud at the same time. I knew I couldn't hide it forever, but still, I tried. I knew though, that she needed to know everything. So I let out a deep sigh and gave her what she deserved to know. The truth.

She sat there, listening, not interrupting me even once, for which I was thankful a lot. After I finished she didn't move and I wondered if she was thinking the perfect way to lash out at me, especially after knowing that the elder sister she did so much for, wasn't worth any of it.

"Look, it's okay if you're angry at me and blame me for it, I do too. I just..." I could feel my throat go stone as it hurt to bring out the words,

"There isn't anything I wouldn't have given to take those words back, to change those seven and a half minutes. Even now I try to keep track of every minute to the perfect second like somehow, it'll bring him back," I said, eyeing the clock behind her the wall. I wanted something to focus on, to keep myself from crying. I was trying to keep my mind on the ticking of the clock when I felt her arms slipping around me and I lost my focus as tears fell from where

I'd been biting back at them.

"Tell me how can I bring you to believe that when I say we love you, I mean it. And I mean it without any terms and conditions. And for what it's worth, you've got to stop blaming yourself, you know there wasn't anything you could've done." She planted a soft kiss on my head and wiped away my tears,

"I love you and so does Zayne and everyone." She paused to pull in a deep breath, "I hope you know how much Zayne loves you," she didn't pause for my answer but I nodded anyway, "I know you've been through a lot. But you need to know this Eea that you deserve to be loved. And I'm happy for you and Zayne." I gave her a weak smile, words wouldn't come out.

"Promise me you won't push me away ever again. You won't push any of us who loves you away ever again," her voice had a hint of deadly seriousness which I knew better not to contradict.

"I promise," I nodded affirming my words, and pulled her into a tight embrace.

Letting the secret, I'd carried for so long go felt light but it also felt empty. But now that it was out, I had more space for letting people in. Maybe I should've done it long before. But however it was, one thing I was more than grateful for was Hella and Eign, and of course, Zayne. I was afraid that whatever happened with Arsh, I wouldn't want to love again, I wouldn't fall again. But he cut off that every point from the list and made me fall even harder. Love even deeper, fiercer.

I was glad I took this risk for letting myself fall for him when I didn't for anybody else.

I was glad I gave me a chance,

I was glad I gave *us* a chance.

CHAPTER THIRTY-ONE

ZAYNE

It was difficult to wave away Zeeshan's constant offer of accompanying me to the airport. I hadn't told him about Iana yet, so his coming meant she wouldn't be able to see me off. Thankfully, the air-conditioning service people agreed to my request for moving our appointment for the gym to a week earlier than planned so he had to be there.

"Hey, all set?" she gave me a brief hug before helping me with my luggage. It wasn't much, just a backpack. Though I missed my home terribly, I had to be back soon, to help Zeeshan.

"Yeah," I stopped, she mimicked me by halting by my side, her eyes searching mine.

"I wish you could come," her mouth drooped a bit at corners but she managed to give me a faint smile,

"It's just two weeks. You'll be back before you even know it. Besides, you should meet your family. They must miss you a lot."

"Look who's saying," I couldn't hide the sarcasm in my voice but I didn't mean it to be sharp, and I knew she knew it.

"Zayne, I'm just... I need time. I'll be fine."

"But you know you can't stay away from your home forever. Plus, I want you to meet my family." Her eyes went wide in disbelief and color rose to her cheeks.

"You what? Oh my god really?"

"Umhm," her eyes were glistening. And even in her usual athleisure, she looked tremendous. Though I doubted Hella would've approved of it.

"Then next time for sure," she hugged me tightly.

"For sure," I kissed her fervently before breaking to check-in. I meant what I'd said and I knew as difficult it'd be, I was positive my family would be happy. Putting my baggage for a thorough search I turned to have one last look at her and couldn't help smiling like an idiot when she stood there, jumping and waving hands with full vigor. She was too far from me to read her expressions but I could see a smile spread broadly across her face while she continued to wave. I too waved back at her, imitating her vigor, smiling stupidly.

#

Papa looked so feeble but when he hugged me, I could feel the same energy and warmth as he patted my back a little too hard. I let go of my bag and let it slip to the floor near my leg, reciprocating papa's warm hug with mine.

"Salam Alaikum, papa,"

"Walaik Musalam. You look..." he took a minute to have a good look at me, holding me at an arm's length. I was surprised by the firmness in her grip despite him looking so fragile. "You look good, happy." I wondered if he could even make out the reason for me being so; if he could tell it was because I finally loved someone and she loved me the same too.

"I am happy." I picked up my bag from the floor, quickly adding, "I'm happy to be home,"

He didn't seem to notice while he sat on the worn-off couch resigning back to his work. Before getting lost again behind the papers he looked up, sliding down his glasses from the bridge of his nose a bit, "Your room's ready. Go have some rest. Your sisters will be here for the dinner. I'll be heading out for some work. Razia will be home. Ask her if you need anything,"

I simply nodded and greeted her, "Salam Alaikum, aunty" she returned my greetings and went back to her work. She wasn't the type to show affection by small gestures. I remembered when she'd first come home after dad had married her after *Ammi*'s death. I was too young. I'd tried being friendly, maybe because I hoped she'd be like *Ammi,* or at least try to be like her. She'd accept me the way *Ammi* did. I remembered calling her *Ammi* and the way she'd shrugged and said to me to keep it to aunty. Since then, we both knew our formal lines. She never tried to erase them and I never tried to push them. It was long ago; we'd been sticking to this arrangement since then.

My room was crisply made, everything was just as I remembered. It felt nice, the hint of familiarity. I discarded my bag in one corner and landed on the mattress stomach first. After laying there, watching the bare ceiling for a while I decided to clean up and took a long shower. I dumped my dirty clothes in the laundry and drying my hair with a towel, took my place back on the bed. I was feeling sleepy and could use a nap, but before that, I fished out my phone and connecting it to the Wi-Fi I texted Eea,

Safe and sweetly home. Already missing you. Take care.

I had to get a new sim card to use services here. I'd get it tomorrow. Right now, I felt too tired to do anything. I looked at the two gray tick marks at the corner of the message and then digging into the gallery, pulled out the weird photo which she'd clicked on the night of Diwali. She looked so beautiful and careless and funny and smart. I let the phone rest on my chest while I smiled to myself. Before long, my eyes felt heavy and I drifted off to sleep with our photo still resting on my chest, close to my heart.

I woke up to a loud knock on my door. Rubbing my eyes I saw the time, it was almost dinnertime, I'd been asleep for more than six hours. My body felt stiff.

"Zayne, are you in there? It's time for dinner," the voice made me jump out of excitement as I hopped down the bed and opening the door in one swift move, swept Huma *apa* in my arms. She was closest to what I could ever have to my mother. She wasn't the eldest but for me, she held respect more than anyone after papa.

"You look so weak, don't you eat there?" she said returning my embrace and smiling at me, her hands cupping my face, wiping away my hair which had fallen in my eyes.

"You always say that. How are you? And everyone at home?" I asked, reaching out for the phone which I'd been too careless to bother about when I heard her voice. Retrieving it, I checked it once to see if there was anything from Iana, nothing. Putting it on vibrate mode, I followed *apa* to the dining room. Almost everyone was there already, only aunty was still hustling to bring in the cutlery and serving bowls, helped by my eldest sister. It felt so happy to be with all of them after so long. Plus, I was glad I had everybody's ears for the news I planned to break.

"How was the journey?" my second eldest sister asked,

"Fine," I said, digging my fingers into a heap of biryani after doing bismillah.

The whole dinner was spent by a series of questions and putting in a keen interest in my answers. Huma *apa* was serving the sweet dish when my phone buzzed as its screen came to light, it displayed Iana's name. I reached out for it immediately. Everybody's eyes shot up in surprise but nobody uttered a word. It wasn't usually my type to use a cell phone while eating. It wouldn't have been so unusual for bhai to do so, but seeing me do that was not obvious for them. The text was short,

Have fun with your family. Give them my regards. Miss you too. Take care.

I could suddenly feel nervousness taking over me, I'd planned to tell them about her, and at that time idea hadn't seemed so stressful. But right now, sitting with all of their attention to me, I could feel my spine go stiff and my body go cold. Aunty was talking about some random topic when I cleared my throat to have their attention. I had to do it, I wanted to do it.

"What is it? are you okay?" Huma *apa* asked, concerned.

"Yeah, I wanted to tell you something," I could feel the heat of gazes on me as everybody paused eating to hear me,

"What is it?" this time papa asked, not taking his eyes off the plate. He was the only one who hadn't left his food uncared for at my words.

"I have a friend I wanted you all to meet. We are close so I thought I'd be good,"

"Oh, that's fine, feel free to invite him over, does he live with you?" my eldest sister inquired, I could feel their interest wearing off as they resumed eating, not looking at me anymore.

"Actually, it's a *she*. We don't live together it's just..." now I could feel lasers being shot at me through wide eyes. Everybody had forgotten about the dessert.

"What?" Huma *apa* asked, confused like she was trying to believe that she'd misheard.

"I like her,"

"And her?" papa asked with a deadly calm voice, eating slowly from his dish.

"She does too."

"What's her name?" my second eldest sister asked,

"Iana," I said softly,

"Iana?" she asked again. It was a sign that she wanted to know her full name.

"Iana Singh," the last name acted like a silent grenade. I could hear everybody gasp as their eyes went wide in shock.

"It's okay," papa said, finally looking at me, "She's just a friend," I could feel the seriousness in his voice and the unspoken words, "I'm not asking,". I could feel the heat rising to my face and nervousness turned into agitation,

"Actually, she's not. She is my girlfriend. I wanted to tell you because we are serious about each other,"

"Astaghfirullah, Zayne. That's how you talk to elders now?" my eldest sister said, controlling the anger in her voice which told that she wanted to yell at me but was holding herself back because of our father being there.

"We should get him married soon. He's slipping out of hand," aunty said in a hushed voice, to my father, everybody nodded except Huma. I could see fear and concern take over his big features.

"You stay out of this," I tried to control the harshness in my voice as I replied to her with sharp words. I turned towards my father expectantly, who hadn't spoken a word till now,

"I love here, papa. We need time together." When he still didn't say anything, I could feel myself bursting from anger and annoyance. I smashed my fists on the table and picking up my phone left the room. Everybody sat frozen, aghast.

#

I remembered how she loved lights, but my eyes were fixed on the source of dim light in the farthest corner of the sky. *Anai*. I don't know why, but I was talking to her like she'd reply to me, tell me something, give me answers to questions which I was too afraid to ask. Deep in my reverie, I felt a hand, warm and sweaty, rest on my shoulder. I rubbed my wet cheeks hastily before turning to face papa. I didn't know for how long he'd been standing there.

"Are you fine, son?" his words were flat, but something in them told me that there was so much more he wanted to say to me. I nodded a brief nod before returning my gaze to *Anai*. I couldn't bear to look straight into his eyes right now. he didn't say anything, but I could hear his footsteps as he slowly walked and stood beside me, staring at the sky without a focus point. After a long pause, he inhaled sharply and finally broke the silence,

"You know I was just like you when was young. So belligerent, my parents had a tough time handling me." He let out a laugh which sounded more like a struggled sigh. I didn't interrupt his narration; I could feel from his words that he was lost in his utopia of memories.

"Your mother, she was an amazing woman." The sudden change of topic to my mother made me a bit uncomfortable. It was for the first time we were talking about her since her death. Papa never could, none of us could, without our emotions taking over the better of us.

"She loved you all so much, but she loved you the most, Zayne," that was at least true. I guess it was one of the implied perks of being the youngest one in the family.

"Yeah, I know. I still miss her," I whispered under my breath.

"Then you must know that she had many plans for you, Zayne. She wanted the best for you," I couldn't help noticing the constriction in his voice. I turned to face him and was surprised by the glimmering tears that were hinting in his eyes. I'd never seen him cry before, not even at *Ammi*'s funeral. He held me by my shoulders and hugged me, and suddenly, I knew what all of this was about. I could feel the onset of protest between my faculties as my reason revolted to take the other path than one which my conscience and heart had till now been walking on. I was torn.

\#

I called her number, not sure if she'd pick up. The phone rang thrice before I heard her voice, full of warmth and excitement.

"Hey, how are you? I was wondering what you'd be doing. How's everybody at home? Say something, why are you mute?" listening to her familiar voice and the emotions that it carried, I almost choked on words, not knowing how to break the news for which I'd called. I decided to let myself have these few last good moments with her,

"Hi, everything's fine. Everyone's good. How are you?"

"I'm good, just missing you a bit," I could hear a giggle before she added playfully, "actually, a lot more than a bit," I could feel my insides ripping apart and I wanted to get over with this as soon as possible, I inhaled sharply and she must've heard it because the next moment her voice was full of concern,

"Hey, what is it? tell me. Is everything okay?" I could feel her standing alert, eyes wide while she waited for me to break the news which she wouldn't have imagined in a hundred lifetimes.

"Yeah, actually no. I wanted to talk about something,"

"What is it?"

"It's that... it's" I couldn't manage to get the words out of my mouth. After an eternity and her nervous call, I finally managed to get it done,

"I don't think so we can be together anymore. I mean it's better that we aren't, given how different we are, you know, our backgrounds. I think it'd be better we get over with this before we get serious," there was a long pause and for a moment I thought I lost her but then I could hear her stifled sobs and had to bite my lip from letting my emotions take over me.

"What is it? Tell me?" She demanded between her tears,

"What is what?" though I knew exactly what she was talking about,

"What is the problem? I'm sure we can figure it out together. It isn't you talking I know. Tell me what is it?"

"It's me Iana. And this is what I think is best for us," I was trying hard to not cry myself but I could feel my voice tremble and I knew she would have noticed it,

"Is it our religion? Because we can totally figure it out, we just need time..."

"Why you don't want to understand Iana. This is what I want," I said a bit too sharply and regretted it as soon as the words were out of my mouth.

"Why can't we just talk it out? Why it has to be like this..."

"Because it is meant to be like this..."

"No, it isn't. You *choose* for it to be this way."

"I won't correct you if you really think it to be this way."

"When did we go like this? What did we do wrong to get here? I just need my answers... I guess I deserve this much at least. You can't just pretend for it to be so normal..." her voice broke,

"It is normal, it is as normal as it could ever be... I don't know why you're trying to look through and find something which isn't even there! Come out of your fictitious world and *see!*"

"Why?"

"What why?"

"Everything..."

"Can you please be straight; I can't understand what you want to say?"

"You *can't* or you probably don't *want* to?"

"Ghosh! Please stop, why do you want to make it so difficult all over again? You know it's best that..." she cut me before I could complete,

"Best that we flee? Take the easier way which let me point out very clearly to you sir is no easier for me, and I won't go too far to say that it isn't easier for you because now..."

"Now what? Say it..."

"...now I don't really know if it is really easier for you."

"I... I can't say anything much now..."

"Did you ever?"

"Why do you want to take it this way? Can't we just keep it normal?"

"For heaven's sake can you tell me even a bit of it which is normal?"

"What do you think, I don't wish for it to be different? I don't want things to be different, to be the way we talked, the way we planned, the way we imagined?"

"Apparently not enough."

"How am I supposed to make you understand, I know it's difficult, but this is how it's meant to be. And we can't help it even if we want to, that's how life goes we don't always get to choose. And God knows could I have been able to choose, it would have been you over and over and over..."

"Then what changed?"

"Because... I don't get to choose."

"We can fight it together, we can, it's just time, I know it'll pass..."

"The thing is, you can fight anyone and everyone and all the odds and all the things but you can't fight your own people. I give up. Am sorry, I just can't..."

"...is that what you really want then?"

"I just... I don't know, it's just too..."

"Is that what you want?"

"I just want you to understand my..."

"For god's sake give me a clear answer now, you can't just keep me hanging like this." I could hear her sobs but her tears were taken over by her angst.

"I don't want to, but I guess I have to..." I heard the line go static before I could even complete. The tears that I'd been biting back for so long started to flow unchecked. I looked at the red heart before her name in my contact list for a bit too long before blacklisting it. How bad I'd wanted this to be right, but apparently, I was proved wrong again, not by someone else, by my own people.

CHAPTER THIRTY-TWO

IANA

It had been over a week and a half since our last call. Though I tried reaching out, he wouldn't answer texts or take my calls. I was still too confused to process all of it, any of it. For days it felt like I'd been dreaming, that he'd be mine once I managed to wake up. It took almost a week for the truth to hit hard and since then, no matter whatever I did, tears wouldn't stop. Like they didn't today when I was trying to complete my leg workout, hoping for the dopamine to help. But it didn't. So, I had to sneak out to the rooftop. It was better here, with lights twinkling, I wouldn't have to hide my tears. I set my gaze to the distant corner trying to converse with *Anai* when I heard the door to the terrace open. I was too startled to look back, but I wiped my face stealthily with the back of my hand. The last thing I wanted was being seen snorting and being a cry baby on the terrace of my gym.

"Not the best place to work out. Is it?" it was Zeeshan. I didn't bother to look at him. He walked slowly to my side and resting his arms on the wall in front of us looked at the red light blinking in the distance.

"No, I... um... I just wanted to clear my head. I was just leaving,"

"Don't bother. Take your time. I guess you wouldn't want to be seen like this." his voice didn't sound sarcastic rather there was something different. Concern maybe.

"What do you mean like *this*? and how did you know I was here?" my eyes were fixed on him, though he wasn't looking at me.

"Eyes never lie, plus you look more disoriented than you think. You can use some fresh air."

"Thank you for your concern but I'm good," I almost turned to leave when he spoke again,

"Do you always cry when you feel good?" he was smiling at me now. but the dead look in my eyes made him go serious again,

"Look, whatever is it, it's your personal life and I don't get to say anything,"

"Pretty much right," I blurted out the words, not moving.

"Still, I'd just say, nobody is worth so many tears and hurt. You're young, pretty, intelligent, you've got a whole life ahead. No love is worth such suffering if they don't understand the value." His eyes were warm on me and though I knew he wasn't saying anything that I didn't already know, he didn't know the situation I and Zayne were in. But then, how could I tell it when even I didn't know more than the fact that we were insanely in love till the day he left, and the next thing I knew was that he didn't want anything that we had anymore.

"Says the person who just cares about *fun*. Pretty ironic," his eyes went wide,

"That was different. I understand what you're going through."

"Oh really? Do you even know what love is? Except, of course, having *fun*," I didn't wait for his answer and started towards the door. My hand was on the handle when I heard him inhale sharply,

"Eesha," he said with what seemed like an enormous effort. I wanted to leave, but somehow my body and mind wouldn't obey me, my legs refused to budge and I stood there, pasted to the ground.

CHAPTER THIRTY-THREE

ZEESHAN

"You are so much like her. But she was more beautiful," I let out a small laugh which sounded more like a sigh. She let go of the handle and slowly turning, walked to join me, taking her old place beside me.

"Your girlfriend? Is she here too?" I could hear the surprise in her voice as her mind nibbled on to the mind-boggling anecdote which I was narrating.

"Yeah, she was, my girlfriend. She isn't here."

"Was? What happened?" I could tell that she wasn't just asking it out of curiosity.

"We dated for four years, she was like this perfect person, the most beautiful soul one could fall in love with the moment you come to know her." I pulled out my phone and scrolled through my gallery to show her a picture of Eesha and mine together. It took all my energy to bite back tears as our happy faces smiled through the screen.

"She definitely is so beautiful. You two look so nice together," she smiled, and the way that smile reached her eyes, I could see she was genuinely into the moment. She wasn't just being modest; she could understand it.

"I know. I always thought how lucky the person would be whom she'll love,"

"And you were that lucky person," she looked from my phone screen to me. I just nodded. Her tear streaks were dry now, and her dark brown eyes shined as they caught the illumination from the lights in the distance.

"I was, that luckiest person," I turned my face away from her gaze and wiped away the hinting tears. I didn't know why I was talking about this with her. I never had. With anybody. Not even Zayne. There was something different about her that made me want to talk to her about it. After all these years, I didn't know why but it felt like she'd understand, and apart from that, the burden of this secret was too much now to bear alone. I didn't know her, but something about her made me want to talk to her, about everything. Something about her tears felt strangely familiar; like I knew that feeling firsthand. I felt her hand on my shoulder and she pressed it a little. Her touch felt like a warm quilt in biting frost. I turned to look at her and she was still there, looking contently at me while her demons ate her up inside. I wondered how someone could look so serene even with so much turmoil going on inside them.

"We loved each other."

"A luxury not everyone gets to feel," she gave a sad smile. "So, did you marry?"

I shook my head, I could feel my throat go dry as tears streaked down unchecked,

"Her family didn't approve of me." She didn't ask why, rather she just added more like a statement than a question,

"Because of your religion." I nodded smiling stupidly, tears still pouring down.

"Damn, I can't fucking believe it." I could feel she was genuinely angry,

"That's why I'm saying, don't waste your time crying over someone. It's life, it happens." I cleaned my face and smiled more fully at her, trying to ease the air between us. But she was still hanging by what I'd just told her,

"Even if life happens," she raised her head to look me straight into the eyes, "you can't just unlove someone. Even if it's not you and them in end, still you can't get your heart to not feel for them, care for them, worse, keep hoping for them to be back even if it's impossible. Can you?"

"You can't. But that ugly full stop at the end of your love story keeps reminding you that you *have* to." Something in her eyes flickered and despite the hurt which was there they beamed when I caught one last look at them before she turned and started to leave.

"Maybe full stops do, but ellipsis doesn't." her voice faded behind her while the words still hung in the evening air. I didn't know what she meant, but to my surprise, I wanted to hold on to her words. I hadn't realized, but I was eagerly praying for her love story to not have a full stop like mine.

CHAPTER THIRTY-FOUR

IANA

There was something that wasn't adding up. And even if it was just my miserable mind playing tricks on me, I had to get to him. I had to talk to him. And though Eign and Hella weren't too keen on letting me go all by myself, especially when I'd been working on two hours sleep and a lot of caffeine for the past four days I could luckily talk them into letting me go at the condition that I'd call them as soon as I saw him. The city was extra busy and roads were wet from last night's drizzle. But wet roads and extra traffic were the least of my concerns. All the argument with Eign and Hella had taken longer than I'd expect and now, I was almost running half an hour. I couldn't miss this chance. I needed to talk to him, and this was possibly the last best shot at it. Despite the crowded roads, I hit the gas, the speedometer needle ascended the arc fast enough to show a hundred miles per hour. I knew I could get a ticket but none of it mattered right now. I pressed the horn, I was sure the frequency of my honking was more than enough to express my desperation.

It had started to snow and despite the heating, I could feel my fingers cold on the steering wheel. The roads had started to become slippery and it wasn't good news. But I couldn't afford to slow down or else I'd lose him. I kept my feet steady on the gas, not slowing down. Suddenly, I could feel the control of the steering wheel going haywire. My mind was too preoccupied that it took me almost a minute to realize what was going on. I reached out to push the brakes but before I could do it, I could feel the car swerving and deviating from the drive. There was a sharp screech as I pressed into the brakes with all the energy, still not sure what was going on. I rotated the steering wheel frantically, trying to regain the position and drive fast to the airport. I wanted to reach for my phone, to see what time it was, how much time I had to reach to him. The wheels made a screeching noise.

Before I could realize it, the car was mid-air, taking three-sixty degrees rotations, my head spun with the motion as I wrestled to get free from the seat belt uselessly. Everything happened so quickly that my mind felt frozen. There was a bright flash of light and awful lot of screaming before I heard a loud crash as I felt my head hit the steering wheel while the car landed upside down where inside I still struggled to get free. I could feel my forehead warm while the cold air rushed into the car through the shattered windows. My whole body was going numb. Sirens wailed in the distance and I could feel people pulling me, ripping my clothes which were stuck in the hook, not letting me break free. There were more than one pair of hands and though my head felt too heavy and buzzed I could make out that something terrible had happened. I didn't know what, I felt sorry for whoever it'd happened with but I tried to get free from the hold of those anonymous people to get to Zayne, I was late, I had to get to him. My head suddenly felt like it was exploding and I could feel the vision at the corner of my eyes going dark. My limbs went limp as my body started to give up on me, I could hear a sharp noise, like an ultrasonic sound which made me feel like I'd explode any second. It felt like forever before it was gone, but with it, everything was gone too. I could feel my body float like I was made of helium, there was no pain, there was nothing, just darkness.

CHAPTER THIRTY-FIVE

ZAYNE

My phone was flooded with missed calls and texts when the service resumed after landing. I still felt jet-lagged. I had been expecting some from her but the sudden dawn of the fact that even if she did I wouldn't get them because I'd blacklisted her made my stomach go in knots as I felt crippled. I knew I shouldn't have been thinking about her but I couldn't help it. I checked my phone, there were texts from Zeeshan and some from my family but there were thirty-seven from Hella. I checked for the missed calls and there they were, twenty-eight missed calls from Hella. My heartbeat almost stopped while my mind raced, going through all the unpleasant scenarios. I dropped my luggage and dialed her number, she picked up on the last ring just before my call could go on voice mail,

"Hey, what happened?" I asked praying for everything to be fine. I could hear the disturbance in the background while someone shouted words like fast, oxygen, lost a lot of blood. My mouth went dry while I waited for her to reply. When she finally spoke, her voice came hoarse, like she'd been crying and shouting for a long time, there wasn't any hint of life in her voice,

"Zayne, come fast please." She'd started sobbing while someone in the background cried, O.T. Now!

"Hella, what is it?" my heart felt like it'd burst out, "Hella, tell me what the fuck is going on? Is Iana fine? Where are you?" I think she might've been shaking her head but then realizing that I couldn't see her, finally managed the words out in a bare whisper,

"It's Iana," my eyes went wide. I didn't care to look for my baggage which had been discarded unguarded. Everything felt too blurry and the only thing I could manage to keep my mind on was to get to Iana soon.

My legs hurt from sprinting and my head was still buzzing while my body tried to readjust. But I just had one thing on mind right now, it was the only thing that mattered right now, Iana.

#

The sterile smell was too hard to not care about. The white walls with red cross marks at intervals were capable enough to make my anxiety worse. I ran to the directed floor and room. A strange rush of familiarity gave me some relief when I saw Hella, her back pressed to one corner, constantly watching whatever or whoever was inside. I paused just for a moment to see what it was. The big words in red O.T spat at me as the red bulb illuminated their viciousness even more. Hella turned to look at me, her face streaked with tears. She nodded at me weakly as new tears started to flow. I reached out to her and the next moment she was cuddled into my arms, breaking into full cry. My mind was still too numb to process everything, the white of the hospital, Hella crying in my arms, Eign, with his gaze sadly fixated on the small glass window, Iana in the O.T., everything.

#

After almost five hours, the doctor came out to break the anxiety and tension that we'd been suffering for the past few hours. His words that Iana was finally out of danger sounded like what could have been the most beautiful words in the world. Hella and Eign looked so drained and even though they didn't want to leave Iana's side I managed to let them have a few hours' break. I needed the time alone with her. When they were gone, I managed to sneak into the I.C.U. She was so cold that her hands barely felt like herself. She looked so pale, lifeless. The beeping of the monitors seemed so brutal that I wanted to shake her awake and rip away the needles piercing her soft skin. The bruise under her jaw was still blue. Her hair spread in fury all over the white pillow, stitches on her forehead still fresh. Seeing her like this made my heart ache. I longed to touch her, to bring her back, to kiss her and tell her how sorry I was. Tell her, that had I gotten a chance to change things, to change the circumstances we were in, I'd have written togetherness for us forever.

#

After almost a week she woke up, and though the doctors said that she was too weak, they let us sit beside her. But it was only after two weeks that she became conscious of our presence and started talking back.

#

Hearing her voice was the biggest relief I'd got in the hurricane I'd been stuck in. She tried straightening herself seeing me walk in through the doors, but I could see it took all her strength not to flinch. She looked so pale, blood drained from her otherwise pale cheeks, her dark brown eyes were bloodshot, hair hanging messily loose on her shoulders. I took the old chair beside her bed, but she shifted and patted the seat beside her, gesturing me to sit beside her. As much as I craved her closeness, it almost broke my heart that I was the reason behind her being here and that even though I wanted things to be so different, I couldn't do anything about it.

She pulled down her oxygen mask. I could see she was having trouble breathing but she won't let it be, I knew she had her questions. Questions I was too afraid to answer.

"Hey," her voice came out in a whisper while she forced a small smile.

"How are you?" I asked, not being able to come up with something better.

"Apart from being banged up, pretty okay I think," she said laughing, holding her stomach and head. I could see that it was hurting her,

"No, don't do that," I said, trying to get her to lie down.

"Laugh?" she laughed some more, more this time, her cheeks had started to get wet as tears started to roll down from her eyes, slowly at first and then with full force.

"Why?" she was almost wheezing with the effort, but she wouldn't put on the oxygen.

"I just... I can't say anything. I'm sorry. Maybe this is how it's..."

"Because of this?" she said, reaching out for my hand and running a delicate finger around the platinum band in my ring finger. She went so still that for a moment that I thought she'd passed out. But then she raised her eyes and met mine, I nodded.

"I told them about you and they went hysterical."

"Wow, that was a surprise. Did we plan it? I don't think so," I shook my head, she was still looking at me, tears had started to dry up on her cheeks, leaving behind streak marks.

"I tried, Iana. I did." It was my turn to let my emotions out. I knew she deserved to know the truth. This girl, who had trusted me enough to love me with all her heart, she deserved to have her answers. I couldn't just leave her wondering for the rest of her life, not when she was the one who *felt* right.

"I wouldn't have done it, but knowing that it was what *ammi* wanted for me, what she had always planned for me, I had to," I couldn't meet her eyes, I had failed her. All those promises, I had failed to keep them.

"You can fight the world *for* the people you love, but you can't fight the *people* who are the world to you, Zayne. It's okay." She tugged the sleeve of my t-shirt lightly and I let her pull me into a soft embrace. My head rested lightly on her chest while her hands caressed my head. She pulled out my phone from my pocket and I didn't protest, I just didn't want to let go of her, maybe if we stayed like this nothing had to change. I could hear her struggle typing on the phone for some time before the words filled in the white room. They felt too harsh yet so soothing,

Loving can hurt,
Loving can hurt sometimes,
But it's the only thing that I know
When it gets hard,
You know it can get hard sometimes
It is the only thing that makes us feel alive,

I could feel her chest rise and fall and I knew she had been crying silently too. I didn't want to stop her this time. I wanted to think that if we cried our hearts out, I'd become easier. But I wasn't fooling anyone, we both knew it'd never get easier.

The music played on loop in the background and we stayed like that, crying, for what felt like an eternity. The way we held each other; we both knew that what we wouldn't have given to not end up like this. I couldn't help but wonder how things would've ended had I not been a what I was and she, what she was. Suddenly, I felt so agitated at the mere thought of unfairness and irrationality of religious vendetta. How bad I wanted right now for it to not be about it. I wanted it to be about us. But now, it'd always be more than us. Like an insurmountable wall. It wasn't fair to her, to me.

"This isn't fair," I spoke my mind aloud, not pulling away from her.

"No, it isn't, but life never is. It's okay, Zayne. I love you,"

"Don't please." I could feel my voice almost begging her. She pulled away and held me at an arm's length,

"Zayne, I love you,"

"Don't, I don't deserve it," she put a soft finger on my lips, she'd pulled free from the clip that'd been tucked onto it.

"Shh, you do. You deserve the world," she let go of me. "I love you, I always will," I wanted to say so much, but she wasn't looking at me now, she'd turned to the other side and I could hear her sobbing more fiercely now. I started to speak but she shook her head and I knew that I'd be making it only worse by saying anything more. So, I turned to leave. My feet felt heavy, cheeks still warm from the flowing tears. I was opening the door when she spoke, with a lot of effort, trying not to break into tears,

"Zayne," I turned to look at her, not moving from where my feet had been plastered, "our story, it won't have full stops or commas. There'll always be ellipsis, possibilities. Because there'll always be a lot more than any of us will ever be able to say and a lot more than any of us will ever be able to hear,"

I opened my mouth to speak but something in her eyes told me so clear that this conversation was over. And all I was left with, and all she was left with, and all we were left with were those numerous possibilities which could've been but they weren't.

We only had this one thing left... our ellipsis...

Epilogue

IANA

It had almost been twelve years. Though, it still felt like yesterday. The hospital sheets, the stitches, him crying in my arms, both of us wondering how we could've made it different. It took all the courage to come back here. It felt nice to see that at least none of this place had changed. I could still see the lights twinkling like they used to, Anai still shining in the corner. How could I forget this day ever? Yet, it had taken twelve long years to muster the courage to finally stand here, on the same day. Though a part of me hurt to see that he wasn't here anymore, we weren't kissing and smiling. His arms weren't around me and I wasn't saying how I wanted to be with him. I wished the *seventeenth of October* back. But I wanted the same day as twelve years before back. Not this one, where I was standing, wondering how anything could make me feel so complete yet so empty. I didn't wipe away tears. I'd hidden them for long enough, not tonight. And somehow, they made it real, him not being here, it not being *us* anymore. But it also made the fact that we were what we were, real too. And God, no one but I knew I wouldn't have traded it for even a fortune. And it hurt to admit but I'd have gone through it all over again to be together, even if it meant being broken over and over again. It felt sadistic to scrape this wound, but no, you can't scrape a wound that'd always been fresh, no matter how long passed by. I just wiped my tears when I heard it, some song playing. At first, I thought it's just some random person listening to some song, but then the sound came closer and I heard it, it wasn't some random song, and now, I definitely knew it wasn't some random guy. The melody became clear as it closed in on me and I heard the lyrics clear now while I hummed with them. I knew them by heart,

When I'm away, I will remember how you kissed me
Under the lamppost back on Sixth street
Hearing you whisper through the phone
"Wait for me to come home"

I knew what it meant, but somehow I was too afraid to turn to only be disappointed. I didn't want to get my hopes high, but I couldn't fool myself, I knew how much I wanted it. I turned, holding my eyes shut, trying to prepare myself for the disappointment but no, I was not. He was there, looking at me, smiling at me sadly. He was hunched a bit, his face lined by age, yet he was himself, handsome. It felt like I was falling for him all over again like it was happening all over again. He stopped the song and stepped in closer,

"Hey," damn, he was real.

"Um... hi," as much as I was happy, all of it felt a bit unreal. But I was shocked that I hadn't forgotten his voice.

"Twelve years ago, same day," he said smiling at me,

"You remember?" I couldn't hide the surprise in my voice, he gave a brief nod before answering,

"It took you long to come here," I couldn't manage the syllables to come out, he remembered. Not only he remembered but he was here,

"You come here every day?" I asked and immediately realized my stupidity. How could he come here every day, why *would* he come here every day. He didn't seem to mind my question though. He just shook his day, "Not every day, but I come here every seventeenth of October," he stepped in closer, trying to gauge how far we could take it without making it awkward.

"I'm sorry, I just couldn't. it..." he looked at me contently, like he always used to whenever I spoke. He never rushed me, still didn't.

"It still hurts," I could feel my cheeks getting warm and eyes flooding from tears.

"It never stops," he said, the sadness in his voice was so excruciating. It felt like I was losing him all over again.

He took another step and we were standing close enough that if I let go, I'd be leaning into him. So, I did, let go. He wrapped his arms around me without a second thought and just like that we were back where it all had started, today, twelve years ago. We stood there, without speaking anything, just crying, and hugging for what felt like an eternity. It took every ounce of our energy to break apart. When we finally did, he wiped away my tears with his thumb and pulling out his phone switched it on, and handed it to me. At first, I could fathom why he had given it to me, but then I saw the wallpaper, two smiling faces peered at me through the illuminated screen. One was him, the other was a chubby kid, must've been four years or so. The resemblance was so striking that I almost gasped,

"Your son?" he nodded,

"Zian," he said, without taking his eyes off me. I pulled out my phone and held it near his'. The screen showed two girls splashed in paints, smiling a full teethed grin. He took the phone and ran a thumb across the face of the three years old little girl.

"When did you..." I could hear the hesitation in his voice. I shook my head lightly,

"I didn't marry, I just... I couldn't. I took her in three years ago,"

"Your daughter?" he asked his voice a bare whisper,

"Ziana," I said nodding.

We both stood there, looking at the happy young faces, who'd someday know the story behind their names, the story of their parents' incomplete yet beautifully complete story. None of us spoke for a long time until he finally broke the silence,

"Iana," he scooted closer to me and pressed his forehead against mine, our lips barely apart,

"Umhm," I could feel my heartbeat racing,

"You were right, our story, it'll never have full stops or commas, it never did. It'll always have..." he stopped to look me straight into the eyes, to see if I was following, I gave him a small smile while we both whispered,

"...ellipsis," just as the words were out of my mouth, I could feel his warm lips on mine and the salt of my tears mixed with his' as they ran unchecked down our faces.

THE END